EMILIE LORING

LOOK TO THE STARS

This low-priced Bantam Book
has been completely reset in a type face
designed for easy reading, and was printed
from new plates. It contains the complete
text of the original hard-cover edition.
NOT ONE WORD HAS BEEN OMITTED.

LOOK TO THE STARS
A Bantam Book / published by arrangement with
Little, Brown and Company, Inc.

PRINTING HISTORY
Little, Brown edition published June 1957
2nd printing .... July 1957
3rd printing .. September 1957
Grosset & Dunlap edition published September 1958
Bantam edition / May 1960
2nd printing .. February 1963
3rd printing ...... June 1964
4th printing ...... June 1964
5th printing .... August 1964
6th printing .. December 1964
7th printing ...... April 1965
8th printing .. September 1965
9th printing . December 1966
10th printing ..... April 1967
11th printing .... March 1968
12th printing ...... June 1968
13th printing . November 1968
14th printing ... August 1969
15th printing ... January 1970
16th printing .... May 1970
New Bantam edition / June 1977

ISBN 0-553-11067-5

Published simultaneously in the United States and Canada

Bantam Books are published by Bantam Books, Inc. Its trademark, consisting of the words "Bantam Books" and the portrayal of a bantam, is registered in the United States Patent Office and in other countries. Marca Registrada. Bantam Books, Inc., 666 Fifth Avenue, New York, New York 10019.

PRINTED IN THE UNITED STATES OF AMERICA

LOOK TO THE STARS

ONE

SCOTT PELHAM strode briskly into the offices of Conrad & Hapgood, Attorneys at Law, and frowned at the deserted desk of their receptionist. Had he not been anxious to conclude his business in New York and catch the five o'clock train for Boston, he might have waited for the girl to return and announce him. But his friend Hapgood's call had been definite; the legal papers were ready, so come right up and sign them. Impatiently Scott pushed through the swinging gate and started down the hall toward the private offices.

A woman's voice, throbbing with restrained fury, stopped him in mid-stride. It came through the open transom of the conference room beside him—

"How can you face me with such a demand? You, my mother and father, who have made me the prey of reporters, legitimate game for every cameraman in the city, a spicy item for the gossip columns! I don't dare go on the street without dark glasses—and now you ask me to stand in court and testify!"

A man spoke, so low that the words were indistinguishable, but Scott Pelham had no ears for him. The first voice held him motionless, as in a spell. Passion. Heartbreak. Contempt. Was there a touch of fear as well? A woman's voice—or a girl's?

It came again, now icy with scorn. "The *judge?* The judge ruled that I must testify before he will grant your divorce? Nothing could make me! Take oath in court, and tell what I know of my father's philandering and my mother's orgies of anger? I'd die first! You'll have to win your *freedom* without your daughter's help!"

The masculine voice protested, soothed, explained, and Scott suddenly came to himself, felt his cheeks burn. He was listening unseen, to a closed-door conference between lawyers and their clients. Eavesdropping! Like one of those gossipmongers the girl despised. Hastily he retreated to the reception room.

The daughter's denunciation reached him even there.

"Lock me up for contempt of court? Is that the penalty for refusing to testify? They'll have to catch me first—and they won't! I have no intention of adding to my present notoriety by landing in jail! Haven't you two done enough to me? Torn my home up by the roots, ruined my life—"

This time there was a muted chorus of protest. The girl silenced it with flaming scorn.

"You have! You and your *'incompatibilities'*—that's what you call them in court, isn't it? There's a shorter word—but it isn't polite, is it! Would a man, the kind of man I could love, marry a girl whose parents had been carrion meat for the tabloids—as you have? Whose father has been notoriously unfaithful—whose mother was a shrew? What a heritage! If any man did marry me his family ought to lock him up in an asylum! But I'm through! I'm walking out, and even when you're a hated old woman, Mother, and Father is a shaky old man whose conquering days are over, you won't get me back!"

Another interruption, but she overrode it. *"Help you?* If you haven't self-respect enough—love enough—for your daughter, to stand together behind her, what can you expect from her? I'm going to Aunt Jane, the one person in the world who loves me, and shows it. We'll disappear together!"

The door to the conference room was wrenched open and a girl appeared. From the room came a woman's pleading, "Faith! Wait—wait—!"

"Good-*by!*" The door banged an exclamation point and the girl came hurrying along the hall.

A slender figure, with dark glasses, low-pulled felt hat and upturned coat collar masking her face. As she entered the reception room and saw Scott she gasped and clutched the collar higher. For an instant she stared at him where he stood by the window, the late October sun streaming in on his bronzed face and broad shoulders. His gray eyes burned, his forehead wrinkled in involuntary sympathy.

Already overwrought, the girl read frightening determination in that look. "I refuse to be interviewed!" she exclaimed in a voice hoarse from emotion. She pulled open the door to the corridor and disappeared.

"Good Lord!" Scott muttered. "She took me for a reporter!" Controlling an impulse to overtake her and explain, he turned to the window and its panorama of crazy-quilt colored roofs and shadowed street canyons. As an architect he never tired of studying the yearly changes in the skyline, the constantly amazing innovations in design which lifted story after story toward the hazy sky.

But today none of these aspects of the world's most stimulating city could penetrate his somber thoughts. The passionate protest he had overheard still beat in dull echoes through his mind. What a mess some people could make of their lives, he brooded. But not only their own lives; that was the tragedy of it. How much more bitterly the innocent had to pay.

Fred Hapgood, the junior partner, banged into the room, banged shut the door leading to the offices. His nickname of "Happy" would be misplaced now; the usually debonair face was colorless, his short, plump figure sagged as with the world's weight. He dropped into a chair and ran a nervous hand over his red crew cut. Sighing, he looked up at Scott.

"I'm too soft to be practicing law," he announced gloomily. "That girl just about squeezed my heart to a pulp! Did you see her?"

"For an instant, as she flashed through here. She mistook me, a humdrum architect, for a dashing and fearless reporter. Seemed to think I was lying in wait for an exclusive first-hand scoop." Scott Pelham hesitated, and then decided to confess. "Not only *saw* her; I heard her laying down the law in there. Afraid I owe you an apology, Happy; there was no one here, so I walked in to look for you. Then I couldn't get away from that voice! I know what you mean about your heart being squeezed; *I* had all I could do to keep from barging in with drawn sword to slay the dragons that menaced her!" He smiled self-consciously, knowing that even the light words betrayed his deep feeling.

It went unnoticed by Hapgood, who was still shaken by the interview. "I'm glad you heard her side of the argument," he said soberly. "It ought to be broadcast on a nationwide hookup! Maybe it would flag some of the couples listening, make them Stop! Look! and Think! before they dragged their squabbles into court." He rubbed his chin, eying Scott questioningly. "Perhaps you heard enough to know that the girl is the daughter in the Randolph divorce case."

"Randolph?" Scott went over to sit on the desk near Hapgood. "Not Bill Randolph's daughter?"

"The same. Know him?"

"Not really. I met him a few times when I was a kid, although I doubt if he'd remember me. Haven't seen him since."

"I've wished I never heard of him," growled Hapgood, "since the newspapers have been having a field day with the juicy details of the Randolph split-up. And yet, in spite of his reputation as a Lothario he's infernally likable. So is his wife, again in spite of a temper which would do credit to the famed Xantippe of old."

Too disturbed to remain quiet he jumped up and paced the floor. "Randolph has been our client for years, so I know them both well. That makes the mess particularly sickening to me. But everyone is sorry for them. I have a hunch that when the judge ordered their daughter to testify in court he hoped it might shock the Randolphs back to sense and decency." He tramped another turn around the room. "Then Faith—that's the daughter's name—asked me to bring her father and mother together here; said she wanted to talk to them. *Talk?* You heard her! The Randolphs appeared stunned, completely bewildered by her point of view."

"Maybe," Scott suggested dryly, "when the shock wears off they'll begin to wonder if she might possibly be right."

Hapgood grunted, drummed restless fingers on the window and scowled out at the city. "Any divorce is bad enough, but the rotten publicity attending this one gives me the creeps." With a shrug he turned. "Sorry to unload my troubles on you, pal, but I always have since we were roommates. You're the sympathetic type under that stern and rock-bound New England front."

"I'm also the business type," Scott reminded. "That's why I'm here, so let's get to work."

Obediently Hapgood led the way to his office, where Scott settled in a comfortable chair while the lawyer leafed through a pile of folders. "I told you the contracts are ready to sign," he said, "but that was my optimism. You may have objections to—"

His telephone buzzed discreetly and he answered. "Mr. Hapgood speaking. . . . You want *Miss* Randolph? I'm sorry, but she left the office some time ago. . . . No, I don't know where you can reach her now. . . ." The phone crackled feverishly. "Oh, Maureen Tenny! Yes, Miss Tenny, of course I've heard Bill—Mr. Randolph—speak of you, but I can't tell you a thing. His daughter has left. Have you tried their house?" He arched a resigned eyebrow at Scott as he listened patiently. "I'm sorry . . . no no! I *don't* think you're a reporter, Miss Tenny! I simply can't give you any help because I have no idea where she was going from here. . . . Good-by."

With a whistle of relief he cradled the phone. "Wonder what's wrong with *her*. This must be my day for frantic females; that was Maureen Tenny, the girl who has been cataloguing Randolph's collection of rare books. And she's howling for the daughter."

"From the clatter of your phone," Scott commented, "she must have been hysterical."

"Too close for comfort. Lovely voice, though, in spite of the tears in it; wonder if she's as good-looking as she sounds. Says she's through with the job there. Mmm—" He eyed Scott thoughtfully. "Did she mean *finished*—or quitting it? I wonder. She's been living at their house while she did the job; an attractive secretary under the same roof with the irresistible Bill, the Great Lover, and his wife who is jealousy incarnate! Couldn't that spell trouble?"

"A fascinating field for speculation," Scott agreed sarcastically. "But you run on so that I'm going to miss my train. Do you suppose the Randolphs *et al.*, as you lawyers say, will now permit us to buckle down to my affairs?"

Grinning, Hapgood opened a folder of papers.

As Scott had prophesied, the business consumed the rest of the afternoon. Not at all reluctantly he accepted Happy's suggestion that he transfer his reservations to the twelve-thirty train and squander the interval in riotous living.

A spaghetti supper, prepared in his apartment by Happy, who proved notably talented as a chef, was a rousing success. To Scott's compliments the lawyer responded with the lofty challenge, "When you find a gal who can cook like me, pal, latch on to her. Or have you roped your One and Only since last we met?"

When Scott smilingly denied it Happy pursed his lips in judicial reproof. "You're not getting any younger, you know. Thirty, aren't you? But I suppose it *is* a job to find a girl who measures up to specifications in family and background for Prescott Pelham of the Boston Pelhams."

"If I thought you meant that," Scott warned, "I'd dump the spaghetti sauce on your head. And cut out that 'Prescott'—I've ducked that since prep-school days." He laughed. "Uncle Phil Pepperell insists on it, but as long as I'm architecting for him I suppose he can get away with it. And also get away with chasing me around the country to close his deals with garrulous lawyers."

Hapgood ignored the jibe; he was smiling reminiscently. "Good old Uncle Pep! How is he?"

"Getting younger every day—and making me sweat to keep up with him. Aunt Patty's fine, too. They sent their love, Happy, and wanted me to remind you that the Welcome mat is always out at their Christmas Eve parties."

"A wonderful couple." The lawyer grunted. "Quite a contrast to the pair we were discussing this afternoon. Remember what a welcome they gave any of your friends you brought from college?"

"They kept it up during the war, but on a wider basis. Had a stream of servicemen dropping in for meals or snacks at all hours, just as we used to do."

"They would do that." Hapgood consulted a pocket calendar. "Less than two months to Christmas! You know, this year I just might surprise them. Revive the good old days!" And the conversation resolved itself into a duel of recollections between the two friends.

Hour later, as the *Owl* prepared to depart for Boston, a redcap hurried Scott with his baggage aboard, his ears still pleasantly ringing with Happy's chatter. Not until he was stretched as comfortably in the berth as his length would permit did his thoughts recur to the girl in the lawyer's office.

Again he heard that searing denunciation of the Randolphs—by their own daughter. Deserved, he felt sure; the fire of scornful truth had blazed in that voice. . . .

The creak and rumble of the speeding train played accompaniment to his memories. Another voice, this one unheard except as an excited vibration of the phone. What was it Happy remarked? "Wonder if she's as good-looking as she sounds." . . . The train whirled on through the night. . . .

Was that a girl's voice outside his compartment ... vibrantly young? . . . He must be dreaming. . . .

Scott sat up with a start. He *had* been asleep; daylight showed gray at the window and the noises of the train had ceased.

Beyond his door a feminine voice was asking, "Is Park Street in this part of the city, porter? I want Number Ninety. I could take a taxi, but it's so early I thought of walking—if it isn't too far."

An accent from the deepest Deep South gave directions.

"I'm sure I can find it. Thank you so much." Evidently money changed hands, and evidently a considerable amount, because the man exclaimed, "Hoo *boy!* Thank you, ma'am! Any time—"

"That's a little extra, porter, so that you'll forget about my question—and forget me."

Scowling, Pelham sat clasping his knees. Ninety Park Street? Philip Pepperell's offices occupied all of that building. Just what in thunder could a girl—especially a girl who bribed porters to forget her—want of fiery Old Pep?

Questions whirled through his mind until he was wide awake; useless to try and snatch another half hour's sleep before he would have to leave the train. Shaved and dressed, he went out into the corridor, where a line of people were crowding from the car. The man in front of Scott was leafing through a late New York tabloid. On one page heavy black letters in a headline spelled "Randolph."

"Ugh!" Scott muttered. "Does he make news every day?" When the man tossed the paper into an empty berth and walked on, Scott picked it up. With growing surprise he read:

TRUSTED SALESMAN GYPS
EDSON & RANDOLPH CO.
$100,000 Securities Stolen

"Well!" he mumbled. "At least this is different." Rapidly he skimmed the brief story. "Negotiable bonds —long-time employee, Walter Tenny, vanished with loaded briefcase—worked for well-known brokerage house before war—made excellent service record—First Lieutenant, decorated for bravery. . . . A sister of the missing man, said to have been employed as secretary in the home of William Randolph, has also disappeared. . . . Police seek Miss Tenny for questioning—"

"Tenny!" At last the name clicked. Scott stood glaring at the paper. Tenny was the name of the girl who telephoned Hapgood—Maureen Tenny! Randolph's secretary—it all fitted! No wonder Hap thought her near hysteria; she must have been trying to reach Randolph's daughter, hoping she would intercede for the suspected brother.

He read the story again, and when he came to "sister of the missing man has also disappeared" he paused, frowning at the memory of that voice outside his stateroom—her question and her request. Scott shook his head in pity and reproof. "Could be the vanished sister," he muttered, "but what an amateur! If she expects to hide, bribing that porter was a supercolossal blunder."

TWO

ON THE BALCONY of his apartment Scott Pelham filled and lighted his pipe, drawing slowly on it while he surveyed the shining expanse of the Charles River Basin. November had slipped away and December, coming in with a rowdy, blustering storm as though to assert its strength, had thereafter subsided into day after day of deceptive summer warmth. The setting sun was veiled by clouds at the moment, but its crimson glow stained half the sky and washed paler rose over the buildings along the shore. With the majestic sweep of a lighthouse looming above jumbled pick coral reefs, a tall office building upheld its daily weather signal, a shaft of lighted windows now bright blue, "Fair Tomorrow."

Beside the azure Basin a scattering of people moved up and down the Esplanade: workers enjoying a walk homeward before cold weather drove them to refuge in the subways, or the inveterate strollers who pursued their daily exercise in unseasonable comfort.

Nearer, on the twin roadways of Storrow Drive, the myriad headlights and taillights of cars drifted past, shifting like schools of minnows in a tidepool, the golden minnows darting always in one direction, the red in another.

At the moment, except for the muted hum of traffic, silence lay over the city—a welcome silence because it soothed Scott's frayed nerves. What a contrast to the uproarious confusion of the interview with Philip Pepperell from which he had just come home! The usual hectic argument, on the same old subject: the names which Uncle Phil had decreed for the two new apartment houses Scott was designing for him.

"They'll be the best I've done so far," growled Scott, "but they'll be tagged The Progress and The Prosperity just to conform to what he calls his 'System'!" He puffed clouds of smoke in his irritation.

Adherence to the Pepperell System was the one drawback to Scott's exciting and remunerative position as Uncle Phil's architect. But it was only a minor annoyance, small price to pay for working with a man who had the magic of success in his hands, as unfailing as the golden touch of old King Midas.

Early in life Pepperell laid a foundation for his fortune by acquiring an almost defunct mill at a bargain. How could a Philip Pepperell, who already suspected a strange omen in his double initials, resist a business opportunity whose slogan was "Perfect Paper for Particular People"? Whether his canny management succeeded by bringing the paper nearer to perfection or by discovering more and more particular purchasers, in true fairy-tale fashion the Ugly Duckling mill blossomed into a Golden Swan of dollars.

Success in that alliterative venture established the System, a lifelong determination to enter only projects which rejoiced in double-P initials. And now having reached a hale and hearty seventy plus he was as excited as a boy over his newest field for investment, the erection of ultramodern apartment houses, designed by his nephew Scott. The first two, in one of which Scott kept comfortable bachelor quarters, stood side by side overlooking the scenic Basin, and others were to follow. There had been, of course, the objection that "apartment houses" failed to comply with the system. Old Pep met that with characteristic shrewdness by building two at once and christening them The Princess and The Pilgrim.

From his balcony on The Pilgrim Scott ran an eye over the twin houses and modestly admitted that, in spite of personal friction, he and Uncle Phil had rung the bell. Warm ivory walls swept in clean curves, banded with floor-to-ceiling windows, and rose to the wrought-steel grille which enclosed a roof garden. Both the metal and the design of the grille were repeated in a balcony for each apartment which overlooked the Basin, not only affording a small outdoor terrace but also shading the windows below from summer heat.

Inside, the apartments represented Scott's dogged efforts to combine up-to-the-minute smartness and utility with Old Pep's ideas of time-tested comfortable living. "There still are a few people," the old man insisted, "who don't want to live in a chrome-plated barbershop!" Proof of the successful collaboration was a full house with an impatient waiting list; the mere rumor of a prospective vacancy was whispered from friend to friend with the secrecy of an inside tip on the market.

Recollection of that "closed corporation" of tenants stirred in Scott's mind as he returned to his living room. After a year in The Pilgrim he was sure he was acquainted, at least by sight, with all the inhabitants of both houses, since they shared a common entrance hall and lounge. And yet, on two recent evenings he had seen a girl he did not know come out of The Princess.

On the first occasion he enjoyed only a glimpse as he descended the stairs into the lounge from which decorative entrances led into each house. The girl stood across from him, silhouetted against the tall glass door etched with allegorical figures and a silvery ribbon bearing the name The Princess.

There, Scott thought, is a picture with a proper title! He watched her walk quickly to the street door. She went out, and the last of the sunset glow threw a red-gold haze over her slender back and proudly carried head. Scott had a distinct impression of bands playing and brave banners waving until she was lost to view.

The second encounter affected him no less agreeably. Again it was early evening when he approached the apartments chatting with Fred Walsh, the policeman on the beat and a friend of wartime. With a parting word Scott left him and strolled up the walk. At the same moment the girl came out on the steps and paused, searching through her purse.

He barely had time to appreciate her beauty; satin waves of dark hair, thick black lashes curving against shell-pink cheeks, sensitive lips without obvious cosmetic aid—

She looked up as Scott mounted the steps, and he thought her brown eyes widened in dismay. Then she saw the officer lingering on the sidewalk, flashed a glance from him to Scott and seemed to freeze. The heavy lashes veiled her eyes; the warm cheeks went pale. She stood motionless as he passed, ignoring—perhaps not hearing—his polite "Good evening." From the elevator of The Pilgrim he looked back. The girl was gone.

Two days since that meeting without a sign of her. Perched on the arm of the sofa beside the fireplace Scott puffed his pipe and wondered. Never mind the encounter on the steps, his first sight of her was the one that lingered; his first sight of the Royalty of Youth and Beauty—with flags and music, he added wistfully. And "lingered" was weak description; the memory had become a too-constant companion, dogging his thoughts, appearing so suddenly in the middle of a drawing that his pen forgot to finish a line and the ink dried in it unnoticed.

" 'I have a little shadow,' " he quoted softly, " 'that goes in and out with me.' Only she doesn't, more's the pity!" Could she be a visitor at one of the apartments? If so, a recent arrival, or he would have noticed her before this. But how to meet her? Knock on every door and, "Pardon me, I'm looking for a princess—"

Impatient with his own nonsense he wandered aimlessly to the window. On Storrow Drive the school of minnows, gold and ruby red, had become solid streams of traffic, the motor hum coming faintly through the heavy glass. A car rolled slowly in from the drive to the quiet side street before the apartments. Scott's attention was caught by the faces which appeared in its front and rear windows—two men, looking up at the buildings. The one in front leaned back to speak to the other, pointed, and went on staring. The car continued its leisurely progress to the corner and turned from sight.

With idle optimism Scott speculated that they were visiting millionaires, preferably in the construction business, who were so bowled over by his architectural skill that they would rush to secure him for their next project. Too bad that the age and unkempt appearance of their car rather thwarted that theory, but—

The telephone's metallic snarl shattered his dreams. He heard John Tinker, ex-marine and now general-utility man to his former commander, answering in the hall. Presently Tinker thrust his round, smooth face of a Rubens Cherub into sight. "For you, sir." Inserting one finger in his ear he massaged it tenderly. "It's Old—ugh, Mr. Pepperell. In good voice!"

Scott returned his grin as he went to the telephone. With the formidable voice deafening him he could picture Old Pep when he undertook a phone conversation. Sparse white hair on end, waving like hay in a windstorm, frost-blue eyes glinting through gold-rimmed glasses perched on a nose as aquiline as the famous beak of Sherlock Holmes. The long fingers would alternately tap impatience and bunch to a slamming fist for emphasis while the ruddy face ran the gamut of expressions from soothing courtesy to ferocious anger.

"That you, Prescott?" Only Uncle Phil used the full name. "Still mad at me?" When his nephew made quick and sincere denial he snorted. "You ought to be, but I'm glad you're not. Any time I get ornery, remember Aunt Patty and I think the world of you—and turn the other cheek. And I'll belt that one, too!" he confessed in an explosive chuckle. "But that isn't what I called for. What're you doing?"

"Nothing, just now. Want me?"

"Take a note out to your sister Nancy, will you? I just discovered that my secretary forgot to mail the check I'm sending for her birthday. And *that*"—with a rousing oath—"is what you get these days for eighty bucks a week!"

"Certainly I'll take it, Uncle Phil; I'm going anyway, to help celebrate her birthday." He called. "Oh, Tink!"

"Fine, boy, fine!" trumpeted Pepperell. "I'd do it myself, but I have to stay home tonight. There's a man coming with a gun."

Tinker, who had come into the hall at Scott's summons, took two catlike steps to his side. The cherub look vanished, half-shut blue eyes glittered in a face like gray steel. *"What's that about a gun?"*

Scott laughed. "Relax, Tink, nobody's after him. Someone is trying to sell him an old gun for his collection." He turned back to the phone. "Quit bellowing, Uncle Phil. You scared Tink."

The instrument rattled to Old Pep's derisive whoop. "I'll *bet!* Can you pick up the note, or shall I send it—?"

"Don't bother. I have to get some plans ready to send to the blueprint shop tomorrow, but Tink can come over."

"Good!" Pepperell's voice gentled to affection. "Give our love to Nancy and all. Remind 'em they're expected for tea Sunday."

"I certainly will; I'm invited too, you know." As he made the commonplace remark Scott was surprised at a sudden feeling of regret that he wouldn't be squiring a pretty girl to that family gathering. What, he wondered, brought that on? And realized the answer at once; the stranger in the other building. Perhaps this was a chance to get a line on her. Carefully casual he asked, "How's business here at The Princess and Pilgrim? Any new tenants?"

There was dead silence on the line. It lasted so long that Scott called anxiously, "Hello—Uncle Phil—?"

"What the devil are you asking *me* for?" bellowed Pepperell. "Think *I* run around there collecting rents? That's what I pay that weasel real-estate agent to do—and if I hear of any empty rooms I'll have his hide!" In a brief pause Scott heard him puffing wrathfully. Then, in honey-dripping tone, "You remind me, though, Prescott; if you balk at Progress and Prosperity for the new houses, what about The Patience and The Prescott? They've both been winners for me!" He was chuckling when he hung up.

Scott smiled in sympathy with the old gentleman's delight, if not with the suggested change, as he turned from the phone. John Tinker had backed off a pace and stood rigidly erect. His face had resumed its usual naïve appearance except that embarrassment heightened its pinkness.

"Sorry I butted in, Captain—*sir*," he mumbled.

"Forget it!" Scott gave him a friendly poke. "And I've told you before—cut out that 'Captain' stuff. We're through with soldiering. *And stop standing at attention!* I can feel silver bars and campaign ribbons sprouting on me every time I catch you at it." When Tinker automatically relaxed to the regulation at-ease position Scott gave up. "O.K.—I've devoted months to breaking you of that, too, but I'll keep at it. You heard what I told Mr. Pepperell?"

"You and him, both," Tinker grinned. "Was he on the phone, or leaning out his window yelling?"

"All right, then." Scott ignored the ribald question. "Get out my car and go to his house for the letter. Better ask for Mr. Pepperell himself and give him one of the extra keys for this apartment. He should have it in case he wants any of our duplicate plans when I'm away. You're out on the town so much—the Lord knows where—when I *am* away, that he might not be able to get them."

"Yessir." Tinker hesitated, then gulped. "About my stepping out—I'll stay in when you're not here, sir—"

"Not a chance! I was kidding you," Scott assured him. "Go out all you want; take the town apart for all I care." Then he added soberly, "That was kidding, too, Tink; keep out of trouble."

The little man, who only appeared small beside Scott's six-foot-one height, nodded. "Don't worry. I wouldn't pay you for what you've done for me, by gettin' your name in the papers." He glanced at his wrist watch. "I'd better slide out on that errand, sir." But when Scott walked back to the living room he followed. "Um—sir, will you want me to stick around this evening?"

Laughing, Scott dropped on the couch and put his feet up. "See? That's what I meant! Johnny Tinker, the Life of Scollay Square! What have you cooked up for tonight?"

"Nothing, sir, honest! Just, me and Fred Walsh—you know, the cop—we're going to Ace Daley's training camp to watch him work out. He's the Number Two challenger for the title; he's fighting Henry Nelson in a couple or three weeks—and after that he'll be the Number One challenger, and the Champ will *have* to meet him."

"*If* he beats Nelson," Scott suggested, smiling.

"Ace will murder him, no kidding! I know Ace, see? He and Walsh and me lived in the same town when we were kids."

"Well, blow me down!" Scott said with amused awe. "You mean that some day I may have a personal friend of a champion living with me? Sit down, Tink, sit down, and tell me more. Have a smoke; there's no rush getting over to Uncle Phil's." He tossed across a package of cigarettes, and when Tink perched on the edge of a chair near the door ordered, "Not over there—sit here."

Obediently Tinker sank into the comfortable armchair beside the fireplace. Dusk was shadowing the room so that Scott saw him dimly as he snapped his lighter, from long habit cupping his hands close to hide the glow from enemy watchers. How many more years, Scott wondered, would that caution govern him? Invariably it woke the memory of a narrow valley between ragged hills, and the whole ablaze with crimson and orange fire and the searing white flare of bursting shells. Tinker had saved Scott's life that night; what return could he ever make that would begin to balance that debt?

"Yeah," Tinker mused, letting smoke trickle from his nose. "Me and Fred and Ace ganged around together in grade school; had a club—the Battlers—that we started. All the kids in it had one idea—to be prize fighters. That's where the big money was, we figured."

His eyes traveled around the darkening room—walls of golden cream, except for the one formed by the tall windows flanking a double door, the whole expanse of glass giving a panoramic view of the Basin. Floor-to-ceiling curtains of pale terra cotta framed door and windows, their tone matched by the thick-piled carpet and accented by the deeper color of the long couch. The shining waxed amber of chairs and coffee table, and their clean-lined contemporary design, complemented rather than clashed with the venerable maple desk which a stubborn Prescott forebear had fashioned for himself when the Revolution cut off English imports.

The room's quiet elegance caused Tinker to shake his head in resignation. "You wouldn't understand, I guess, but kids like us didn't wonder what per—profession we'd study for; we just prayed that some fight manager or big-league scout would notice us before we had to go to work in the mills." There was no envy in the words, only a desire to make his friend comprehend the desperation of an underprivileged boy.

"And," Scott prompted, "Ace Daley got the lucky break?"

"Yup. He'd have been Champ long ago, only for the war; in the Army till the trouble was over, then back to the ring. Undefeated, so far, with a string of knockouts. I used to see the name in the papers but never caught on it was him; there's a million Daleys. I'd sort of forgotten Ace; he had a kid brother who was pretty wild, got into a jam and ran off, and then the family moved away. But the other day I ran into Daley on the Common and recognized him right off—by his eyes. One is blue and the other a kind of washed-out green. Believe me, they don't make him look soft!"

"Have you ever considered going back to the ring, Tink?"

The man rubbed his straw-colored hair in doubt. "I tried it before the war, but I was no Ace Daley, and I don't want to end up punch drunk. But, gee, sir—it's all I know except being a marine, and they don't want me, even in peacetime."

"Not quite all you know, pal," Scott corrected. "I can testify that you're a Number One cook."

Tinker made a wry face. "Maybe, but I ain't in love with it. Not forgetting, sir," he added hastily, "that you took me on when I was at the end of my string, and I'm lucky to be working for you! But if the Doc ever passes me for active duty—and you don't need me—me and the kitchen stove is done! Holy cats! I only picked up cooking after the war, bumming around the country. Seems like those years were just one cheap restaurant after another, every one worse than the last, and me going downhill with 'em!"

The two men sat silent a moment, and Scott felt sure that their thoughts were racing back over the same memories. After Tinker had saved his captain in that nightmare battle for a miserable hill, Scott found him in a base hospital. Could he ever forget the wracking ordeal of that visit? Johnny Tinker, of reckless ferocity in a raid or mop-up, this ghost-pale, dazed boy who lay mumbling and shaking on a tumbled cot? Suffering from wounds and battle fatigue when he reached the hospital, he had collapsed heart and soul after a careless medic read him a letter from home.

Not a letter from his mother, this time, but from a doctor who fumbled in vain for gentle words to tell him that his whole family, mother, father and sister, had been wiped out by an epidemic.

Scott left the hospital swearing at a fate which could so heartlessly batter a helpless man. A few years later, the same revulsion sickened him when he met the ghost of Johnny Tinker, gaunt, unshaven and close to prostration, stumbling along a downtown street. The bitter saga of those years between came out later; on that day it was enough for Scott to discover that the man had conquered his spiritual illness, and needed only a helping hand for physical recovery. From that meeting on, Tink had a home and Scott Pelham a devoted servant, and friend.

To shift the depressing mood of memory Scott turned on the lamp beside the couch. "I suppose I'd better get to work on those plans while you run over to Mr. Pepperell."

"Yessir." Tink stood up. "All right if I stop in at the doctor's and let him look me over?"

"Good idea, you are due for another checkup. He's built you up so rugged, Tink, that I bet he'll say this is the last call and turn you loose."

"That'll be something."

Tinker was on his way down the hall when Scott called, "By the way, any new people moved in that you know of?"

He came back shrugging on his treasured battle jacket. "None in The Pilgrim, sir. One in the other house. You know this apartment right next to us, Number Three in The Princess?"

"The Jordan sisters' place? A new tenant there?"

"Nope. But there's a lady staying there while the old girls are abroad, so the housekeeper tells me."

"A *young* lady?"

"I guess so." Tink buttoned his coat. "Haven't seen her myself, but the housekeeper says she's 'real snazzy!" He grinned. "Honest, sir, when that nice little old dame gives out with slang she snows me! Anyhow, she says the lady is doing something to them old books the Jordans are always buying." He departed whistling.

THREE

TOO STUNNED to move, Scott listened to the cheerful whistle until it was muted by the closing door.

She's doing something to them old books—

That girl in New York who called Hapgood—Maureen Tenny?—had just finished cataloguing Bill Randolph's collection, and now a young lady was doing similar work for the Jordans, equally avid bibliophiles. It would have seemed only a coincidence if Scott had not known that the seventy-year-old sisters were cousins of Randolph. That being so, what was more natural than for Cousin Bill to recommend a secretary who completed satisfactory work for him? Probably he did it while the Tenny girl was still on the job and before her brother disappeared with the Edson-Randolph securities.

But wait a minute! Scott sat up frowning. Only yesterday he had called Hapgood on business, and during the ensuing chat had idly inquired about the robbery. The passing weeks, Happy reported, had left the situation unchanged. Walter Tenny still among the missing. Ditto sister. Police, as usual, predicting a break in the case at any moment. Newspapers, as usual, rudely doubtful.

Considering that news Scott sank into deeper confusion. "A serious flaw in our deductions, Watson!" he muttered. "If Bill Randolph arranged the Jordan work, he knows where she is. So what's all the talk about her vanishing?"

"Pelham," he reproved himself, "as a dumb detective you are wasting a brilliant architect's time. There's work to be done!" He jumped up and went to his workroom, pulling a notebook from his pocket. A roll of tracing cloth, the plans which he was to prepare for blueprinting, lay ready on the table. Perched on a stool he opened the notebook to the list of minor changes Uncle Phil wanted.

He read the list without having one single item register in his busy mind. That "lady" in Number Three—a "real snazzy" lady—hmm! If she was the girl he saw come out of The Princess, he could easily coin more appreciative descriptions. But perhaps she wasn't; there might be other newcomers in the two houses—

Restlessly he abandoned the plans and wandered back into the living room, crossed to the balcony door. The crimson west had faded to translucent aquamarine, with a single star hung like a guiding beacon near the horizon. On the far side of the Basin an electric sign flared and faded with pulse-beat regularity. Scott opened the door and stood for a moment feeling the cool breeze which carried the salty taste of the ocean across the city and rippled the water to shimmering sapphire and emerald, like a carpet of jewels flung down by a giant's hand.

A small white object landed with a soft thud on the balcony and rolled almost to his feet. Scott picked it up; paper wrapped around something hard and held in place with adhesive tape. Now where the dickens did that come from? Stepping outside he looked up. No one in sight on any of the balconies above his. He went to the railing. No one below, except a man standing at the edge of the grass plot. He could have thrown it, but he seemed absorbed in tugging at a rope or leash attached to something among the shrubbery. He finally succeeded in hauling a small dog into sight.

A dog? Not with that queer, rocking gait! Scott stared. "A monkey!" he exclaimed when the animal stood upright and carefully settled a miniature overseas cap on its head. He set it at a cocky slant which reminded Scott of every soldier in his company. The man walked slowly away, a thin, drooping figure with listless, shambling steps. The monkey skipped beside him, then climbed the leash hand over hand to perch on his shoulder.

Scott rested his elbows on the railing, unwrapped the paper from the fragment of brick it enclosed, and smoothed out the wrinkles. Amazement furrowed lines between his brows as he made out the scribbled words:

"You're watched."

Someone, he guessed, had gone mildly crazy. Who would watch him, and for what? Whether the mysterious benefactor who sought to warn him was the man with the monkey or an unknown, he was barking up the wrong tree. A joke? Offhand, Scott couldn't recall any of his friends who wasted time in practical joking.

The sound of an opening door on the next balcony startled him—and switched his thinking. The lady in Number Three! If she was Maureen Tenny, as he was beginning to suspect, someone might well be trying to put her on guard, and either through ignorance or poor aim delivered the message to the wrong balcony.

He straightened and turned. The girl he had twice seen downstairs stood in the doorway looking off toward the clustered lights on the Cambridge shore. Had she come to the door at that moment, or had she been standing observantly inside? For how long?

She drew a deep breath of the evening air, then started to return to her apartment. That broke the spell of bewilderment which held Scott in a state of suspended animation. "Don't go! Please!" he called, extending his hand. "Not until you have read this message. It fell on my balcony, but it isn't for me. It may have been intended for you."

She stood hesitant, one hand on the open door, while eyes brilliant as brown jewels studied his gray ones. "A message?" she repeated in mingled surprise and skepticism.

Scott moved to the edge of his balcony and held out the scrap of paper. Would she accept it, or ignore it—and him? While he waited he could find no reason to alter his first snap judgment of the girl—a princess! Even in the gathering dusk her loveliness was breathtaking, not at all lessened by a vivid red dress whose close sleeves and full skirt conjured a vision of medieval Italy and the court of the Medicis.

He continued to offer the message, glad of an excuse to prolong his admiring appraisal. "You'd better read it," he insisted.

Although the girl moved nearer she clasped her hands behind her and eyed the paper cautiously. "Why should I?"

Scott shrugged. "You know the answer to that better than I. This didn't drop from the sky, I'm sure; it was thrown here. And it seems to be a warning. Since it couldn't have been meant for me, I thought it might be for whoever lived next door. However, if you aren't interested—" He crumpled the paper.

"Don't tear it! Please! I'll read the message because—oh, because this situation reeks of melodrama." Her clear voice fell to a stage whisper. "On a lofty balcony of the palace in Baghdad a mysterious stranger appeared!" She laughed. "That might fit into an Oriental thriller, but who would expect it in Boston, where you all live staid, conventional lives? Quite out of character. That's why I find it intriguing. Bloodchilling, in fact! Of course I want to see the message; one of my reasons for being in this city is to study its peculiar customs." She leaned across the railing and took the paper.

"You don't sound favorably impressed with us Bostonians," Scott complained. "And you also sound like an author."

"An aspiring author only—up to now," she smiled. "Plodding a long, hard road. If you don't think so—try it! While waiting for the lightning bolt of fame to strike me, I am cataloguing books for my bread and butter."

"But why in Boston? Couldn't you do your plodding to better effect in New York, where the editors grow?"

"Oh, but I couldn't stay—" She bit the sentence off, but if it was an admission she covered it swiftly. "How could I stay camping on their doorsteps, presenting a manuscript every time an editor appeared—hurrying to lunch with a celebrity, no doubt."

"If I were an editor," Scott assured her, "I would stay on the doorstep. But I still wonder, why Boston?"

"Persevering, aren't you?" There was a hint of chill in the girl's comment. "Very well, there is no secret about it. First, I came to Boston because I was sure of work here. Secondly, because I wanted to know the city of Sam Adams and Paul Revere, the Tea Party and Bunker Hill, Longfellow, Emerson, Cabots and Lowells, the Proper Bostonians—" Smiling, she spread her hands to end the list.

"Do I detect a descending climax?" he bantered.

"Possibly. I admit I have been disappointed in that phase of your city. I expected the average citizen to look like a cartoon in the *Boston Herald* and act as though he believed only in Heaven, Hell and New England. Instead he seems no different from a New Yorker: wears the same suits, watches the same movies and television programs and plays—"

"Enough!" Scott laughed, holding up a defensive hand. "I'm thoroughly put in my place. But all of us are not like that all of the time. I'd like to show you some of the Boston you want to see. Why, tonight I'm going to supper in a house which for two hundred years has looked out on a village green where the Revolution began. It's not Boston, but it is the spirit you are in search of. Wouldn't you like to see it—well, er—sometime?"

The pause, and the lame conclusion, were due to Scott's sudden realization of how completely he had fallen victim to alluring feminine charm. Carried away by it, he was within a word of proposing to escort to his sister's home a girl of whom he knew nothing—not even her name. And yet, even in his confusion, it was remarkable that regret mingled with relief when she said flatly:

"Thank you, but I'm much too busy."

"Oh?" With masculine inconsistency he resented the dismissal. "Working all day and writing all night? Genius must really burn!"

"It does! My typewriter smokes like a four-alarm fire," she exclaimed in delight. Her constant change of mood did nothing to dispel his enchantment. "That diatribe against your Boston was only in fun; truly, there is atmosphere here—atmosphere by the yard!

More, I think, than in any other city I have seen. But, of course," she qualified hastily, "being a working girl I haven't seen many. It surprises me that more novelists don't use Boston for a setting."

"Probably they think us too slow."

"Slow?" she echoed with a ripple of laughter. "They should meet *you!*" She turned toward her door. "Thank you for this Mysterious Message," she said, waving the slip of paper. "Who knows? There may be a story in it."

Scott made an impulsive effort to detain her. "Did you see the monkey?"

"Yes. Cute, wasn't he?" The girl peered over the railing. "Do you suppose he climbed up with the note? We're only two floors above the street."

"I'm sure he didn't. It was wrapped around a piece of brick and thrown. Anyway, I looked over and saw him on the ground much too soon for him to have climbed down—even if a monkey could climb this smooth wall."

"Could a—a person—climb down?"

Scott laughed. "Back in the twenties or thirties there was a publicity-hungry maniac who climbed up the face of buildings. The newspapers dubbed him the Human Fly. Maybe he could have done it."

"Please be serious. There is a drainpipe, or whatever it's called. Couldn't one climb down by clinging to that? If someone—well, I mean in an emergency?"

There was a tremor in the question that hinted of panic. Scott felt a dismaying conviction that she had contemplated the attempt if the need arose. She must be truly desperate! He would smash that mad idea, and smash it hard.

"How can I be serious," he scoffed, "when you ask such absurd questions? Yes, you could go down there, just as you could simply step off your balcony into space. The result would be equally stunning—and that's putting it mildly."

"It does look ticklish," she admitted. "But I still believe it could be done."

"Persistency, thy name is woman!" Scott misquoted grimly. Then he forgot that question, noticing for the first time that her long lashes were wet and her eyelids betrayingly pink. Severity melted to sympathy as he accused, "You've been crying! Anything I can do to help?"

Deeper color warmed her cheeks and she retreated. "You are a keen observer!" she said scornfully. Before he could protest she repented her curtness and acknowledged, "I was crying, for the first time in years. While I was about it, I indulged myself prodigally." With a defiant little nod she disappeared into the apartment. The glass door shut with a determined clang.

Scott frowned at the closed door. Was she angry? Had he antagonized her by commenting on her tears? And what did her reckless idea of climbing down that wall imply?

If she worried about an emergency exit from a building most thoroughly equipped with elevator, stairway and fire escape, it suggested that she wanted a quick way out when some caller came knocking at her door. And the drastic measure she contemplated further suggested that the dreaded caller would block every other exit—an exhibition of power or authority which pointed inexorably in one direction—the police. With that startling thought Scott's memory called up the picture of her standing—rigid with fright?—when she saw him break off his conversation with a uniformed patrolman and stride toward her.

Only one girl he knew of was dodging the authorities: the sister of a missing New York bond salesman. That knowledge aroused no condemnation, he discovered, but instead an instant protective urge. Sympathy for the hunted? More than that, he admitted. An urge born of the certainty that he had met a rare person, gallantly gay when she could forget her troubles, facing those troubles stanchly, and—far from incidentally—quite the loveliest girl he had ever seen.

FOUR

IN NUMBER THREE of The Princess, the object of his reflections drew heavy satin curtains tightly together on the balcony door and windows. Crossing the room to switch on a single lamp beside the Victorian rose sofa she sank down and read the ominous message in her hand.

That hand was shaking until with fierce contempt she clenched it, crushing the paper. *"You're watched."* Only two words, yet she felt almost a physical sickness at their import. Who could have written them? The tall, brown-haired man on the next balcony? Surely not he; his smile had been friendly, his pleasantly deep voice sympathetic and breezy in turn. A man to depend on; more so than any she had known. If at times he appeared unduly inquisitive, honesty forced her to admit that she often had that effect on impressionable young men.

Who knew that she was here? Until this moment she had been confident that only three trusted friends shared her secret. "Only two, really," she corrected in an apprehensive whisper. Then with a positive shake of her head, "No, *three!* Not even this bolt from the blue can make me doubt Philip Pepperell."

"Bolt from the blue?" she echoed in derision. "Whoever sent this note might as well have thrown a hand grenade in at the balcony door!"

Still breathless with consternation she stared around the room, a haven suddenly transformed into a prison. A beautiful period piece, she had considered it, steeped in the personalities of the Misses Jordan. Their treasured books lined the walls, serried ranks of vellum and morocco, dim with age or bright with unchanging gold. A vast and priceless oval hooked rug, its riot of pink roses and apple-green leaves dulled to a monotone by a century of trampling boots and slippers, stretched between the corpulent red-lacquered mandarin cabinet filling half a wall and the grand piano of white mahogany almost as old. They, and the rose couch on which her dress now made a blood-red splash against dark crimson brocade, where the dominant furnishings of a room packed with the Jordans' trophies from half a hundred voyages abroad.

The girl sighed. Lovely as it was, it had become a cell from which she saw no escape. Even with some unknown spying on her she must stay or else vanish beyond the reach of her only friends. And how would the stately but diffident Misses Jordan react if they learned that their beloved apartment stood in a state of siege? Take the next boat home, no doubt. Or, more probably, fly! To arrive, brandishing umbrellas, in time for the kill.

Her spirits a little lifted by the absurd idea the girl concentrated on the note still crumpled in her fingers. "Don't get panicked, silly!" she reproved aloud. "For a twenty-six-year-old, you act like a child." There was enough unhappiness in her heart to condone a lack of courage, but she sturdily rejected any excuse.

On quieter second thought it seemed reasonable that the warning had come from a friend, since it was meant to put her on guard. But except for Philip Pepperell her confidants were many miles away, and she simply could not picture that elderly, irascible citizen coyly tossing a note to her balcony. More likely, if he thought she was in danger, to burst in waving a club. She enjoyed the imaginary scene.

Without conscious intent, she substituted another figure in the heroic role, the man next door. A much more formidable ally, she was sure, from the steadfast gray eyes and the uncompromising set of his mouth when she evaded his questions. If he were on her side—!

Impatiently she thrust the thought away. Although he showed eagerness to continue the acquaintance, and in different circumstances she would have been equally willing, this was not the time. The more people who knew her secret, the more talk—and the greater danger. And her sense of decency and integrity rebelled at the idea of meeting him under false colors.

"You conceived this Disappearing Lady act," she reminded herself sternly, "and it's up to you to play it out." Slowly she tore the note to minute scraps and dropped them in the wastebasket. "Only," she whis-ered, controlling an hysterical impulse to scream it to the world, "I get so darned lonely!"

As though perfectly timed to a stage cue, a gentle rapping sounded from the hall door.

The girl stood listening with held breath. She tiptoed to the door and waited, hearing the thud of her heart.

Again the hesitant rap—rap, and this time a murmur came through. "It's Martha Beddle, miss."

A gasp of relief bubbled to soft laughter as she pulled open the door. The housekeeper stood smiling, her gold-rimmed spectacles twinkling, brown uniform freshly starched, brief white apron spotless. Gripped in her wrinkled hands two polka-dotted holders supported a silver teapot which breathed enticing aroma.

Mrs. Beddle, for years a housekeeper in England to what she fondly styled "the landed gentry," had been one of Philip Pepperell's happiest contributions to The Princess and The Pilgrim. Endowed with a sunny dis-position and the motherliness of a setting hen, "Mrs. B.," as the tenants called her, had enlarged her nominal duties of housekeeper until they included watching over the general health and well-being of every one in the two buildings—especially the younger set. This was not her first visit to Number Three.

"I thought you might welcome a cuppa, miss, it's that late in the day." The soft accent of Scotland hummed in her voice. "Cheer you up," she suggested after a darting look at the girl's face.

"How wonderful, Mrs. Beddle—if you'll join me!" She closed the door and hurried to clear some papers from the low table before the couch. "Set it here while I get the cups. I'm sure there are some of your scones left, although I've nibbled them constantly."

"I did just what you told me, miss," the little woman announced complacently. "Knock—and wait—and knock again and tell who it is. A clever scheme, I must say, though it's a dreadful pity you have to stay so close in this apartment. Like a dungeon in that old Tower of

London! Mr. Beddle took me there once; gave me the shakes, I must say!" She trotted around the room snapping on lights until the girl returned with cups and scones. "That's better, isn't it?"

"Definitely!" The thrill of a visitor to break her constant solitude added an extra sparkle to the girl's natural vivacity. "I put on this particular dress to counteract a fit of the blues. And, oh! I now revise a recent estimate; I have *four* good friends. Shame on me for forgetting you!"

"I'm sure you have many more than that." Mrs. Beddle firmly removed the teapot from the hands of her hostess. "Just you sit back, my dear. I've waited on tea tables more years than you could count. In the Old Country, of course. Not often, any more, though Mr. Pelham—next door to you at The Pilgrim—likes to drop in on me now and then for a cuppa. Or so he says, anyway. Maybe it's just his kindness; he is the kindest man!"

"I believe you, after talking to him today. Odd that you should mention my neighbor, because I meant to ask you about him sometime."

The housekeeper drank tea, her sharp eyes studying the girl's face. "No time like the present," she agreed briskly. "And there's no one I'd rather talk about than young Mr. Scott Pelham!"

Back in his living room, seated on the arm of the couch, Scott filled his pipe. As he struck a match he looked up at the portrait of an eighteenth-century governor which hung above the fireplace, the only picture in the room. Even by the light of the single lamp he'd turned on, it glowed like a precious stone in its ornate gilded frame, the ruddy, stern face, the plum-colored velvet coat and white satin waistcoat heavily embroidered with gold.

The governor's descendant addressed him with half-humorous gravity. "Your Excellency, I want you to be the first to know—at last I have met *the* girl. So far, she is known to you and me only as the Princess, but I'd bet my favorite pipe against that gold snuffbox in your hand that to a hotly pursuing world she is known as the sought-for Maureen."

"What did you say?"

The hoarse demand exploded from the hall. Scott sprang to his feet, humiliated at being caught in the demented act of talking to a painting. Speechless, he scowled at John Tinker, who stood leaning in the doorway. One hand clutched his jacket, the other gripped the door casing as he stammered, "I thought—I was hanging up my coat—I thought you said a name—?"

Quick premonition shocked Scott. Good Lord! Somehow—somewhere—Tinker had heard of the New York case and the girl connected with it! Had he seen an item in the papers, or—? But no, simpler than that! His pal, Officer Walsh, had been talking. Of course the Boston police would be alerted by New York. Now he himself had put Tinker on the alert. He must throw him off the trail, somehow, at least until he could give the matter some cool deliberation. He gained a moment by carefully rapping out his pipe.

"I mentioned a *name*, Tink?" Pursing his lips doubtfully Scott shook his head. "Don't know why I should, although I was daydreaming when you bounced in. Perhaps you misunderstood me." Dismissing the subject as unimportant he asked briskly, "Did you get the letter from Mr. Pepperell?"

There was enough formality in the tone and question to snap Tinker to business. "Yes, sir—and gave him the extra key. Here you are." Red of face he presented an envelope. " 'Scuse me for barging in like that, sir—"

"Skip it." Scott pocketed the note. "O.K., pal—you're on the loose for this evening."

Tinker hung his jacket in the hall closet. "Nope. The Daley excursion is off. We were going in Walsh's car, but he pulled extra duty tonight."

"In his *car?* Where is your friend's training camp?"

"Out in Acton. There's this feller runs a boarding camp—"

"Well, great day!" said Scott. "I thought it was in the city. Come along with me; you can drop me off at my sister's and come back to pick me up about ten-thirty."

They had crossed the Charles and headed into the

country before Scott thought to ask, "Did you see Dr. Towle, and what's the word?"

"I'll say!" Tink chuckled. "He gave me a checkup like I was trying to join the Marines, and he couldn't find a thing. Sound as a dollar, he says. Holy cats! Sir—I'm in the clear!"

Scott matched his happy grin. "Best news I've heard for years! So it's time we did some serious thinking about your future. And I'll tell you what! Why don't I talk to Uncle Phil about it? He's bound to have some ideas."

"Would you? That'd be swell." Tink hesitated, took out a cigarette and lighted it. "Look, would you ask him how he likes an idea I had? I got no education for any business, see? But do you think I might do some physical training? You know, line up some fellers—businessmen—to let me put 'em in condition, and keep 'em in shape?"

Scott slapped the wheel. "Bull's-eye for John Tinker! I have a hunch you've rung the bell. Plenty of my friends could stand working off a few pounds, especially in winter when their golf is curtailed. You could open a sort of gentleman's gym." He slid a curious glance at Tinker. "Where did you get the idea?"

"Well, sir—" The little man squirmed in his seat, drew rapidly on his cigarette. "I picked up training tricks while I was boxing, and more in Marine boot camp—as you know. And running a—a gentleman's gym, like you called it, would be better than being just a punk fighter, wouldn't it? I mean—" the fingers holding the cigarette trembled—"I mean—more dignified?"

"Much more," Scott agreed, unsmiling. "What's the pitch?"

"Well—you remember that time you came to see me in the hospital?" Tink kept his face averted; he was almost whispering. "Didn't I babble something about—about a girl?"

Scott tensed with interest; in all their conversations this was the first reference to a girl. "Yes. You seemed worried because you hadn't heard from her for a long time. You didn't mention her name." Hesitantly he suggested, "Have you heard?"

"No, sir—not yet." As though a dam gave way, words poured out. "I kept shooting letters to the old address, but they all came back. She lived in our town, her brother was one of us Battlers I told you about. He went all the way through high school, though, and during the war I heard he got a commission. The whole family was higher class than us. Gee, she ruled our gang like a little queen. Don't know why she ever went for *me*, but from the seventh grade, she had me hooked solid! Pretty—gee! And the way she'd look at me and say, 'Johnny,' made me feel warm all over!" Tink grunted. "Aw, I can't say it right! You must think I'm nuts!"

"I never heard it said better, Tink. Go ahead."

"That's all," he muttered. "When I started fighting at smokers and stag parties—that did it. Her folks wouldn't stand for their little girl going round with a *prize fighter*." He rubbed his face with both hands. "I left town to make my fortune in the ring." His voice was harsh with bitter disappointment. "Then the war. By the time I got back they'd moved a couple of times, and I couldn't trace her. Never had money enough to go find her, anyway; I couldn't thumb my way, and walk in on her lookin' like a bum." He chewed his knuckles. "I'll bet her family never gave her my letters! She'd have answered *something*—unless that flu epidemic got her, too!"

"Don't you believe it, Tink!" Scott put all the certainty he could into the assurance. "She'll answer yet." Inwardly he saluted the devotion which could sustain itself through year after lonely year with *nothing*. Nothing but love.

"Well, sir," Tink shook off his momentary discouragement and grinned, "that's why I thought up this physical-training racket. If I do find her, maybe her folks will think I'm a better prospect."

They were silent until Scott pulled up beside his sister's house and got out. Tink slid behind the wheel. "Much obliged for the car, sir—and for letting me bend your ear with my troubles."

FIVE

SCOTT PELHAM halted abruptly at the threshold of his sister's living room, then retreated with a smothered exclamation of dismay. A shrill, breathless voice was speaking, a voice which for him had the nerve-wracking properties of a dentist's drill. Lucy Wheeler had invaded the Selwyn home, and as if her mere presence were not enough to daunt him, she was holding forth on a subject too much in his thoughts already. He thanked his stars that his sister, for the moment, bore the brunt of the oration.

"Nancy Selwyn!" the Wheeler tirade ran. "*Have* you seen the young woman who is camping in the Jordans' apartment? At The Princess, I mean. Uncle Philip finally admitted that she is there to catalogue their books—but I had to practically *pump* to get *that* out of him. *My dear!* Don't you think he's out of his mind to let some person of whom he knows absolutely nothing into their rooms? I mean, think of those books! A *fortune!* And all their lovely things. That's what I ran out here to talk to you about, Nancy—well, that and the new dancing class for which I am sponsor!"

From the hall Scott watched Miss Wheeler pout and preen, her expressions shifting with the change of subject. Even while she was silent to catch her breath she managed to remain the one jarring note in the Selwyns' otherwise restful room. The too-masculine cut of her tweed suit fared badly against the graceful mahogany furniture which, like the house itself, dated back to Minuteman Joab Selwyn. His likeness, rough-hewn by an earnest if untrained traveling artist, hung at one end of the low-beamed room where the painted eyes could look out the window toward the Battle Green.

Today, however, his granite face seemed bent to censure the cackling female seated by the fire, and the twentieth-century Mrs. Selwyn's manner assumed some of the portrait's severity as she protested, "Why do you say that Uncle Phil knows nothing about this young woman, Lucy?"

"My dear! He *can't,* because he simply will not answer questions. If he knew anything about her he'd tell it, wouldn't he—if only to nip conjectures in the bud? He only says that she is employed by the Jordans, and if her credentials satisfied *them* it's nobody's business who or what she is!" Miss Wheeler bounced indignantly and lifted her voice to a higher key. "He said that to *me,* Nancy, when I merely asked for information because I'd heard of her from Molly Todd, in the apartment above. And when I suggested that the Jordan sisters might be—well, a little—I mean, after all they *are* over seventy!—he shouted that as long as they paid their rent they could do as they pleased without interference from him or *anyone else!* And he glared at me until I almost felt insulted."

By the time she ran out of breath Scott was seething with anger. Why should that little snoop poke her nose into this affair? He knew why; because Lucy Wheeler was never happy unless she found someone she could stick her knife into! High time, he decided, to step in there and—and what? Convince the woman that her suspicions were unfounded? Confusion quenched his anger. How could he honestly attempt to give the suspected girl a clean bill, when half the time he himself had grave doubts about her?

With his mental conflict unresolved Scott stalked into the living room, and thereby at least succeeded in stemming the Wheeler monologue in mid-word. His sister greeted him with equal parts of enthusiasm and relief, he guessed from the smile which lighted her lovely face and twinkled in her blue eyes. He managed a courteous nod to the other woman, and a lukewarm, "Hello, Lucy."

Her thin face flushed. Perfectly aware that all the family loathed gossip, she had been caught red-handed, or red-tongued, by the one she most admired. The Witch, as the collateral male members nicknamed her —partly because she hailed from Salem, but more for certain personal attributes—was an in-law graft on the Pelham family tree, endured because she was "family," but only endured. Although she was in her thirties the severity of her dress, the lines of permanent ill-humor on her cheeks and the black eyes nervously squinting as though for closer examination of a juicy rumor made her appear almost an old woman. Many an invitation had been most reluctantly tendered from fear of those eyes and their attendant censorious tongue.

Scott avoided his sister's warning glance. Nancy knew how he detested the Witch; the humor of the situation was quirking her mobile lips. The firelight glinted sparks of red and gold in her auburn hair; a larkspur-blue dress, the deep silver bowl of chrysanthemums in shades of bronze, the glow of a lamp reflected in a gilt-framed mirror above the fireplace made warm accents of color in the charming room. The unfailing source of the charm was Nancy Selwyn.

Scott was sure that she was shaping a gentle remark to quiet his obvious annoyance, and without giving her the opportunity he rushed to the defense of a girl he had met only once.

"I heard your—complaint—as I came in, Lucy," he growled, "and I'm sure that the *tenants* at The Princess—" he mimicked her in stressing the word—"may trust in the judgment of Philip Pepperell. But you don't live there, so what has any of this to do with you?"

Miss Wheeler bridled at the implied reproof and contemptuous tone. Her face glowed like a ripe tomato. "My dear boy, if the tenants are satisfied, of course—" She hunched her shoulders unbecomingly, a more infuriating end to the sentence than anything she might have said.

With difficulty Scott controlled an atavistic urge to wield the poker, and his sister rushed into the breach with an affectionate command.

"Sit down and be sociable, Scott. Don't stand glowering."

He laughed, kissed her and then dropped an envelope in her lap. "That, from your kid brother, with the usual wishes. And this, from Uncle Phil, with many happy returns of the day."

"What a dear he is—and you, too, Scott. I loved that gorgeously extravagant box of candied fruit you sent.

Box? It's more like a trunk! I feel pounds added to my buxom figure just from looking at it!" To Lucy Wheeler she apologized, "I'm not offering any because I'm determined to keep it out of my daughter's clutches until after dinner." She laughed brightly. "That assumes, of course, that she hasn't already ferreted it out!"

Scott listened, amused. Nan certainly was rambling with unusual abandon, no doubt to sidetrack further discussion of the mysterious tenant. She must sense his close-to-explosion temperature.

"Lucy came out to tell me about a dancing class which is being organized, Scott." Nancy smiled invitingly.

"My dear!" Miss Wheeler eagerly accepted the gage. "If you could have heard Miss Carpenter describe her project! She is to be the instructor, you know; comes *highly* recommended and has had a world of experience in training the younger set. I do hope you will enroll Ellen, because the course will include not only dancing but general *deportment*, too—if you know what I mean."

"Dancing?" Scott queried with counterfeit enthusiasm. "Ballroom or tap?"

"I am sure," Lucy answered coldly, "that Miss Carpenter is qualified to teach any form, but since the entire course will emphasize *refinement,* I imagine that—"

"Hi, everybody!" A young girl bounded through the doorway, accompanied by twin boxers of such size and vitality that the room seemed swarming with dogs. She gripped a collar in each fist to restrain them as she demanded, "What have you got to eat, Mother?"

"The 'younger set' of whom you were speaking," Scott remarked to Lucy, who had cringed back in her chair and eyed the obstreperous animals with aversion.

Nancy Selwyn's tone reproached her fourteen-year-old daughter with the reminder, "Ellen, Cousin Lucy and Uncle Scott are here."

Ellen tossed a fragmentary bow in the general direction of Miss Wheeler before she linked arms with Scott and grinned up at him adoringly. "Old sweetie!"

He had no chance to return the greeting until Major and Minor, the boxers, had pawed and snuffled over him in ecstatic welcome. When they flopped down before the fireplace in panting relaxation he said solemnly, "Good afternoon, Niece."

"Stuffed shirt!" She thumped his chest with a grimy fist.

"A little more deportment, please!" Scott begged in mock disapproval while giving her arm a surreptitious squeeze. He could not quarrel with those who said Ellen should take more pride in her appearance, but how he would hate to see her grow up, he thought, patting her tangled brown hair flat. Her boyishly slender body was attired in an outgrown T-shirt, the sleeves the worse for stains of ink and chocolate. Her fashionably faded dungarees and cracked saddle-shoes were a bit more grubby than usual. But beautiful eyes shone startlingly blue in a face which caused Nancy's friends to predict that some day she would wake to find herself the mother of an acclaimed beauty.

Scott could see no echo of that thought in his sister's expression at the moment. Instead, from her perturbed frown, she was wondering what verbal bomb, loaded with gaucherie, her child would fling into the rarefied calm of convention. Scott appreciated her anxiety; Ellen and Lucy Wheeler never met without fireworks. Match to fuse; it was only a question of time . . .

Disregarding bitter experience Lucy made a point of ignoring the girl and resumed her first subject. "About that matter we were discussing, Nancy, before the interruption, I feel that I must *make* it my business to find out more about dear Uncle Philip's new tenant. In spite of Scott's remark I think I owe it to the Jordans to make certain *who* that girl *is!* If there is a mystery, as I suspect, I will let you know. My dear, if *I* had an attractive bachelor brother living next door to her—" A smile of sickening coyness left the sentence hanging in mid-air.

"What girl?" With the abrupt question Ellen flung herself across one end of the couch. Propping her chin on her hands she fixed Lucy Wheeler with an inquisitorial scowl.

Scott groaned inwardly. His niece had an abnormal development of the bump of curiosity, and in addition, an uncanny memory for faces and names. There had been occasions when the combination functioned to the embarrassment of her family, so that now they were solidly aligned against her attempts to investigate their personal concerns. To his relief, Nancy rather breathlessly forestalled an answer from Miss Wheeler.

"A secretary, dear, who has been engaged to catalogue the Jordan collection. Lucy, why don't you tell us more about Miss Carpenter's class? I do think Ellen ought to go somewhere this winter. She has been every season, until last year, when she wheedled her father over to her side and—"

Miss Wheeler interrupted with a contemptuous sniff. "Jim is too indulgent with the child! I quite agree with you, Ellen should go somewhere." The venom in her tone betrayed how shaken she was by the girl's relentless scrutiny. "At least, she could be taught how to enter and leave a living room!"

Ellen slid off the couch and patted back a yawn. "Leave a room, Cousin Lucy?" she drawled, blue eyes big with surprise. "But I *know!* I learned at camp. G'by now!" Like a released spring she whirled into a series of perfectly executed cartwheels which carried her to the door. The boxers sprang up and raked the rug into peaks and valleys as they tore after her. The trip disappeared, whooping and barking joyously.

Scott doubled up with laughter, but Nancy was crimson with mortification. Lucy Wheeler, speechless but glaring disapproval, flounced to the doorway, where she turned and drew breath for a parting shot.

Again Nancy anticipated her. "I hope you'll ignore Ellen's nonsense, Lucy, and stay for my birthday dinner."

Scott's spirits sank below zero at the woman's hesitation, rebounded when she shook her head. "I mustn't, thanks. Molly Todd is expecting me for supper at The Princess. I wouldn't *dare* disappoint Molly. Besides, I may find out more about that girl in Number Three. I have a feeling there's a story there!" Her glance flicked to Scott. "I *also* have a feeling that your brother knows more than he's telling."

She left Scott with a brand-new worry, born full-grown at her "there's a story there." Lucy had once or twice managed to sell an article on some social function to the newspapers, a tenuous connection which she liked to magnify into a journalistic career. Perhaps she did hobnob, as she often hinted, with editors and columnists in the newsrooms and at cocktail parties. Suppose her wagging tongue took to mentioning a "mystery girl"; how long would it be before some reporter grew curious? And then—?

Happily, Nancy derailed that ominous train of thought when she returned from speeding the parting guest and appealed to him in despair. "What am I going to do with Ellen? She is always at her worst with Lucy Wheeler. Now I suppose our peculiar cousin will parade my daughter's atrocious manners as a horrible example of the need of this dancing class!" She sighed. "Jimmy is actually coming home from college tonight to take his sister to a dance at the country club, hoping to interest her in social affairs, but I doubt if he has any success."

"She could make a show-stopping entrance, cart-wheeling across the dance floor," Scott laughed. "Don't worry, Nan, some fine day she will burst her chrysalis and emerge as a gorgeous heartbreaker—or a prim career woman, with horn-rimmed glasses. Her present rawness is only a passing phase."

"Old Dr. Pelham's Advice to Young Mothers!" Nancy bantered, joining him in front of the fire. Carefully she corrected the set of his tartan necktie and fastened another button of the gray sharkskin suit. It gave her opportunity to look up at him closely. "How come you are so wise about females and their 'phases'? Was Lucy right when she insinuated that you know that girl at The Princess?"

Scott avoided a direct answer. "If you're going to swallow everything the Salem Witch says—"

"Don't you believe it! Goodness knows, she's a pain in the neck with her perpetual snooping and gossip. Just the same, I'm beginning to wonder if there was a grain of truth in her last spiteful accusation." Nancy took the poker and gingerly prodded the fire, then impulsively set it aside and faced him. "Do you know anything about that girl?"

Scott shook his head. "I really don't."

"I don't mean ever to—to butt into your affairs, Scott, but I'm older than you, and may be able to see trouble where you don't. We're the only ones left of our family, and I worry about you." She laid a placating hand on his arm. "This isn't a lecture—but—you're so good-looking, and successful, that some girl who isn't good enough—isn't right for you—might—"

Scott patted the hand. "Don't be silly. As though worrying would get you anywhere. My dear sister, I have a hunch that when I see the *right* girl I'll go tearing after her without one instant's consideration as to whether she measures up to specifications for the Pelham family." He grinned. "That last is Happy's sarcasm, not mine."

She administered an affectionate shake. "You don't mean that—about your hunch! The Pelhams have too much background for you ever to marry an undesirable."

"You're a snob." Scott was still smiling.

"I am *not!*" And you needn't laugh at me; you have as much regard for respectability as I have. Hasn't he, Jim?" she appeared to her husband as he entered the room.

Selwyn kissed her and slipped a possessive arm about her waist. "Hasn't he what, Nancy?" He nodded to his brother-in-law. "How are you, Scott? Is she giving you the third degree, boy?"

"You saved me in the nick of time!" Scott declared solemnly. A grand guy, Jim Selwyn. The lines which problems of his own and of his clients had etched around keen eyes and drawn deep from nose to lips, the silvering of his dark hair at the temples, even the increasing fullness of his waistline would never alter the cheerful confidence of his youthful days.

"Call off your wife, Jim!" Scott begged. "She was launching her bimonthly cross-examination as to the state of my young affections. She's afraid that, as old age catches up with me, I'll marry something exciting, like a gangster's moll."

At the words his smile faded. He had meant to ridicule Nan's anxiety by offering the most absurd example that popped into his mind. But how absurd was it? Too much of the time his thoughts were centered on the most attractive girl he had ever met. And who was *she?* Supposing his suspicions to be correct, if she wasn't exactly a "gangster's moll," she was the sister of a criminal and a fugitive from justice. He shook his head in irritable bewilderment. Evidently Nancy's apprehension wasn't too far-fetched, after all.

SIX

SCOTT had no idea that his preoccupied silence extended to noticeable length until Jim Selwyn sank down on the couch, drawing Nancy beside him with the dry remark, "You'd better rest, dear. Your young friend seems to have fallen into a trance. I can't imagine what causes that sickly grin of his, but I might hazard a guess!"

Fortunately Scott was saved from further embarrassment by the entrance of Ellen, who squeezed onto the couch beside Jim. Perhaps in repentance for her recent misdemeanors she had made a complete change of costume, appearing now in a swirling, frosty-pink dress and short mandarin jacket of dusty rose.

Hugging her father, and dropping her voice to a shamelessly ingratiating purr, she pleaded, "Darling! you won't let Mother send me to dancing school, will you? It's a crime to waste hours scuffing around a stuffy old hall, when there's all outdoors to enjoy!"

"Dancing school?" Selwyn looked inquiringly at his wife. "Who is starting this one?"

"A Miss Carpenter. I believe I've heard of her, and if Lucy's report is true, she's a wonder. Like Miss Sophy Wackles in *The Old Curiosity Shop*, she teaches 'dancing, music and general fascination.' "

Ellen thought it wiser to switch the subject. "Cousin Lucy's all haired up over a new girl who's moved into

The Princess, Pappy! Suspects that she's not all she might be. I mean, *think* of it! she mimicked. "Uncle Phil must be absolutely *senile* to let her in there! Mother tried to shut her off, and Uncle Scott looked daggers, but there was no stopping her—"

Nancy intervened. "Ellen, will you ask Betty if she can hurry dinner? She is later than usual tonight. Jimmy will be raring to go when he gets here; you know how he hates to be late."

"Jeeps!" the girl muttered, slipping on her discarded pumps to limp away. "I could stand being so late we'd never get there! Mother," she wailed as an exit line, "why can't I wear loafers to a dance?"

"Exit the disturbing element," said Scott, amused.

Nancy breathed a troubled sigh. "I didn't realize, Jim, how much she took in of Lucy's babble about the secretary in the Jordans' apartment."

"The *Jordans'?*" Selwyn's hand lifted toward the breast pocket of his coat, but was at once withdrawn.

Only Scott noticed the involuntary gesture, and he with mild interest. Nancy's attention was on the fire, which she regarded with half-shut eyes. "Yes, the *Jordans'*," she repeated. "You sound surprised. Why? Do you think there is a mystery about this girl in Number Three, Jim? Do you know anything about her?"

"Know anything?" Selwyn leaned to take a cigarette from the table. "I didn't even know there was a secretary there. What's all the excitement? Philip Pepperell wouldn't let anyone in those houses unless he was satisfied that they were one hundred per cent." He lit the cigarette and fingered his lighter. "For heaven's sake, Nan, don't you be taken in by our Witch-cousin's foolishness. It's bad enough when she sets Ellen's curiosity complex bubbling."

Scott chuckled. "And how it can bubble! Remember that open house at Judge Graham's, when Ellen asked Lucy to show her the broom-stick she came on?"

"Please!" Nancy implored. "Let's forget it—"

"Soup's on!" announced Ellen's polite bellow from the dining room.

Selwyn raised an eyebrow at his wife. "Let us discuss this charm-and-dancing school further, my dear," he suggested with ominous gravity as he escorted her to the door.

The gay birthday dinner ended with blowing out candles, gorging on cake, and a round of healths. Afterward Scott and Nancy were alone in the living room, Ellen having allowed her brother to drag her away to the dance, and Jim Selwyn having left with what Scott considered a self-conscious mumble about a business appointment. An unusual proceeding, Scott thought, for a brother-in-law who was notoriously hard to budge from his hearth in the evening. Was Nancy wondering about his going, too? She sat quietly in the wing chair, thoughtful eyes on the fire.

Then she spoke. Coincidence? Or mental telepathy? For she answered his unspoken question. "A queer thing, that 'business' of Jim's. It almost seemed as though he were sneaking out."

"Whoa, Nan!" Scott advised in a shocked manner. "Don't distrust Jim!"

"*Distrust* him? I couldn't! We adore each other!"

"I know it. Maybe I've never told you, but Jim Selwyn is about my ideal of what a brother-in-law should be. And your devotion to one another," he went on soberly, "and to your children and home, steadies my faith in marriage when I see some people flunk out in the endurance test. Lord! The stuff I heard in New York about the Randolphs made me sick."

His sister nodded. "We've heard the stories about Bill Randolph, but I simply cannot believe them. Spiteful rumors, I hope. Of course he had too much money—too suddenly—when he came of age. Uncle Phil never approved of that but couldn't prevent it. He was guardian to Bill as well as to my Jim, you know, and he and Aunt Patty considered those two orphan boys the sons they never had."

She reached for the poker and prodded the fire unnecessarily, a habit of hers when meditating. "Bill married Sally Kendall before he graduated from Harvard, as soon as he came into his inheritance. That was years before Jim and I took the plunge."

"Have you seen Randolph lately?" asked Scott.

"Not since I married. I've never met his wife and

daughter, only the son Kendall. He entered Tech the year you were abroad, and Aunt Patty used to have him at her house for teas and week ends."

"The hospitable Pepperells, always on the lookout for lonely boys."

"And he," Nancy reminded, "was the son of one of their favorite lonely boys. Besides, young Kendall became the apple of Uncle Phil's eye on his first visit—he was equally mad about old guns. The hours those two spent in the Gun Room, discussing flintlocks and matchlocks and Lord knows what other kind of locks! I never understood half they were saying. But Ellen! She was a child, then, and couldn't have comprehended any of it, yet she would sit on Uncle Phil's lap or on a footstool between them, completely spellbound and turning from one to the other as though she were watching a tennis match. Sometimes I wondered whether she was fascinated by their talk or by Ken Randolph. She was at the hero-worshiping age."

"Sounds like quite a boy," Scott said. "How did he take to his father's philandering?"

"I doubt if he knew much about that," Nancy suggested, "because he was at college and then in the Army when the worst of it was going on. But his family life must have been unpleasant enough with a mother who indulged in frightful outbursts of temper on any excuse. Kendall was the only one who could handle her then. He had picked up some Down East expressions and accent on summer vacations, and his drawling 'Naow, Maw—steady daown!' usually jolted her into laughter."

The authentic Maine timbre she herself gave the words would have brought amused comment from Scott had she not looked so unhappy. He knew that she was contrasting the Randolph boy's dreary world with her own home, forever filled with love and laughter.

In the silence the deep-toned church bell across the green clanged its first stroke of the hour. The final jarring beat roused an ancient tall clock in the Selwyn hall to neglected duty; it wheezed, whirred and ran off nine echoes in apologetic haste.

When the house settled to quiet Scott asked, "If you

haven't seen the Randolphs for years, how do you know so much about them? From the Pepperells?"

"More through Bill's sister, Jane. When he was in college she used to come up to football games and dances, so I saw a lot of her, and we've corresponded faithfully ever since. Her letters were always full of 'little Ken's' doings; she adored the boy." Nancy stood up, moved to the mantel and needlessly straightened a silver candlestick. "Then Ken went in the Army, went overseas, saw action—" Her voice choked; in a moment she whispered, "Then word came that he was gone—nothing came back but a decoration."

"Hard luck," was all Scott could find to say.

Nancy sat down and lighted a cigarette with shaking fingers. "I can't help thinking of my own son—Poor Sally Randolph! She lost her boy in the war and now she has lost her daughter."

Scott paused in filling his pipe, remembering a girl's voice raised in passionate denunciation from Hapgood's conference room. "Lost her? Is she dead?"

"No, no. But she has left home for good, I'm afraid. As usual, her Aunt Jane is my news source. She wrote some time ago that she and Faith—that's the daughter—were sailing to Europe for an indefinite stay. Actually, fleeing the country so that Faith couldn't be forced to testify in the divorce proceedings."

"Hooray for her! I heard about that from Happy—"

The ring of the telephone in the hall interrupted.

"I'll go." Scott waved Nancy back to her chair and strolled out. Picking up the handset he announced with sonorous dignity, "The Selwyn residence," and winked at his sister. Then his face sobered, his voice went flat. "Yes, she's here. Just a minute." He put down the phone and returned to the living room. "Lucy!" he reported sourly.

With a grimace of distaste Nancy went to sit at the telephone table. "Yes, Lucy? . . . *What?* . . . Well—well, what of it? . . ."

Scott saw her knuckles whiten as she gripped the phone. She swallowed convulsively, turning to stare at him, wetting her lips before she said brusquely, "Of course I knew that he had met her! . . . But, Lucy, why *should* I tell you? . . . No, I won't! Good-by!"

She banged the handset in place and stood up. Her eyes were deeply, angrily blue as she faced Scott. "I was lying like a trooper! Do you know what that—that *witch* said? That she was coming down from the roof garden at The Princess just now, and—and she saw Jim! My Jim!"

Scott's nerves tingled as he leaped to a snap conclusion, but he produced a soothing smile. "Why get worked up over that? Probably he was checking on something for Uncle Phil. Jim handles all his legal business, doesn't he, including the leases at those buildings?"

"But Lucy said—or intimated—that he had come from the apartment of that—that girl we've been talking about. The mysterious female in Number Three! And Jim told us that he didn't even know there was a girl there!"

SEVEN

BY SUNDAY afternoon, when Scott walked past the Public Garden toward the Pepperells', his habitually sunny disposition was in partial eclipse. Added to a constantly gnawing perplexity over the girl in The Princess was anxiety about John Tinker. Late the night before, Tink had departed for an unnamed destination with the suddenness of a jet-propelled plane. And although Scott knew the reason for the expedition he was dubious as to its success.

On Scott's evening with the Selwyns Tink returned crestfallen from his Acton trip to report complete failure; only the day before, Ace Daley had broken camp and moved into Boston, leaving no forwarding address. For the next days Tink's spare time was spent in calling sports writers on the papers until he secured his friend's new location, and on Saturday night went off to run his restless fighter to earth. He had not returned when Scott went to bed at eleven.

Sometime during the night, however, the wanderer made a flying visit, for when Scott awoke he found a terse communiqué slipped under his bedroom door.

Evidently greatly excited, Tink wrote:

Captain — Just to tell you what this is about, I got some news from Ace about my girl and got to go away to check it.

Sorry to dump you this way, but I got to go.

J.T.

Below that in a feverish scrawl:

P.S. I took the cash for the grosseries—about $12—but the Frigadare is loaded. Sorry. J.T.

"The poor kid!" was Scott's immediate reaction. "Why didn't he wake me up and ask for money?" A foolish question he realized; John Tinker would never disturb his captain on a personal matter. "Doesn't tell where he's headed—just away," he muttered. He turned the note over. Nothing further, only a series of penciled phone numbers, the trail of Tink's quest for his friend Daley. His new address was there, too; at least *17 Breen St.* was scrawled under the last phone number.

Scott tossed the paper on his worktable. "I certainly wish him luck," he said aloud. "Now that he's in good shape again, finding his long-lost love will have him walking on air."

Reviewing the situation as he approached the Pepperells' home on Mount Vernon Street, he decided that Tink's chance of success, after so many years, was slim indeed. Gladly Scott shelved his problems at sight of the Selwyn car pulling up to the curb ahead of him.

Scarcely had it stopped when Ellen leaped out like an arrow springing from a bow. Flinging a careless, "Hi, Scotty!" in his direction she raced up the iron-railed steps and attacked both knocker and bell.

Nancy Selwyn wore a puzzled frown when Scott opened the car door. "I'm a mean-minded creature," she told him, "and unjust to my offspring, no doubt.

But just *why* did Ellen come here so willingly today? As a rule she rebels against dressing up on Sunday afternoon, even though she really does love Uncle Phil and Aunt Patty—and their spreads—but today there wasn't a word of protest."

Her husband echoed the sentiment as he joined Scott and Nancy on the sidewalk. "Unjust or not, any time our young juvenile delinquent acts semihuman I get suspicious. Look at her! What is she cooking up now?"

At the Pepperell door, Ellen was whispering excitedly to their elderly Negro butler, who legally rejoiced in the fantastic name of General Wilson. Thirty years before when the Pepperells engaged him, Aunt Patty insisted that she could never accustom herself to ordering, "Serve coffee in the drawing room, General," so they would rechristen him "Gerald" for domestic use. The tall Negro bowed with childlike obedience, and with equally childlike ingenuity simply failed to hear any remark addressed to "Gerald." Such a battle of wills being too inconvenient to endure, the Pepperells learned to call for "General" without a qualm, and to depend on him without question.

Now he detached himself from the eager girl to bow with dignified courtesy. "Good afternoon, Miss Nancy. Proud to see you here, Mr. Jim, and Mr. Scott. Tea will be served in the Gun Room." Very like a general he was, gray haired but straight of back and shoulders, as he led them along the hall. At a doorway he paused and announced ceremoniously, "Mr. and Mrs. Selwyn. Mr. Pelham. *And* Miss Ellen."

The affectionate emphasis on the last name made Scott smile in sympathy as he entered the room where Philip Pepperell's hobby was enshrined. Viewed as a whole, and discounting the effect of an armory of weapons displayed on its walls, it was a room to delight the eye. Its graceful proportions had been conceived by a master architect of Beacon Hill's lush Georgian period, but the décor was pure Pepperell.

As one of his many enterprises Old Pep had chanced on a pile of seasoned cherry wood, originally cut and laid aside for the manufacture of church pews. Captivated by the delicately grained tawny surface, he lined the sitting room with floor to ceiling boards, and from two of the widest formed a single panel above the original fireplace of rough red brick. Even the interior shutters of the tall windows were fashioned from cherry, their color melting into the deeper cinnamon curtains and the cushions on the long window seat.

But Pepperell had not left the paneling bare; on all sides, muskets, rifles and pistols from every period in the long history of gunpowder hung one above the other, or stood upright in racks, arranged so that their gleaming barrels of varied lengths resembled miniature pipe organs.

In keeping with the pioneer air of the collection, random-width flooring, scrupulously waxed by General, formed a fitting background for the twin braided rugs whose dominant geometric deigns were a rich forest green, the scattered pine and maple captain's chairs, and two green denim wing chairs set like Darby and Joan on either side of the hearth.

From one of these chairs darted Philip Pepperell to meet his guests. White hair bristling, blue eyes dancing with pleasure, he shook hands with Jim and Nancy, nearly drove Scott's breath from his lungs with a stabbing forefinger and chucked Ellen under the chin with a wicked leer. All this with a running fire of welcome, ending, "Elly, if you can act like a lady for five minutes, General has something to show you—but you've got to behave!"

Aunt Patty, enthroned in the other wing chair, made a perfect foil for her strenuous, talkative husband—slender and dainty, where he was chunky and angular of body and mind, soft-voiced yet compelling attention, while he must roar to assert authority. White hair made a flowerlike halo above her scarcely lined face; his wiry pompadour reared up from a wrinkled, russet face like the crest of a fighting cock.

Guns to the right of her, guns to the left of her, thought Scott, and Uncle Phil discharging a volley a minute—yet her personality dominates the room, and everyone in it. She sat placidly serving tea, and although she wore a simple gray silk dress and no jewelry except a diamond cross on a hair-thin platinum chain, she suggested to him—not for the first time—Queen Victoria presiding at a function in Buckingham Palace. . . She did have the advantage of presiding at a carved teakwood table whose appointments held fast Ellen's hungry gaze and drew an approving smile from her father. Over a steady flame the enormous tea urn, encrusted with the garlands of fruit and blossoms dear to the heart of the Victorian silversmith, emitted a promising jet of steam. Flanking it, silver platters bore piles of sturdy sandwiches, cookies and frosted cakes. A smaller brother to the tea table offered a decanter of sherry, the Pepperells' only concession to any modern-minded guest who felt that "afternoon tea" should consist of alcoholic refreshment.

Ellen, mindful of her uncle's warning, tended solicitously to the wants of all. When she had served the last cup of tea and glass of sherry she arched an inquiring eyebrow at her host. Uncle Phil nodded approval. Daintily, then, she appropriated two sandwiches in each hand and minced from the room.

No sooner had she left than Patience Pepperell gave Scott's arm a fond pat and asked eagerly, "Have you seen the girl at the Jordans'?"

If, with that ladylike gesture, she had dropped a bomb in his lap he would have been less disconcerted. He spilled some sherry, wondering if his hair might be standing up, in King Hamlet's phrase, like quills upon the fretful porpentine. In spite of his efforts there was a tremor in his voice when he asked, as though surprised, "Have you sublet the Jordan apartment, Uncle Phil?"

Perhaps that gentleman was as startled as Scott. He braced his back against the mantel, twirled his glass and rubbed his long nose violently. "No, I haven't sublet it. Not exactly," he evaded, and in the next breath confessed, by demanding testily, "How'd you know?"

"Mrs. Beddle told Tink that someone had come in there to list their books. 'A real snazzy number,' to quote Mrs. B. I saw a girl on their balcony the other night, so I suppose she's the one."

"Is that the first you've seen of her?" jeered Uncle Pep. "Boy, you're slowing up! Plenty of people have beaten you to it; that Lucy Wheeler has been buzzing around me for information like a human gadfly. All I can tell anyone is what I told her—the woman was authorized by *them* to catalogue their collection." He sipped his sherry with deliberation, as though the subject was closed.

Nancy studied him over the rim of her teacup. "The lady must have made an immediate impression, if you installed her in their rooms."

"*I* didn't!" Pepperell growled. "*They* cabled instructions—said she was to live there. She appeared at my office one morning. I—she—she presented her credentials. I liked her at once; hadn't talked to her five minutes before I felt I'd known her for years." Casually he drained his glass. "A very attractive personality—if I'm any judge. Although," he added musingly, "she didn't seem happy. Lonely, perhaps; it's no joke to land friendless in a strange city, even if you have a job waiting. As a matter of fact, my dear," he said to his wife, "I felt sorry for her, and invited her for tea today."

Scott repressed an exclamation of astonishment, but the others chorused anticipation, and it seemed to him that Uncle Phil's eyes glinted with deviltry when he punctured their balloon of enthusiasm with a dry, "She isn't coming." Carefully he set his empty glass on the mantel and selected an anchovy sandwich. "She turned quite pale as she refused the invitation, politely but firmly. Got a will of her own, if I'm any judge."

"Most young women have, these days," Mrs. Pepperell reminded him. "Did she tell you anything about herself?"

"I didn't grill her!" snapped Old Pep. "I'm no Lucy Wheeler!" Prodding the plate of sandwiches with a bony finger he demanded testily, "Anything here but that darned fish paste? Almost skinned my tongue!" Again there was a noticeable twinkle in his eye at his guests' unconcealed impatience. "Well, she did mention that she's only doing this secretarial work to earn a living while she tries to become a writer."

"Writer? Not an artist?" exclaimed Jim Selwyn. "I

thought—" The sentence ended in a mumble as he met his wife's startled gaze.

"Go on, Jim." Nancy was carefully casual. "Can you tell us anything about this mystery at The Princess?"

"What *mystery?* That girl? Just because she is a beauty—" As before, he stopped and hastily drained his glass of sherry.

"Then you've seen her?" his wife probed sweetly.

"I have heard comments," he parried. "Scott, fill my glass while you're at that bottle, will you?"

Shaking his head in silent sympathy, Scott complied. Old Jim had never been an accomplished dissembler; he must be deeply involved to act so upset; imagine calling the elegant cut-glass decanter a bottle! Were he *and* Uncle Phil mixed up in the affair?

The suspicion was not lessened when Pepperell shattered the awkward silence with a burst of talk. "Writer—that's it. A budding author, b'gad, because she asked if the apartment was near our public library, and seemed to know a little about historic Boston. Hmm, we got quite chatty over historic Boston, so I told her about my guns"—he looked fondly around the room—"and how I collected 'em while my wife collected young men whom we called 'Patty's boys.' She seemed to warm up at that, so I asked her to tea again." His grunt was admission of defeat. "She thanked me, and said, 'If you are satisfied that the arrangement with the Jordans is in order, please just forget about me.' "

Another unpleasant jolt for Scott. In almost those words the unseen girl in the Pullman had beseeched the porter. If she was trying to escape notice, why arouse suspicion everywhere?

Jim Selwyn proved the point when, with a worried frown, he suggested, "An unusual request. Remember, Uncle Phil, there are plenty of sharks who wouldn't be particular how they got their hands on some of the Jordans' choice items."

"She only meant I wasn't to bother about her," protested Old Pep. "You're all the darndest suspicious people—"

The rest was smothered under a whoop of laughter from the hall and a clatter of feet. Ellen catapulted into the room making frantic snatches at something trailing on the floor. In vain. A brown monkey bounced across the room, his leash whipping behind him, and sprang lightly onto the tea table. Sandwiches, cakes and lumps of sugar flew in every direction. The animal followed them to the rug and gave an inspired imitation of a vacuum cleaner.

"Isn't he darling?" cooed Ellen. "General said I could play with him awhile."

"What has caused this sudden invasion of Boston by monkeys?" Scott demanded of the room in general. "He's the second I've seen."

Selwyn smiled at his wife. "The mystery is solved, Nan. Now we know who telephoned Ellen this morning, and why she came so willingly."

Uncle Phil nodded. "I heard General on the phone: 'Great Day of Jubilee, missy—come see what we got here!' " When the monkey switched his leash out of the girl's hand to prospect further under the table Pepperell barked, "Watch out, Ellen! Hang on to him before he breaks anything!" At her futile grab for the leash he ordered, "Get hold of him, I tell you! Quick!" and slapped the arm of his chair for emphasis.

At the pistollike crack the monkey stood erect to stare. Even to his tiny brain it was clear that the noisy, red-faced man was upset. The permanent melancholy of the hairy visage wrinkled to greater sadness. He flung himself into Pepperell's lap, gripped his jacket with little paws and protruded black rubbery lips to press his cheek with a loud, sucking kiss.

For a split second surprise and outraged dignity turned Old Pep to stone. A burst of laughter from the enthralled audience roused him to action. "Get the beast off!" he roared, flailing his arms.

The animal vaulted easily to the mantel, but his leash tangled with a threshing hand and dragged him off balance. With a squeak of alarm he groped for any hold to keep his place and by bad luck fastened on the flintlock gun over the fireplace. Supported only by wooden pegs, it followed him to the hearth with a crash. The monkey squeaked again, bounded clear and flew to refuge in Ellen's arms, where he buried his head under her chin and uttered soft sounds of remorse—or amusement.

The amazed stillness which had greeted the animal's first appearance was noisy in comparison to the petrified horror of the present moment. To touch one of Old Pep's treasures was sacrilege! Even Aunt Patty's perennial calm broke in an audible gasp of dismay.

Scott crossed to the fireplace and picked up the gun. His movement broke the spell.

"O-o-oh!" moaned Ellen. "Is it broken? Oh, Uncle Phil, I'm so sorry—"

Scott interrupted, sensing the flood of tears forecast by her tragic tone. "Ellen, take your pal back where you got him."

"Yes, *please!*" The choked prayer was Nancy's contribution. As her daughter trailed dejectedly away she stammered "Uncle Phil—I—don't—just don't know how to apologize—"

"Skip it, Nan," Scott ordered with a brother's directness. "She didn't do anything except bring the little devil in here. She wanted us to see him, and I don't blame her—he is cute." He dusted the gun and scanned it for damage. "Didn't hurt it, Uncle Phil, as far as I can tell."

Pepperell sighed with relief. "Hang it up again, will you? First time it's been off that wall for years. I guess the last time was when young Kenny Randolph was here; he was the only one I ever let handle any of 'em." He scanned the crowded walls and shook his head. "Too bad Kenny didn't come back; I've added some beauties to the collection. He'd have loved 'em."

A moving shadow in the hall caught his eye. "Come in, Elly, nobody's going to eat you," he called. "But don't bring that imp!"

"I won't," was her fervent promise. "Honestly, I never *dreamed* he'd hurt anything. But you frightened him, Uncle Phil!"

"I should have strangled him!"

Ellen giggled. "Didn't you *love* it when he kissed you?" Wisely she waited for no reply but knelt beside the tea table, explaining, "Dizzy left his cap here. His name is Dizzy, General says; isn't that darling? Here it is! Dizzy will be so relieved!" She skipped out of the room, swinging in her hand a diminutive overseas cap.

Scott experienced all the sensations of a knockout punch. While the company resumed the even tenor of a social gathering he, like a prize fighter floored by an unexpected blow, struggled to collect his scattered wits. One day he saw a monkey trailed on a leash by a man who, he felt sure, had tossed a warning note onto his balcony; today a monkey was installed in the Pepperell home. The same monkey; Scott would have staked a substantial wager on that. While it was possible that there were two of them in this section of the city—both small and brown and lively—it would be stretching coincidence to absurdity to believe that each wore an identical cap.

"Aunt Patty," he demanded, "where in blazes did that animal come from?"

"Thereby hangs a tale," she said—and blushed when the others roared with laughter. "Oh! I made a joke, didn't I! But it's quite true in the way I meant it. Wait until I give you all some tea, and I'll make it strong. We all need stimulant after what happened!"

"*I* need it," agreed Uncle Phil cheerfully. "Sherry won't fill the bill at this point! It's a wonder I didn't have a stroke. Over the years, 'Patty's boys' have presented her with about everything, but this latest offering threatens to wreck the household."

"I gathered from the remarks," said Jim, "that General is the proud owner?"

"A lawyer shouldn't pay attention to hearsay evidence," Old Pep advised. "General is one of the victims. He is longsuffering, but he's near the end of his rope."

"So is Susie, the cook," Aunt Patty added, handing him a cup of tea as dark as coffee. "Dizzy escaped from his cage yesterday and hid in the washing machine. When she went to put in a wash he leered at her—her own words—through the glass door. She screamed her head off. Then he tracked dirty footprints over the plates and napkins General had laid out in the pantry."

Scott fidgeted, impatient to learn the origin of the monkey, but unwilling to betray noticeable curiosity by repeating his question. To his relief, Nancy pressed the subject;

"But *where* did you get him, Aunt Patty?"

"Well—" Patience Pepperell settled comfortably to the story. "You remember, Nancy, that nice soldier, Albert Daley, who came here several times on leave during the war? A sweet boy. Do you know, he took the trouble to write me his bread-and-butter letter, all the way from the front!" She sipped her tea. "I know he must have had a nice mother."

"And she'd be glad he remembered his manners," Nancy agreed. Refusing to allow her aunt to wander from the main topic she prodded, "Did he bring the monkey?"

Aunt Patty beamed. "He appeared yesterday morning with the animal in a cage and asked us to keep it for a few days. I didn't recognize him until he told me his name: he's grown older of course—more mature—and—and harder. But he was as sweet as ever—"

"Let me tell it," growled Pepperell, "you get lost in admiration! This Albert had quite a story," he assured them. "Got captured in some battle—told me where, but I can't pronounce it—and was in a prison camp for months. And, by the Lord, he found his own brother in the same camp! How about that? They weren't from the same outfit; in fact Albert hadn't seen him for several years; but they end up together. The brother was in bad shape, though, Al told us. Shell shock? Something like that?" He looked inquiringly at Scott.

"Shell shock, battle fatigue—call it anything. It's hell!"

Aunt Patty murmured, "I'm afraid he still has something a little wrong with his mind. Albert's voice was quite gruff with tenderness when he spoke of him."

"Anyway," Pepperell went on, "they escaped somehow, just before the war ended. He didn't give any details or clear account of what they'd been doing since. Seeing the world, I judge. Mentioned different countries, you know, but nothing definite."

Scott thrust his hands deep into his pockets to keep from waving them in exasperation. Forcing a casual tone he asked, "And where did they pick up our friend Dizzy, with the long tail?"

"He didn't mention that, only explained that he bought it for his brother; hoping it would get him interested, give him something to look after, keep him occupied when Al was busy."

"Busy at what?" Scott demanded.

"Didn't tell us that, either. But the brother had been restless and unhappy, and the monkey did seem to help that."

Scott hammered another question. "Then why is he depriving him of this charming companion?" Too late he was conscious of his sister's speculative regard.

"You sound," she marveled, "as implacable as Jim when he has a witness writhing under cross-examination."

Aunt Patty rushed to his defense. "That is Scott's way when he is interested, Nancy. Albert explained that the monkey was very unpopular where he lives. He gets out in the hall, hides behind a newel post and jumps on the tenants when they come upstairs. Some of them objected."

"The understatement of the year!" chuckled Uncle Phil. "*All* of them objected—and at the top of their lungs. Don't blame 'em!"

"So," Aunt Patty continued serenely, "Albert asked us to keep his pet here until he found another apartment. He assured us that it was gentle as a kitten and quite harmless." Pepperell snorted, eying his cherished flintlock. "Well, dear," she reminded, "this is the first real accident we've had. Oh—and a perfectly dreadful thing was that Albert warned us to keep the monkey out of sight because several of the people at his rooming house had sworn to kill it." She turned. "Did you speak, Scott?"

What she had heard was his involuntary grunt when she told of the request for secrecy. "I was wondering," he replied thoughtfully, "if I remembered this Albert Daley. I met some of your boys here." For a moment he concentrated on his impressions of the man with the monkey outside The Pilgrim. "Is he short with a droop to his shoulders?"

Pepperell gave an explosive snort and Aunt Patty exclaimed, "Goodness, no! You're thinking of someone else. Albert has nary a droop anywhere; he's quite burly and carries himself with bullish assurance."

"Had a shiner, too," Old Pep added. "Old, but still a beaut!"

"Yes, he did," sighed Aunt Patty. "I'm afraid he'd been fighting. You know," she announced with ladylike horror, "he was my idea of what a prize fighter looks like! But what a dreadful thing for me to say!" She hurriedly switched to a more suitable subject for conversation. "Jim, you've hardly said a word. What's new in the legal world?"

EIGHT

". . . MY IDEA of what a prize fighter looks like." The words echoed in Scott's mind as he walked home, glad of solitude in which to marshall the evidence thrust on him at the Pepperells' that afternoon. So the monkey was owned by an ex-soldier who looked like a boxer? Making due allowance for the fact that any man with a black eye would suggest that to demure Aunt Patty, it was still thought-provoking. At the time Scott had been tempted to ask if the man had parti-colored eyes, and restrained himself to avoid probing by his already curious relatives. It was pretty obvious that Aunt Patty's "sweet young man" must be Ace Daley, Tinker's friend—

Cometlike, the discovery flashed a trail of light across his mind. The man with the monkey under Scott's balcony was probably Ace's brother. A disturbed mental condition might contribute to the listless manner and droop Scott had noticed. But granting all this, and assuming that the message thrown to him had been intended for the girl, where was the connection between a prize fighter, his deranged brother and gorgeous Maureen Tenny?

"Whoa, stupid!" Scott chided himself. "And slow

down! You don't even know that she *is* Maureen Tenny!"

Speculation continued while he waited at a crosswalk for the lights to change. Twilight made the Common a shadowy prairie stretching to the clifflike buildings on Tremont Street, where golden windows and neon lights glowed and winked, but Scott saw only his jumbled puzzle. Jim Selwyn, now—where did he fit in? Perhaps Bill Randolph had sent Jim to the girl's apartment. The two men had been close friends years ago. If Maureen Tenny's late employer learned—or suspected—that she was in Boston he might ask Jim to contact her. But earlier Scott had decided that Randolph was instrumental in placing her with the Jordans. . . .

Still fruitlessly theorizing he entered his apartment, hung up his coat and called, "Tink!" before he remembered the little man's absence. "Hope he isn't on as much of a wild-goose chase as I'm carrying on," Scott grumbled. "But I'm going to untangle it somehow. Not in here, though." He passed up the topcoat in favor of his long-discarded marine jacket, as more suited to the hand-to-hand struggle he meant to have with his problem, and took the elevator to the roof.

From the car he stepped into the sunroom which occupied half the top of the two buildings, with another elevator opposite his for the use of Princess tenants. The room itself, softly lighted and gay with colorful tile floor and scatter rugs and an even more polychrome assemblage of cushioned chairs and lounges, eased the tension in his mind. Too much so, Scott felt; warmth, the fragrance of violets and gardenias massed along the southern windows did not fit his mood.

He opened the door to the roof garden and stepped out into a maze of moonlight and shadows. The gracefully curved steel framework, where in summer an azure canopy was stand-in for the sky, and the Italian blue trellises with their masses of ivy cast grotesque shapes of inky black across the cream-tiled floor. Picture-tiled, too, with naïvely painted Dutch scenes, was the end wall which concealed the elevator housing. In the wall a niched fountain stood waiting to drip its crystal thread into the pool below—when summer came again. Tiled paths led between flower beds covered with evergreen boughs to protect the bulbs set deep to bloom in the spring. Only the wrought-iron furniture with cushions of plastic defied the calendar.

A gust of wind from the river rustled the dry branches and snatched the door from Scott's hand. It banged shut. An exclamation, quickly suppressed, drew his attention to a corner of the garden. Silhouetted against the interlaced steel railing and the sky stood—the girl from Number Three! With quickening pulse Scott was certain of her identity before she turned so that the light from the sunroom showed her white face.

In an instant he was beside her. Below the gold and white kerchief binding her hair, dark eyes in their fringe of black lashes were wide with alarm. She put a gloved hand on the railing as though to brace herself.

Scott hastened to reassure her. "Did I frighten you? I'm sorry. I'm your neighbor in The Pilgrim."

Color swept back into her cheeks, her eyes lost their startled look. Her voice registered relief as she explained, "It was that army coat which s-surprised me. I used to—there was someone I cared for—"

As she hesitated, before Scott's inner eye flashed a line from the newspaper account of the bond robbery; Walter Tenny had been an officer. Another fragment of the puzzle which seemed to fit, although it irked him to find it. Would he ever be able to forget that story—a smear of dirty black type on dirty paper? Would she, poor hunted girl? His voice was tender as he sympathized, "Tough luck that you had to go through that anxiety so young. I hope that 'someone' came through all right."

When she looked away and turned up the collar of her long coat without answering, he groped for a commonplace subject. The best he could offer was a light, "By the way, have you decided whether that cryptic message was for you—and genuine—or merely a Bostonian's flair for eccentricity?"

"Evidently *you* have a flair for questioning strangers."

He flushed hotly, but preserved his casually friendly manner. "Strangers—you and I? Not a chance! This roof garden is sufficient introduction, because Old Pep—as some of us disrespectfully dub our landlord—allows no tenant in these apartments who could possibly be *persona non grata*. And, after all, we've met before. I had to offer *you* that message, didn't I, since I knew it wasn't for me?"

The girl's lips widened in a tentative smile, only a trace of disapproval lingered in her eyes. "I suppose you are right, but—"

"Still bothered by the proprieties? Then we will go through the proper formalities," he proposed, and gestured toward the sky, "with the stars as witnesses. Convention, of course, requires that the gentleman be presented to the lady, so—may I present—"

"I know who you are," she protested, still smiling. She drew a quick breath and said hurriedly, "I am—Maureen Tenny."

At that voluntary declaration all his suspicions and doubts evaporated; what possible mystery could there be about one who so frankly acknowledged her name? Before he could speak she rushed on:

"And you are Scott Pelham, architect extraordinary, former captain of Marines, and 'Dearie, you should see his decorations!' " The last was delivered in imitation of Martha Beddle's throaty Highland burr. The girl lifted wide eyes to study him, one finger tapping her full red lips in pretended reflection. "I don't see any ribbons on that jacket, but I understand there are two Purple Hearts, a Silver Star—which isn't given for excellence in paper work—and—"

"Hold everything!" Scott growled in embarrassment. "Don't believe all that Mrs. B. tells you; she's apt to gild the lily where her affections are concerned."

"You are equally apt to misquote, aren't you?" she chided lightly. "Try to remember—one *paints* the lily—*gilds* refined gold."

"So one does!" Scott experienced an inner glow at her increasing friendliness. He leaned beside her, elbows on the railing. In companionable silence they viewed the city, from nearby shadowy buildings to the horizon outlined against the pink radiance of more distant lights. The moon silvered sloping roofs and pointing steeples. Almost overhead blazed Orion, mighty hunter of mythology, his stars seeming nearer and brighter than the man-made imitations which jeweled the water front below.

Irresistibly Scott's eyes were drawn to the girl, and he pursed his lips in a soundless whistle. Maybe, he conceded, it was the moon's influence, but each time he saw her he was more impressed. This, though, was hardly the moment to give way to impulse.

Aloud, and with commendable restraint, he remarked, "What a view from up here!"

"All of Boston—old and new," she agreed.

"Some of the old so little changed," Scott mused. "See that long shadow on the water at the foot of the Basin? That might be one of the British men-of-war past which Paul Revere rowed stealthily on his way to Lexington and Concord."

"And, being a Bostonian," the girl added with an impish grin, "I'll wager that Mr. Revere looked back on the sleeping town—hardly more than a village then—and thought, 'What a wonderful city!' "

"How right he was—if he compared it to the scattered huts which made up Boston a hundred and fifty years before that," Scott reminded. His face was sober. "Remember, he and his friends believed it was worth fighting for. If they hadn't—how would we be living today?"

She raised her gloved hands. "I concede defeat. But it isn't a fair contest; you probably had to recite Longfellow's poem in school!"

"No, only learn it by heart. We had a teacher who couldn't stand amateur treatment of the classics. *He* used to tell it—not recite it—and send icy chills up the spine of *one* ten-year-old!" Scott touched her arm, pointing to distant Charlestown looming against a backdrop of gray mist. "I told you some things haven't changed," he said. His voice dropped a tone, vibrant with feeling and memories:

"It was twelve by the village clock,
When he crossed the bridge into Medford town.
He heard the crowing of the cock,

And the barking of the farmer's dog,
And felt the damp of the river fog
That rises after the sun goes down."

The girl was silent a moment, before she said softly, "That chased a few shivers along *my* nerves. You should be a poet yourself."

"Under favorable circumstances," Scott dared an admiring look, "I might be." At once, lest she resent the implication, he waved toward the sky. "What a star-studded show! When I build my model city, the roofs of the houses will be their living rooms—glass-enclosed for comfort, of course—and my model citizens will look upward. Faith from the heavens will be the fashion."

"Then you will create a sane, optimistic people."

"You talk," said Scott uncertainly, "as though you were a thousand years old, Princess!"

" 'Princess?' "

He laughed, not sorry the name had slipped out. "Yes—Princess. I've thought of you by that name since the first day I saw you, crossing the lounge downstairs, and christened you after your residence. But to fit the name, you should be young, carefree, gay."

"Should I?" Chin on hand she stared out across the city. "A girl who stands alone in the world soon loses her exuberant spirit. Mine flew out the window some time ago."

"Alone? But, surely you have your—"

"Suppose," she cut in, "we change the subject back to the stars, to whom I always bring my problems. As you plan for your model citizens—look up to the stars, and try to feel depressed. It simply can't be done!"

In spite of the gentle tone, Scott was fully aware that he had been slapped and stood in a corner. Evidently any reference to her family or background was out of line. He managed a conciliatory laugh, charging, "Who's quoting now? You cribbed that weighty observation from an editorial in today's paper; I saw it, too."

"I deny the accusation!" she retorted with quick resumption of her gayer mood. "Although it is possible that I did remember it from some reading. Too bad! I thought it original—and quite clever. But I didn't read it in your editorial—I haven't even looked at a newspaper since—since I arrived in Boston."

Mentally Scott filled in that broken sentence—"since I heard of my brother's trouble." She need not have worried; the Boston papers were too occupied with their own local bandits and muggings to give space to any but top New York crimes.

But why should all that matter to him now? Here he was in the moonlight, with the girl he had waited for most of his life, having a wonderful time as long as he kept his mind cleared of doubts and unanswerable questions. Better make the most of this enchanted hour.

Smiling, he faced her. "My ignorant princess! Do you read anything?"

"Do I? Could anyone live for even a day surrounded by the Jordan collection and not become a bookworm? Just between you and me—and the stars, of course—when I come across a treasure—why, they have one of the original Audubon portfolios; the most beautiful paintings of birds!" Laughing at her own enthusiasm she sat on a vividly striped glider in that corner of the garden. "Won't you join me, sir?" she invited demurely. "If I bore you with talk of my work you can always flee."

"I am anything but bored!" Scott needed no urging to take his place beside her. He leaned back so that he could watch her face, delectable in the moonlight, even though she was frowning as she rummaged in a plaited leather bag slung from her shoulder.

"Here!" She produced a cigarette case. "I understand —again from our mutual friend, Mrs. Beddle—that you smoke a pipe like a chimney in Glasgow, but will you have one of these?"

"Pipe while I'm working—cigarettes on a date." He waited apprehensively for her to crush the romantic suggestion, busying himself with opening the case. Either she missed it or preferred to ignore it. Relieved, he lit a cigarette apiece. "So you found the Audubon book?" He picked up the thread of her monologue. "Notice its condition?"

"Some of the pages are stained."

"Peach-plum jam," he confessed gravely. "One of my earliest recollections of the dear old ladies is being allowed to look at the 'Big Bird Book' when I visited their Duxbury home."

"And you smeared jam on it? I could shoot you! You see, next to books, birds are my ruling passion. Have you ever been to Franklin Park?" The question came so abruptly that Scott could not follow her train of thought. "Or," she scoffed, "are you one of those Bostonians who has never bothered to visit even Bunker Hill?"

"Certainly I have been to Franklin Park!" Preferring to duck the second question he answered the first with pretended indignation. "Uncle Phil took me there on my tenth birthday."

"And never since? I knew it! *I* have gone there repeatedly, on half holidays from my clerical labors; it takes an outlander to appreciate your city. Especially the aviary, with every sort of bird, from stodgy, plodding ducks to exotic tropical marvels, attracted me."

Scott was worried, remembering the warning note. If she was being watched, regular trips to the zoo could bring disaster. She shouldn't wear a beaten path in any one direction. If only she would allow him to advise her—help her—"Princess," he began.

"Pilgrim!" The retort was tinged with amusement. "You tagged me from the house in which I live, I'll return the compliment. It has such a dependable, friendly sound, that name *Pilgrim*." She was silent a moment; eyes and voice were turbulent with suppressed emotion when she admitted, "It is humiliating to acknowledge it, but—I'm so horribly lonely that I'm ready to grasp the first friendly hand that's offered."

Scott's heart leaped with eagerness, but he said nothing, only extended his right hand. With a soft laugh she placed hers in it. He tightened his clasp. "Princess," he whispered, "you can count on me for anything. Tell me about your troubles, and whatever I can do—"

The girl twisted her hand free and jumped to her feet. Back against the rail she faced him, alarm dilating her eyes. "You misunderstood me! I am not looking for a champion. There is no trouble *you* can do anything about." She pressed tense fingers against her eyes, drew a long, shivering breath, before she continued more steadily, "I'm not usually so silly, but tonight you caught me in a depressed mood. I don't believe I've talked to half a dozen people since I've been in Boston, and you were so friendly—"

Scott stood beside her. "Others would be, if you'd let them. Why not go out more, meet people—"

She shook her head, and the intriguing curve of her lips thinned to a line of determination. Her eyes on the stars, she said slowly, "I decided on a course because I thought it was the right thing to do, and just because it is harder than I expected is no excuse for quitting! I'm not the passive type, Pilgrim; I'll battle the current with my last breath, and if I'm swept under it won't be because I've given up the fight. There's always a chance to win out, even when things seem hopeless."

To Scott she had never looked more a princess than in this moment of gallant defiance. And never, he thought, less in the mood for impertinent, although well-intentioned, questions. Gravely he saluted her. "A truce between fighters, then. We are all fighting for something, aren't we? For our lives, for a living—for ideas or ideals. The weakling goes down to defeat, or compromises to save himself—and loses after all. The strong fight on, in spite of failure."

He felt himself flushing under the girl's steady gaze. "I don't often mount the pulpit," he apologized with a wry grin. "Evidently you do something to a normally tongue-tied pilgrim. But now I do solemnly promise to go on being friendly, and swear off being inquisitive, if you'll come back and sit down." Although he made the vow in good faith he had a premonition that it would prove worthless; never again could he ignore anything which seemed to concern this lovely girl. Whether she wanted a champion or not, she had a willing one in Scott Pelham.

"Truce accepted." She returned to her seat and offered a contrite smile. "I must be overtired—"

"Think nothing of it! Anyone as nosy as your pilgrim would irritate a saint." Scott settled back comfortably. "Let's see, we were at Franklin Park, weren't we? I told you Uncle Phil took me."

"Is he the 'Old Pep' you mentioned?"

"Yes, Uncle Phil Pepperell. He and Aunt Patty—short for Patience—are like parents to me now; mine died years ago."

The girl whispered, almost to herself, "Losing one's parents is the most tragic—" The murmur faded to silence.

"You've met Mr. Pepperell, I believe," Scott said.

"I have indeed. A really wonderful person, with his delightful enthusiasm for the rusty old guns decorating his office—"

"*Please!*" Scott admonished, lifting a cautioning finger. "Antique firearms is the term. He collects them."

"I know. But his taste in office decorations is a little unusual. Guns, and queer pictures—an old tumbledown shack which might be the first mill built in America, and a group of odd-looking people grubbing around a field or pasture—"

This time Scott's interruption was a whoop of laughter. "Don't ever mention his projects to Old Pep in those colorful but contemptuous terms!" he warned, enjoying the smoother progress of their friendship. "I see that I must indoctrinate you with the System. Philip Pepperell—notice the double P—invests his money only in projects which bear those same mystic initials." Humorously he described the golden rise of Perfect Paper for Particular People.

"You're making this up!" she accused with an incredulous giggle.

"Cross my heart! You mentioned the people grubbing in a field. Another memento of success. Uncle Phil joined a combine who imported potato pickers to Maine, moving them from one district to another as a general shifts his divisions in battle, and the combine—and Uncle Phil—reaped their own harvest from a series of bumper crops." He rubbed his chin thoughtfully. "Then there was Paris Perfumes, photographic products, a flyer in Plastic Pearls. Shall I go on?"

"My brain reels now. But why," she asked shrewdly,

"does he jump from one to another, if each is so successful?"

"Why—and when—only Old Pep knows. But he seems to leave each project at its peak and emerge dripping dollars."

Ruefully the girl announced, "I apologize to Old Pep's office decorations. For him they are positively perfect. Oh!" she laughed. "You have me doing it, too!"

"You're swamped by a flood of words from a silent Bostonian," Scott comforted. "Now—let's hear from you."

There was no trace of restraint as she answered, "Then I must return to Franklin Park and my bird watching. Studying them, rather—for a purpose. But it is frustrating at times, they are so quick and—and *flitatious*. Is that the word?"

Scott laughed. "If it isn't, it should be; it packs all sorts of meanings—flitting, and flirtatious, and maybe capricious."

"What Humpty Dumpty called a 'portmanteau word,' " she suggested happily.

"Exactly. But look here, what you want is our Museum of Science, down there at the end of the Basin." He pointed at the white domes gleaming in the moonlight. "Plenty of mounted specimens who will stand still as long as you like."

"That sounds ideal!"

"As a matter of fact," Scott went on, too deeply enchanted to remember caution, "I'm supposed to drop in at the museum tomorrow. The director asked me to look over some plans for a new addition. Why don't I take you down and introduce you; he'll give you carte blanche."

"Thank you, but that would be impossible." The girl's manner chilled him as she stood up. "I'll have to drop in on impulse, some day when I'm fed up with cataloguing. Good night, Mr. Pelham."

Scott struggled to his feet. Another rebuff, but this one, he realized, brought on by his own stupidity. A fine champion he had turned out to be, proposing to publicize her from one end of town to the other! Groggy from disappointment he petitioned humbly, "Not even—'Good night, Pilgrim'?"

At least that called back her smile. "Of course—Good night, Pilgrim." She held out her hand.

Scott was reaching for it, as a drowning man clutches a straw, he thought bromidically, but she avoided his touch and mutely pointed to his hand. Only then did he discover that he still held her cigarette case. It was then, too, that he noticed how the moonlight winked from it in fiery sparks. He had not been aware that the yellow metal case was deeply chased and studded with brilliant stones. As he returned it, unobtrusively he hefted it on his palm. Weight, and the scintillation of the gems, told the story. Gold and diamonds, if he had ever seen any!

"That's a gaudy bauble," he remarked, keeping poker-faced.

The girl laughed. "What a polite way to call something choice 'a piece of junk'! I fell in love with it in Par—" She shut her lips on the name and color darkened her face. Then, "Why should I try to pretend?" she confessed pathetically. "It was given me by a doting relative, but I do think it looks quite real, don't you? Good night, Pilgrim."

NINE

SCOTT accompanied his preparation of breakfast with a particularly doleful whistling, thoroughly attuned to his state of mind as he considered last night's interlude with the princess. The pleasures of that meeting were clouded by his former doubts and suspicions, now augmented by additional problems.

"A big help last night was!" he grumbled, carrying coffee and cereal to the kitchen table. "Here I had her pegged as the missing sister, and now look at the facts. *Facts?*" he snorted in disdain. They were as scarce as hen's teeth in the stew of conjecture which his imagination had concocted. The girl had given her name without hesitation; even the stupidest person wouldn't do that if she was hiding from the law, and hoped to escape detection. Could it be possible that there were two Maureen Tennys—and each with some loved one a veteran of the war? Well, why not? Wasn't he annoyed at times because there was a Dr. Scott Pelham right next to his own name in the telephone directory? No relation, either.

He finished breakfast with no consciousness of what he had eaten. Tying on one of Tink's aprons he sloshed water on plate and cup. How about that fabulous cigarette case? He was perfectly sure that Maureen had barely checked herself from saying that she had bought it in Paris; and then pretending that it wasn't real! Scott slapped the plate on the counter. An act; trying to play him for a dope! If she *had* bought it, how could a hard-working secretary afford such a costly item? How do I know, he asked himself savagely, that it wasn't a gift from Don Juan Bill Randolph—?

Scott straightened and glared at the sink. "How crazy can a man get?" he asked in a shocked whisper. "Even to wonder such a thing about that lovely girl is an insult. I'd murder anyone I heard hint at it—and I'm the one who ought to be shot!" He shook his head. "How crazy can a man get?" he repeated slowly. "As crazy as I am, I guess—when he's in love."

It was the first time he had said the word, even to himself. Oh, he'd thought, "She is for me!" and mentally called her "the girl I've waited for all my life!" Now he said, under his breath, "I love her!" The phrase gave him a wonderful happiness; he sat down at the table, smiling broadly. "I love her, and by the Lord Harry, I'm going to marry her, whoever she is!" There was a thought to savor at length: years and years of living with her, loving her—

The doorbell pealed its musical chimes.

For an instant Scott still floated on clouds of blissful imagining. The chimes sounded again, and this time penetrated to his roseate heaven. Damning the interruption he strode out and flung open the door.

A tall man with a rakishly canted midnight-blue Homburg hat lounged against the door casing, hands thrust into the pockets of a powder-blue topcoat—suit a delicate smoky gray, shirt of shocking pink with a watered-silk gray tie held in perfect alignment by a broad clip. Awaiting Scott's approach, the vision had been yawning widely; he concealed it daintily with a hand on which gleamed a signet ring as wide as a cigar band.

Cold, slightly bloodshot eyes took in Scott's apron and dish towel. The man grinned, shifting his weight to lean against the other side of the doorway. "Kinda late with the housework, ain't ya, Mary Ann?" he jibed. "Boss in?"

Scott disliked on sight the long, heavily seamed face and bristling black eyebrows. "I'm alone here," he evaded.

"You'll do, I guess. Mind if I step in?"

Accepting his role as man-of-all-work, Scott growled, "We're doing all right here. What's the pitch, Jack?"

"Just looking for information, pal. I'm making a survey of this neighborhood, trying to get good-looking society girls to endorse our products. Nationwide publicity, see—pictures, write-ups, an' all, like that."

Scott hoped his skepticism showed. "What are *you* selling that society dames would fall for?"

"Beauty preparations—all kinds." The man grinned with nauseating friendliness, baring a set of teeth which never grew where they were. "All I want to know, is there any good-looking da—young women in this dump? I been ringing bells all over the place, and nobody showed."

"How did you get in, anyway?"

"Aw, the door was open, but nobody's around. Where is everybody?"

Scott had his doubts about the alleged unanswered bellringing, but caution made him play along. "Maybe they're not back from their weekends yet."

The stranger produced a file card and an ornate pen. "Guess you're my only hope, then. Be a good guy and help me out?" He studied the card. "I copied a couple of names off the mailboxes downstairs. Miss Helen and Grace Jordan. Number Three, The Princess. Jeez—what a name for a swell dump!"

"You can say that again!" said Scott, for the first time able to approve of his visitor's taste.

"Yeah. Hey, wait! Your boss—any pretty daughters or beautiful wife?"

"Nope, not married." To himself Scott added, "Not yet."

"Well, let's hear about them Jordan girls."

Scott filled a thought-packed pause by carefully folding the towel. This man acted strangely insistent on discussing the Jordans. He *might* be making a survey, but not for beauty preparations. There was plenty in that apartment to interest a sneak thief. "They aren't what you want," Scott assured him. "Maiden ladies—in their seventies."

The black eyebrows bunched in a scowl. "You giving me a ride? The girl I seen on their balcony wasn't no seventy!"

Scott's heart skipped a beat and went into double time. He experienced, too, an angry satisfaction that his premonitions had been correct; this furtive-eyed stranger was out of character. No beauty preparations nor possible loot brought him here; he was spying on the princess.

Assuming indifference far from his inward anger Scott put his hand on the door to close it. "I don't know who you *seen* on the balcony," he grumbled. "All know is the Jordans hire that apartment, and I ain't got time to keep tabs on who else is there. And speaking of time, Jack—" he moved the door suggestively—"the boss don't pay me to shoot the breeze with every drummer that rings the bell."

Blue Homburg blocked the closing door with his beringed fist. "O.K.—pal, but get wise." He jingled some coins in his pocket. "You find out anything about that young dame, it might be worth a few bucks to me. I'm covering this section for the next few days; you'll see me round; so make yourself maybe a fiver by getting me some worthwhile dope on her." Snapping a finger against his hat brim in jocular farewell he strolled toward the stairway.

Scott went back to the kitchen, and in a moment

realized that he should have tried to follow the stranger. Too late now?

The chimes sounded again.

"Do I get a second chance at that thug?" he exclaimed eagerly, and hurried to the door.

"Good morning, Mr. Pelham!" This time it was Mrs. Beddle, her eternally prim and spotless self: neat uniform, starched apron, not a white hair out of place. "I've just finished giving my rooms a real good do," she announced, "so I thought I'd step up here and see if I could lend a hand. With Mr. Tinker away things will be in a pretty state no doubt!"

"Well, thank you, Mrs. B., but—"

"It's no trouble, really, sir—I do love to clean up." Smiling till her wrinkled cheeks bunched into rosy apples she rustled past him. "There—I knew it!" Glasses or no, the brown eyes missed nothing in kitchen, bedroom or living room. "Dust, dust! Oh, I mind well how Mr. Beddle used to pig it when I was away! Now just you settle down in your workroom and I'll put things right."

"Glad to have you take charge, Mrs. B. But how did you know Tinker was away?"

"Left a note for me, bless him. *He* knew you'd never manage by yourself."

"Adjudged incompetent," Scott grinned. "Know where he's gone?"

"Not where, nor why." That, her crisp tone indicated, was that.

Gingerly, Scott ventured on other ground. "Tink tells me that you know the girl in the Jordan suite. Maureen Tenny, isn't she? Cataloguing their books?" When the housekeeper did not answer, but dusted busily, he persisted. "Do you know where they hired her?"

"Mr. Pelham, sir!" She folded her arms and faced him squarely. "You've been wonderful kind to me and I'd do anything for you. But if I learned one thing in service—and I did for some proper, well-born families—it was to keep my tongue behind my teeth as to their affairs. I do *not* gossip, and I never will!" No faintest blush accompanied this statement from the teatime confidante of the girl in Number Three. "Now, run along to your work, and leave me to mine, sir."

"Yes, ma'am." Obediently Scott went to his drawing table, but knew in advance that he could not work. Too many questions—too many mysteries. His princess—the sneak in the Hollywood costume—Tinker's absence—

His note lay on the table—*17 Breen Street.* Perhaps Ace Daley knew where Tink had gone, or at least when he might return. Scott flung on his topcoat in the hall. "Thanks for everything, Mrs. B.," he said. "I'm going out for a while."

"That's nice." She showed him her smile again. "A breath of air will do you good. You've looked peaked lately."

"Wasting away for love," Scott joked.

Mrs. Beddle nodded. "I wouldn't be surprised," she said.

Scott went out, wondering.

On Breen Street, Number 17 was no more dilapidated than the other houses nor any more attractive. In its narrow hall, stale air smote him with the ghostly odors of a hundred boiled dinners. Above the battery of mailboxes a large square of cardboard proclaimed in surprisingly skilled lettering:

ACE DALEY
In the Flesh
2nd Floor Back

Scott mounted the stairs by the light of a single dim bulb in the ceiling. Except for the continual creaking of the treads under his feet the house was quiet. The rap of his knuckles on the door at the rear of the dark hallway sounded like muffled shots. From the room came the quick scraping of chair legs on bare floor, then a long-drawn but subdued squeaking. Someone opening a window—with extreme caution? Scott knocked again.

The door jerked open, but the entrance was blocked by the figure of Ace Daley. There was no hesitation in Scott's identifying him. A lurid bathrobe only partly hid a remarkably hairy chest and purple trunks which, like the brown gym shoes, were battle-scarred veterans. The face of this apparition, topped by close-cropped red hair, must have been worked over by experts in the art of demolition. One eye still sported the yellowing bruise which had disturbed Mrs. Pepperell.

Daley's brows bristled aggressively as his blue eye and its green mate swept the caller, taking in cashmere topcoat, unwrinkled charcoal-gray suit and conservative navy-blue tie. In a throaty rumble he drawled, "You're in the wrong corner, Mac! This ain't the Ritz."

Scott laughed. "You're the one who's off base, Daley. I'm looking for you. I'm Scott Pelham—Tink's friend."

The boxer's thick arm shot out and pulled Scott into the room. He shut the door, backed against it and transformed his battered face with a friendly grin. "Captain Pelham? Swell! I'm glad to meet ya!" Then the scowl returned, the strange eyes slitted. "Anything wrong?"

"Not that I know of. Just looking for information."

"Oh, yeah?" Daley rasped a fist across his jaw, still eying his visitor with a frown. "Well, grab a chair and let's hear about it."

Scott sat in the nearest, glancing around the room. It was littered with towels, boxing gloves, discarded clothing, and over all hung the pungent smell of rubbing alcohol. Having overheard what he guessed to be someone's stealthy departure at his knock, Scott was surprised to discover that he and Ace were not alone. In one corner stood a rumpled studio couch and on it slumped a man who, chin in hands, seemed absorbed in an account book open on his lap.

"Why, hello there," said Scott. "Sorry I didn't see you—"

"Hold it!" Daley growled, stepping between them. To the man he said quietly, "Hey, Gent—run down to the corner and pick up a pack of smokes for me, will ya?" He held out a coin.

The man looked up, blinking—a young face, but hollow-cheeked and pallid, with shadowed eyes and lines of strain around them and the mouth. He took the offered money, studied it, then smiled up at the fighter. "Sure, Ace—glad to." His dark eyes shifted to Scott. "Want some cigarettes, Captain?"

The voice gave Scott a prickly tingle, as though skeleton fingers brushed his spine—flat, wholly devoid of life and hope, he thought, a voice coming from the depths of a tomb. "No, thanks," he said smiling. He watched the man shuffle slowly from the room, and recognized the listless gait and drooping shoulders he had seen from his balcony.

Daley closed the door and faced Scott, jerking a thumb over his shoulder. "The Gent's absolutely O.K. It ain't that I don't want him listening in, see—but he gets nervous round strangers." Hands on hips, lifting a little on his toes, he demanded, "Now, shoot!"

Equally brief and to the point, Scott asked, "Where's Tinker?"

"If he ain't at your place, I wouldn't know."

Scott explained, "He left Saturday night—"

"He's back. Pulled outa here a while before you came."

"Oh—do you know where he's been?"

Daley examined a scarred knuckle. "Why don't you ask *him?*"

"Good idea," said Scott, smiling, and stood up. "Waste of time, bothering you, after all."

"No bother, Captain Pelham."

As long as he was here, Scott thought, he might as well check on a few questions which had been seething in his mind. "I meant, I'm sorry to make you chase your brother out, for nothing," he explained. He saw Daley's parti-colored eyes narrow. "I assume, from what Mr. Pepperell told me, that the Gent *is* your brother?"

"So what?"

"Wonderful luck that you found him in that prison camp." Scott's manner was warmly friendly. "Makes you believe in some kind of Divine Providence, doesn't it! I'd like to hear the details of how you escaped, sometime. And how did you manage to get him discharged, in his condition?" When Daley scowled, Scott read his mind and chuckled. "Don't worry about me,

Ace. I'm not Intelligence, checking up on you; I'm long through with the Service. I'm curious, that's all."

"O.K." The fighter relaxed. "Tink says you're on the level—I'll buy it. The way I got the—my brother discharged, well, that was luck, too. I didn't want a disability rap filed on him, see—he'd never get loose from the Army then! So I kept him under cover while I put through my own discharge. They never knew about him."

"But then he's still listed—"

Daley waved a fist negligently. "Maybe—but I knew some dirt about the officer in the discharge department —" He paused, eying Scott warily. "Anyway, he was glad to get rid of me in a hurry, see? Then I picked up the Gent and we started bumming our way home." He shook his head. "It was a long haul!"

"But why, Ace—why? You know the government will do everything possible for a soldier disabled in any way—"

"I'd rather do it myself! I've looked after him ever since I found him. Sir, he's got *something* that makes you want to help him!" Daley scrubbed his red hair and spoke softly, so that Scott caught the undertone of tenderness which had warmed the Pepperell's hearts. "He's a good kid—and smart in his way. Suppose I'd let the Army stick him in one of their hospitals with a lot of guys who were really off? It would have finished him! Alone, in a crowd of nuts—nobody knowing who he was—"

"But you could have told them," Scott protested.

"*Me?*—oh, yeah!" Daley furrowed his scarred brow and rolled his eyes around the room. "Sure, but I couldn't stand to think of him on his own, and helpless —after I sprung him from that stockade, and steered him clear of red tape—and then clouted my way through a string of fourth-rate fighters halfway round the world to bring him home. He's staying with me!" he declared with sudden intensity. "And when I take Nelson next week and head for the big money, I'll hire a real hot-shot doctor to put him on his feet."

"Don't wait too long," cautioned Scott. "Or do you think that he has improved since you got him home?"

Daley lifted his fist for emphasis. "A hundred per cent! The minute we hit the U.S. he begun to look different; all them foreign places worried him, sort of. Why, right now he's keepin' my books—I'm my own manager, see?—and can he keep books! And he made that sign downstairs. He's smart, Captain!"

"Good luck to you both," said Scott. "And if you don't want to wait for the big money, I could give you some doctors' names—brain specialists—who wouldn't press you for payment."

"I said I'd do it myself!" growled Ace. "I mean, thanks, sir, but I started this—"

"And you want to see it through." Scott nodded, starting for the door. "I don't blame you, Ace. But if you should need help, give me a call." He paused and turned. "One other thing I meant to ask you about, that message your brother threw onto my balcony—"

"Yours?" Daley snapped, and then flushed. "I don't know what you're talking about."

His awkward attempt to cover the break amused Scott. "Then you wouldn't be interested in what I did with it? Because I turned it over to the young lady in Number Three at The Princess."

Daley opened the door suggestively. "Still don't get your drift."

"You don't know anything about that girl—?"

"I don't know nothing!"

Scott nodded as he went out. "That makes two of us, then, Ace." Going down the stairs he looked back. Daley still stood there, watching him with a troubled frown.

Scott was relieved, when he reached home, to find John Tinker seated at the kitchen table, carefully sealing a large envelope. "Welcome home!" he said.

Tink gave a convulsive start and stuffed the letter in his pocket before he stood up. His face was white with sooty patches under his eyes. "Gee, Captain, sir! I'm sorry about running out—"

"Don't apologize, Tink! Damn it, I've told you often enough—this is *your home*; you come and go as you please. Any luck?"

"Well—I don't know for sure yet, sir. Guess I went off half cocked. Over at Daley's—he wasn't there—his brother showed me a letter Ace got from a guy in New York, and he was the man I've been looking for. He's—well, he knew the girl I told you about. So I lit out for New York. I should've waited for Ace, 'cause he knew the guy was coming right up here. In fact—" Tink raised a hand to feel of the letter, then checked the motion—"we came up together on the bus. I took him to Daley's and came home."

He wet his lips. "Sir, he says my girl—isn't dead or anything, like I was afraid of! She never did get my letters but she—the fellow says she isn't married, and he knows she hasn't forgotten me." He drew in a hissing breath. "Sounds good, doesn't it?"

"Sounds wonderful!" Scott encouraged. He noticed that Tinker snapped his fingers, softly but incessantly, a habit of his illness which Scott had hoped would be banished permanently by returning health. Usually it indicated that Tink wanted to unburden his mind on some subject, but was uncertain how to approach it. Scott tried to help him. "You haven't seen the girl yet?"

"No, sir, but I know where she is. I mean, I can write now—and she'll get it."

"Good!" Smilingly Scott tapped Tink's pocket. "You didn't waste any time, and I don't blame you!"

Tinker clutched that pocket. "Aw, no, sir! This is something else. And it's got to get to New York quick. I was just going to whip out to mail it, but I'll be right back—"

"Take your time, and I won't need you tonight. I'm meeting a contractor for lunch, dinner with the Pepperells and bridge till all hours, probably. And Mrs. B. 'did up' the rooms."

"Yeah—I found her here." Now Tinker's white face reddened. He walked slowly to the door, hesitated and then swung round.

"Here it comes," thought Scott. But he was completely unprepared for it when it came.

"Sir!" Tink spoke hoarsely. "Don't you have nothing to do with that girl in Number Three in The Princess! I could tell you were interested, the way you asked about her. I didn't know anything, then, like I said—but I do now! Mrs. Beddle took me up there—I talked to her. And I know she's not for *you*, Captain!" When Scott started to interrupt he made anxious pushing motions with his hands. "Wait a minute, please! I know it's none of my business, what you do—but you've been so—so damned swell to me, I don't want to see you walk into any trouble!"

He stopped, to clear the huskiness of emotion from his voice, but Scott was too taken aback to seize the opening. "That girl," said Tink rapidly, "told Mrs. Beddle that she didn't want to meet any of the other tenants. She don't get any mail, won't answer the doorbell or the phone, and she hardly ever goes out. She acts so queer that some of the people are beginning to talk about her!" Fixing Scott with a scowl of mingled distrust and anxiety he added, "No kidding, sir! This place is too high-class for any Mysterious Female racket! The old gentleman never ought to have let her in!"

He stalked out and shut the door decisively before Scott could get his breath to speak.

TEN

BLISSFULLY unaware that she had been the subject of John Tinker's philippic, "that girl in Number Three" roamed happily among the wonders in the Museum of Science. Ending prolonged study of some mounted bird specimens, she caught her reflection in their glass case and noted with approval that the breezy walk down Charles Street still colored her cheeks. How wise she had been to yield to sudden temptation and escape, even for an hour, from the oppression of that apartment!

She wondered if her encounter with Scott Pelham on the roof garden, the brief interludes of amiable conversation in a distinctly hectic half hour, had sharpened her realization of all that she missed by her self-imposed exile. In spite of her work and the solace of typewriter and piano, there were too many hours when she conquered an hysterical urge to beat against the walls and batter her way to freedom.

The museum made a welcome break in her confined life—not too crowded for comfort on this weekday afternoon, but still far from deserted. A scattering of visitors moved about singly, in arm-linked couples or low-voiced chatting groups. There was so much to see: a miniature diorama showing a Pacific coral reef, complete with sharks and a dark-skinned pearl diver; a single drop of water magnified to giant proportions to exhibit the somewhat frightening microscopic life within; a small boy instructing, with studied nonchalance, his smaller brother in the operation of a push-button microscope. The girl smiled companionably at them as she went down the stairs to view other wonders.

At a huge glass-enclosed diorama she stopped with a gasp of sheer delight. "Shore Birds on Crane's Beach, Ipswich." A stretch of sun-warmed sand, driftwood, shells and ragged beach grass sloping to the sea, and birds everywhere—brown and white, black and white, gulls, tern, unfamiliar species, and the diminutive perky sandpipers so real that she waited hopefully for the one whose slender bill was probing the sand to withdraw it in triumph. The actual sand, on which the birds were mounted, merged imperceptibly into painted sand and a painted sea that blended from inshore green to distant azure smudged with hazy, far-off islands, and lifted its blue at last into a sunlit sky flecked with cottony clouds.

The beauty of the scene was enough to hold the girl enthralled. Then, from the other end of the hall, a huge lighthouse lens on exhibit added the final touch of realism. Slowly revolving, it flooded the girl and the birds with blazing golden light, and for that passing moment she *knew* that she smelled the salt breeze sweeping the beach.

That proved the spur for an imagination already urged to a canter by the birds observed upstairs. Now it galloped. She hurried to a chair in the corner of the lounge. Her pencil raced across line after line in the notebook.

At what precise point enthusiasm gave way to vague uneasiness she never knew, but gradually the pencil slowed and stopped. Without raising her eyes she became unhappily conscious that someone was watching her. Her heart pounded. The fingers holding the pencil trembled. "Why, oh, why did I come here?" she whispered. "After that warning note I should have been more careful than ever! Am I caught?"

Gritting her teeth to forestall any quiver of her lips she forced herself to look up. The lounge was only a corner of the exhibition hall enclosed by six-foot walls containing glass-fronted displays. Only a handful of people were visible. Two elderly matrons relaxed, recuperating from their tour almost to the point of napping. A long-legged youth sprawled on a couch opposite, also apparently resting his feet. No one else? Yes! Lounging against one of the partitions, near the entrance, a tall, gaudily dressed man remarkable for the rakish slant of his blue Homburg hat. A stranger, and, she was reassured to find, not interested in her; his attention rested on another man standing in the doorway. Following his gaze the girl felt her throat contract in panic; the second man *was* watching her!

A slender drooping figure, he stood as though halted in mid-stride, one hand plucking at his lips so that it concealed the lower part of his face. She saw only deep-set eyes above hollow cheeks of an ivory pallor, and unbrushed blond hair thickly streaked with white.

The expression in his eyes soothed the girl's consternation to uneasy perplexity. There was no menace; rather they held wistful pleading, as though a captive soul were begging for help. That, and something in the pale face, gave her a twinge of regret, as though she had failed him in some way, and a disturbing sense of familiarity. Was it a wraith of memory indeed, or only some chance resemblance to an acquaintance in the past? She bent her head, shutting her eyes in an effort to force the elusive picture into focus, but it faded. When she looked up again, both men had disappeared.

The first glow of relief was followed by an instant compulsion to get away—to flee back to her apartment, which all at once seemed a haven. After a moment's delay to be sure that the men had gone she stuffed notebook and pencil into her bag and walked rapidly across the exhibition hall.

In the main corridor she knew another instant of dismay. At the moment it appeared deserted—but not deserted enough. The blond man was nowhere to be seen, but near the front door stood Blue Homburg. And this time his chilling stare rested unmistakably on her.

The nightmare series of shocks set her mind racing wildly from one surmise to another. Blue Homburg represented the police! Not the police, but some far more sinister organization! He was a maniac who had done away with the other man and selected her as his next victim!

With a scornful sniff she reined in her imagination and dismounted to practical thought. She would ignore the waiting menace, walk briskly past him, congeal him with a look if he dared to speak—"But suppose he refuses to congeal?" she murmured, mocking her fears. "Shall I scream, or topple over in a ladylike swoon?" Assuming the most theatrically regal pose of which she was capable she went forward, chin up, eyes front—and heart in mouth.

She reached the halfway point in the corridor, passed the ticket collector's stand. Why wasn't he on duty? Now the information booth. Where was the girl who should be sitting there? Where was *everyone?* Only closed doors of private offices, now, and the bare tiled floor where his feet tapped loudly.

The man in the blue hat stepped to the middle of the entrance. Blocking her way? Ignore him! Stare right through him! If ever you acted a part—do it now!

Beside her an office door opened suddenly. The tall figure which emerged almost collided with her. With a startled gasp she backed away, then recognizing a familiar face, clutched the man's arm. There was nothing theatrical, nothing assumed in her rapturous greeting, "Scott—Mr. Pilgrim! Am I glad to see *you!*"

Scotts lightning recovery from stunned surprise was truly remarkable, considering that he had not thought of his princess for over an hour, and considering also the dizzying nearness of shining eyes and lips parted in a joyous smile. He returned the smile, closed his fingers over the hand on his arm and unhesitatingly manufactured the required chivalrous falsehood. "Sorry I'm late, my dear."

The girl flashed a nervous glance past him. Blue Hat had vanished. "Please," she whispered, "get me out of here, *quickly!*"

Realizing her uneasiness without comprehending it, Scott nodded. Disengaging the shaking fingers from his elbow he linked arms companionably. "O.K., let's go," he suggested calmly.

Outside the museum the girl wavered, looked up at the gray eyes regarding her with a speculative twinkle and flushed. "Could I get a taxi? And I want to be sure that nobody follows me home!"

"A taxi, Princess?" Scott smiled. "Not while the royal coach awaits you." He guided her to his parked car, opened the door with a footman's bow, and installed her in the maroon and chrome convertible as if she were indeed royalty. "If you'd like the top up," he offered as he slid into the driver's seat, "your wish is my command."

"Thanks, but the more fresh air the better. . . . *Oh!*" she gasped, shrinking against him.

Seemingly from nowhere a man had materialized at her door. His long, seamed face under the blue hat leaned in. "Just a minute, lady," he growled. "I was following a guy that acted like he knew you."

With repugnance Scott recognized his morning caller, but before he could speak the girl whispered, "Go, *please!*"

"Out of the way!" Scott warned, starting the motor.

"Just a couple of questions." A muscular hand sporting a gold ring fell heavily on the girl's knee. "All I want from you—"

Rage blazed in Scott. He snatched the man's hand up and slammed it against the side of the windshield with a crack like a snapping whip. "Keep your paws off her!" he rasped.

Blue Homburg swore, nursing his fingers. "Listen you—!"

"Stand clear!" Scott ordered, restraining a furious desire for further action. A brawl in public would do the girl's cause no good. He drove out of the lot, across the drawbridge, and headed up Storrow Drive.

"Thank you, Pilgrim," she said softly, and added with attempted lightness, "a wholly inadequate, but truly heartfelt, expression of gratitude."

"And wholly unnecessary." Scott copied her airy tone. "My only regret is being pinned behind the wheel so I couldn't swing at his ugly mug."

"I was so relieved, when you stepped into the hall—!"

"*I* was surprised," he countered gravely. "Last night you were quite indefinite as to when you'd be free to visit the museum."

She flushed at the rebuke. "I wasn't very nice, was I? But truly, Pilgrim, this afternoon I couldn't stand that apartment."

"Then we won't go back there." He swung off the drive and turned into a quiet street behind The Princess and Pilgrim. "Here we abandon the car," he announced, "and venture on foot into the wilds of Commonwealth Avenue. You've been cooped up with books too long. A brisk walk will do wonders for your complexion—lovely as it is."

Hurriedly she demanded, "Tell me how you happened to be at the museum—in the very nick of time."

"Have you forgotten that I offered to escort you, because I had to examine some plans this afternoon? I assure you, I wasn't spying."

They were both silent then, until they reached the path which led down the middle of the avenue. On either side of the wide street houses began to glitter with early lights as twilight neared. An east wind brought chill and the smell of the sea, stirring the bare limbs of the trees along the path. Leaves drifted and whirled.

Covertly Scott studied the girl at his side. Her well-worn blue suit, except for the delightful figure it enclosed, looked to him as like a thousand others as are the kernels in an ear of corn. The brim of her green hat was drawn low, its perky feather slightly worn along the edges. One of her yellow pigskin gloves showed a rip on one finger. Curious, he mused, that a secretary who had been employed by William Randolph—and who owned a gold cigarette case—should wear such a shabby outfit.

Questions, problems, puzzles; were they all he would ever know of this girl? Abruptly he drew her to a bench overlooked by the bronze dignity of William Lloyd Garrison's statue. "Sit here," he invited, "and tell all. Or at least all you can. First, what frightened you in the museum? Were you afraid someone would recognize you as—as a New Yorker?" He had almost said *fugitive* but changed in time.

"Now, why should they? What is the matter with me?" Her appeal was charged with mischievous surprise. Reproachful eyes challenged him as she brushed the lapels of her coat. "I'm wearing a navy-blue suit; I understand that every Boston woman has one in her wardrobe even if she doesn't always wear it. "What *do* I look like"—words properly demure, but tone laughing—"in my working clothes?"

"We won't go into the matter of what you look like to me—not *now*. There's hardly time for me to do justice to such a delectable picture." Scott steadied his voice as he caught the expression her eyes flashed to his. It was as though the spirit in their brown depths poised for instant flight. "What happened at the museum?" he insisted.

"I wonder if you'll understand. It was the curious sequence of disturbing events, I suppose, rather than any one thing. Or nerves—the reaction from weeks of loneliness. The moment I stopped before the bird exhibits you spoke of, my spirits soared like an eagle. Not waiting to reach home I sat down in the lounge and let genius burn and guide my pencil!"

Her voice tingling with remembered excitement she gave him an account of the watching men and her own confusion. "At first," she mused, "I thought the tough-looking man had been spying on me, and that the pale, inoffensive one was trying to warn me. But I'm sure that wasn't it; that thug said he was following the other, didn't he? So I needn't have been so nervous when I saw him waiting in the hall." She attempted to laugh. "It all sounds foolish, doesn't it? I told you it was probably tired nerves. But then I met you—and felt safe—and here I am!" She sighed contentedly.

Scott conquered a passionate impulse to crush her in his arms, assure her that she would be safe with him—always. Instead he pleaded, "Tell me why you are hiding, Princess. The course of deception is full of uncharted rocks; don't try to sail it alone. Let me help."

"No!" She turned to face him, one hand gripping the bench. "You must not try to help me. I can't tell you why I am hiding, you might be forced to report it. Please, Pilgrim, be only—friendly—and nice! Promise that you will not ask questions—not of me, or about me of anyone else. Otherwise I can't, I won't see you again. Promise?"

"All right," he sighed. "But only with reservations. If ever you are in danger, I'll smash that promise! And that's final."

Her frown was dubious. "That isn't quite the hand-on-heart, hope-to-die vow that I expected, but since I can't foresee any *danger* I'll accept it." She made a wry face at him. "I want to ask you a question, but how can I if you glare so?"

"Was I? It was worry, then, not bad temper. Shoot—I'm listening."

"Suppose—suppose a man is accused of a crime." She hesitated, biting her lip.

Exultant, Scott held his breath. She intended to confide in him after all.

"Suppose," she slowly repeated, "he is accused of theft—the theft of jewels, for instance. He was taking them from—from his firm to another when he was held up and robbed. But suppose that he knows the bandit, a man who was a sergeant in his old command in the Army—a man whom he, as an officer, had to discipline repeatedly and finally break. That's reduce to private, you know—"

"I'm familiar with the term," Scott admitted dryly.

"Of course!" The girl was too intent on her story to return his smile. "This man had sworn to even the score when they got out of uniform, had nursed his grudge for years until his chance came, and with some friends robbed the—the jewelry salesman. The salesman knows that if he gives himself up, with no proof for his story, he will land in jail while the real thief goes free. So he disappears."

Scott groaned. "The worst thing he could do!"

"But that's what he did. Wait, that isn't the whole story. His—a girl, a friend of his—knows all this and is being sought for questioning; she is supposed to know where he is hiding. What should she do? Come out in the open, tell what she knows—or is suspected of knowing—or keep out of sight until the man can clear himself? Because he is sure that he can expose the real thief in a short time."

Scott repressed his inclination to stand up on the bench and cheer, from experience he feared that if he gave too-free rein to his elation the girl would freeze him again. But his heart leaped with relief; her brother was innocent—the victim of a long-held grudge. He had seen the beginning of many during his own service.

An afterthought somewhat dampened his enthusiasm. Was he too ready to believe this story? Scowling, he stared down at his heel drawing meaningless hieroglyphics on the gravel path. What devil had insinuated that sinister query in his joyful mind? After all, she might be trying to shield her brother. Excusable loyalty; even commendable loyalty! On the other hand, he stubbornly insisted, suppose the brother was a crook, even the king ripple on a crime wave—what was that to Scott? *She* was—herself! She was, as he had already learned, the girl he loved. He looked up at her.

Dark and inscrutable, her eyes watched him; sensitive lips quivered as if she read his thoughts with inner amusement. Decidedly this was no time to tell her what she meant to him. His intonation was completely sympathetic when he said, "Too bad you didn't come here under an assumed name."

"But I didn't know—I mean the girl didn't know—" She threw up her hands with a resigned laugh. "All right, it becomes too complicated if I try to keep up the pretense. *I* didn't know about all this trouble when I came here. And now that I have announced to the world that I am Maureen Tenny, I must take the consequences, and I won't quit! Remember, last night I boasted that I'm not the passive type?"

There was no need to remind Scott of a conversation whose every word he treasured. He was occupied with another problem: if she had not known of Tenny's difficulties when she came, who had informed her of them? No letters, no phone calls, Tink had complained. Tinker! He had seen her a few hours ago; had he told her? But if he did know the truth about her, what the devil had he meant by that ruthless character assassination delivered to Scott?

"You haven't advised me, Pilgrim," the girl reminded, now openly amused at his furrowed brow.

Strangely, an earlier guess flashed back to him—that there were two Maureens in his maze of puzzles. The idea might be worth adopting.

"Why not stick to the name you have announced," he suggested, "but spread it around that you are from—from Oklahoma, say—anywhere but New York. There must be more than one Maureen Tenny in the world." Warming to the plan, he elaborated on it. "You are from—well, Tulsa is the only city I can think of out there." He grinned. "Bostonians are weak on foreign geography. And, look here—have you a middle name?" When she shook her head he brushed the lack aside. "We'll give you one. Er—h'm—Portia! M. Portia Tenny. Not bad. Hello, Porty!" He shuddered visibly. "Not so hot after all? But perhaps that recommends it, in this case. No one would suspect you of assuming that name! And with the Tulsa story, it just might divert anyone from checking up on you."

A shadow of uncertainty clouded the eyes raised to his. "I suppose I could do that, but"—her voice trembled—"if you knew how I hate the thought of living a lie!"

"For a good cause? And perhaps no one will bother you, dear—I mean, Princess!—so you won't need to play a part—"

"Scott Pehlam!" The shrill voice slashed across his reassuring words. "Is it really you? And *Miss Tenny!*

Maureen Tenny, from New York, is it not? *Unusual* name!" Lucy Wheeler stalked up to the bench, sending her greeting ahead of her with the nerve-shattering pitch of a police siren.

ELEVEN

SCOTT gritted a forceful expletive between locked teeth as he rose to meet the malicious advent of the Salem Witch.

"Miss *Portia* Tenny," he corrected, "but not from New York. From Oklahoma—where the oil grows," he paraphrased flippantly. Lucky they had agreed on details in time! "Porty"—he turned with gallant deference—"this is my cousin, Lucy Wheeler." Without giving either lady a chance to acknowledge the introduction, he exclaimed, "Aren't you a long way from your bailiwick, Lucy?"

"My beat is the world!" she gushed. "Wherever I can find a bit of atmosphere—for my next novel, you know." She gestured vaguely.

Scott's annoyance tempted him to ask what novel she had ever written to make this one "her next," but Lucy drove the question from his head with her customary malice.

"I felt sure that I had stalked a sensational scene," her harsh voice prickled with innuendo, "when I spied an obviously romantic couple on this secluded bench while a man skulked in the shadow of the statue. A rejected suitor, perhaps?"

The girl's gasp of alarm was quickly smothered. Scott patted her shoulder soothingly, attempting a careless laugh. It was not a successful effort, because as he turned he glimpsed a tall figure in the too-familiar hat and light-blue coat hurrying off along the path. How long had he been at his listening post? Had he followed them from the museum, or happened on them just now? Too late to worry about him. Get rid of Lucy, then whisk the girl back to her place without delay. This locale was suddenly far too thickly populated.

"Now, Lucy!" he rebuked. "A man skulking? Your imagination has the bit in its teeth today. Your new novel must be a thriller, so that you view life only in ominous purple and hectic red!" With a premonition that she was drawing breath for a barrage of prying questions he tried to divert her with flattery. "But I'll bet you put the new story across, as you do everything!"

"There isn't much I can't put across." Her unsmiling agreement held a threatening undertone. "But you really have surprised me this time, Scott. To think of finding one of *the* Pelhams with an assignation on the avenue—and practically *after dark!* Nancy will be stunned when I tell her."

Scott folded his arms to resist a near-murderous impulse. His jaw ached from controlling a furious snarl. The Salem Witch never failed to aggravate him, but today she was outdoing herself. "I doubt if my sister will be as surprised as you *expect*." The last word he altered from "hope"—but it took will power.

"Indeed? You mean that she has already met Miss—Miss—?" Lucy peered past him like a searching vulture. Her cackling laugh dripped venom as she sneered, "What *has* become of your friend?"

Scott whirled, incredulous. The bench was empty. Was that Maureen disappearing down the street? In the dusk he wasn't sure.

"Pretty, isn't she!" was Lucy's gloating comment. "But watch your step, dear boy. I always say, you can't tell a book by its cover."

"An original phrase!" Scott growled.

"And how well it fits this situation," purred Miss Wheeler. When he glared she heaved an exaggerated sigh of patience. "You men are blind. Be reasonable, Scott; how can a girl who earns her living cataloguing books—if we believe Uncle Phil—how could such a girl afford those obviously expensive clothes, to say nothing of that fabulous La Tour model?"

Later, on the sidewalk in front of the twin apartments, Scott loitered irresolute. He had deserted Lucy at the high tide of her vitriolic dissertation on modern girls, but she had added to his puzzlement. Trust a woman to instantly recognize costly tailoring in a suit which a mere man would dismiss as showing signs of wear.

Hardly the appropriate time to pursue his investigations, though. The balcony door of Number Three, The Princess, stood ajar. From the room shone a dim light and from it, too, drifted the notes of a piano played with every indication of taut nerves. Anyway, she had made it plain that she didn't trust him enough to confide in him or accept his help. His obvious course was to dress and proceed to the Pepperell dinner, putting his princess out of mind for the evening. A completely sensible solution, he told himself sternly—and completely impossible.

A ponderous tread thumped the sidewalk behind him and he saw Officer Walsh bearing down like an attacking tank. "Good evening, Fred!" said Scott, barely in time to prevent a collision.

"Oh, it's you, Mr. Pelham." The patrolman doffed his official severity. "You joining the Peeper Society?"

"What's that?"

Walsh grunted with either contempt or impatience. "The guys that walk by, or ride by, or hang around—looking at them apartment houses."

"Many of them?" Scott camouflaged his interest by lighting his pipe.

"Enough so's you wonder what they're up to. That's why I drifted over here when I saw you doing it. Didn't recognize you, of course."

"What do they look like?"

"All kinds," said Walsh with the boredom of a man whose time is occupied in checking on the activities of "all kinds." When he shifted to a more interesting subject his face lighted. "Hear Tink's been away."

"Got back today. Did you see him?"

"Nope." Walsh grinned. "I heard about it from New York—and was it funny! They've been looking for a guy down there, on a robbery charge, and last night they thought they had him. A detective picked him up at a bus terminal—with John Tinker! How d'you like that?"

"*Tink* was with him?"

"Yup. But it wasn't the guy they wanted after all! This feller was Ace Daley's brother. Daley the fighter —you know—Tink's pal."

"But Daley's brother is here with him," Scott objected. "He's recovering from a bad siege in a concentration camp—"

"Not that one—his older brother, Dick. I guess he gave the detective who stopped them a bad time. He's a master sergeant, see—Regular Army since he was eighteen, and no city dick impressed him."

"And he came to Boston with Tink?" asked Scott.

"Listen, let me tell it; the pay-off will kill you!" Walsh shook with inner laughter. "Back at Headquarters, the detective takes another look at the wanted man's description, and still thinks it's the guy he had his hands on. So he puts the word on the teletype to Boston, and *we* are supposed to barge into Ace Daley's and put the pinch on his brother! Wow! Glad it isn't my detail—I'd as soon stick my head in a cage of gorillas!"

"A rugged assignment," Scott agreed, and departed wrestling with new confusion.

Tink went to New York because "a guy" knew about his long-vanished sweetheart. Then he returns with Daley's brother, whose description tallies with that of the missing salesman. *Was* it Sergeant Daley—or someone else with Daley's papers, enough of them to satisfy the detective for the moment? Because the detective would have demanded some identification, surely. Scott pictured Tinker in the kitchen, sealing a large envelope of a size to contain nicely an enlisted man's travel papers. If the sergeant *had* come to Boston, why should Tink mail his papers to New York? Answer, obviously, someone had used them to travel incognito, and a "Wanted" description fitted him!

Scott whistled. So Walter Tenny was in Boston. And he must be a friend of Ace Daley, or the fighter wouldn't send a warning to the sister in The Princess. Scott went thoughtfully up to dress for dinner.

Tinker sat in the kitchen, bolting a sandwich washed down with hasty gulps of milk. His face was wind-blown pink, his hair ruffled. "Been out for a walk, sir," he explained unnecessarily. "Sort of trying to settle things in my mind. But I'm too tired, I guess. Didn't get much sleep on that bus."

Scott leaned against the table, relieved that the subject had come up of itself; he didn't want Tink to believe he'd been snooping. "I saw Fred Walsh outside. He says you had a little trouble in New York."

"I hope to tell you!" Cautiously Tink delayed further speech by a long drink of milk while he weighed Scott's expression. Nothing but friendliness in the smile. He returned it with interest as he chuckled, "I wish you'd been there! We walked into the bus station, and this dick—you could tell he was a cop a mile away—grabs old—er—my friend and says, 'Hold it, bud!' plenty tough. My pal gives him the old judo stab on the biceps"—Tink's hand flickered expertly—"and the guy swears and starts nursing his arm. 'Resisting an officer!' he says.

"My friend says, 'Oh, excuse me, officer—I thought it was a stick-up.' With that he flashes his papers. He's an Army sergeant, see, but in civies, and did he give that dick the works! You never heard a hotter bawling-out!"

Scott laughed with Tink. "Walsh said it was Daley's brother."

Tink sobered, blinked. He nodded. "That," he admitted, "was what floored the cop. You never seen such a blizzard of papers; identity card, special assignment, travel orders, a letter from some woman thanking him for helping her boy—I don't know what else!"

Scott felt a timely warning was in order. "Walsh thinks he isn't in the clear yet. That New York detective wants the local gendarmes to pick him up at Ace's."

"Yeah?" Tink finished the milk with an air of unworried pleasure. "Too bad to bother 'em, because Sergeant Daley won't be there."

"He won't?"

"Nope."

The simple negative hung in the silence. When Scott was sure that nothing was to follow it he walked to the door. There he paused. "Anything on your mind that I can help with, Tink?"

"No, sir." Unconsciously he stiffened to attention. "I—ain't in any trouble, Captain, sir."

"If I *can* help, you can count on me."

Tink grinned. "Don't I know it!"

"Don't ever forget it. *At ease!*" Laughing at the prompt obedience Scott retired to prepare for dinner and an evening of contract. Plus, he apprehended, a running fire of complaint from whoever was his unlucky partner, at the errors his wandering thoughts would commit.

That foreboding had been full realized, he admitted at the end of the evening, safely back in his apartment. Not one, but two successive partners had struggled to drag him from his bog of mental paralysis, with equal lack of success. Pretty girls, too. He had assured his hostess of that as he left, but Aunt Patty was not mollified.

"I don't know what to do with you, Scott!" she worried, disappointed at the failure of her campaign against his bachelorhood. "Lovely girls! Either one perfectly suitable—"

"And perfectly charming, Aunt Patty. I liked them both." What he did not tell her was that neither had deep-brown eyes veiled by enchantingly heavy lashes, slim, erect shoulders, and a light-footed gallant stride to set bands playing in his heart.

That was the picture which had clouded his card sense and was with him now while he smoked a last pipe on the balcony and stared unseeingly at the silver night stretching away across the river.

A distant clock boomed. Only eleven? An early party! There was no doubt that his lovesick stupor had hastened its untimely end. He returned to the living room. The eyes of the portrait above the fireplace seemed to observe him with a critical expression—as if wondering how long this modern Pelham would go on wavering between attraction and suspicion. Gad, man, make up your mind! It was only a trick of the wavering smoke from his pipe, Scott hoped, that ruddy-faced

Governor Pelham's brow contracted in a frown and his satin waistcoat swelled with indignation.

Shrugging, Scott wandered to the piano and dropped a tentative finger on a key. Maureen had been playing when she returned from their interrupted walk—always back to Maureen! Scott tramped to the fireplace and emptied his pipe. On the hearth lay a twisted yellow envelope. A telegram. He picked it up—empty. It must have arrived while he was among the Pepperell flesh-pots, so faithful Tinker, making sure that it was not urgent, had tacked it to the drawing board in the workroom, as was his custom.

Scott strolled in, unhurried, and inspected the drawing board. No telegram. He prospected in Tink's domain, the kitchen. A crumple of yellow paper, plucked from the trash basket, unfolded in his hand. His eyes narrowed and his fingers gripped tighter as he read:

JOHN TINKER
NO. 3 THE PILGRIM BOSTON
BRING GIRL TO SILK HAT CLUB TONIGHT
ELEVEN DON'T FAIL

D

Numb with surprise Scott went back to the living room. He reread the message. "GIRL"! It must be Maureen who was wanted; Tink didn't have a girl, all his thoughts centered on the dream of long ago. John Tinker was asked—no, commanded—to produce Maureen at a night club on the disreputable outskirts of the Back Bay. Scott was familiar with the Silk Hat only as a name; some of his acquaintances professed interest in the hot bands which performed there, and amusement at the boisterously tough patrons of the place. Fights were run-of-the-mill, riots not unusual. For anyone to take Scott's princess into that—that dive—!

Scott's jaw set, lines of determination creased from nose to thin-lipped mouth as he visioned possible results of that visit. But certainly Maureen, by embarking on this foolhardy mission, had canceled his promise of hands off. Grimly he said aloud, "All right, 'D'—I wasn't invited but I'll be there."

Quickly he changed to slacks and sport coat as more suited to the Silk Hat than evening dress. As he crossed the living room he saluted the governor's portrait with a wave and a meaning grin. "Relax, Your Excellency! You needn't worry about my delaying tactics now. And thanks for reminding me that the Pelhams never have been quitters!"

TWELVE

FESTIVITY at the Silk Hat was approaching crescendo when the girl from Number Three settled at the table to which John Tinker led her. She sent a comprehensive look around the small, low-ceilinged room and was far from favorably impressed.

Curtains of poisonous green shrieked against walls of painful orange, stained and scarred but each adorned with a top hat in black silhouette. Naked plastic-topped tables, plastic chairs. A few pendant lamps whose art-glass shades reduced their light to a nightmare glimmer of red and yellow. From an elevated platform across the room a Negro band pumped out throaty moans and piercing squeals which perfectly matched the decorations.

The semidarkness and a shifting fog of tobacco smoke mercifully obscured many details of the Silk Hat's habitués who crowded the dance floor or lounged around it. Enough was revealed, however, of those nearest the girl, to make her heart go into double time. Setting her teeth gamely she clutched her evening bag close and confined her attention to her escort. He at least looked human.

Human as to face, she qualified, if not as to apparel. John Tinker, she decided, had dressed carefully for this expedition, with the sole object of mingling unobtrusively among the regular patrons. The very blatancy of his mauve and chocolate sport coat, yellow silk shirt and white, hand-painted tie made him unremarkable here. The girl acknowledged his wisdom with a shudder, and concentrated on his smooth pink face and steady blue eyes.

There was a quality in those eyes, and in his sturdy bearing, which had invited confidence the moment he appeared at her door in The Princess—even before Mrs. Beddle's fluttery introduction of "Mr. Tinker—Mr. Scott Pelham's friend." Somehow that characterization banished all possibility of doubt. Rather a disturbing indication, she reflected, of her increasing implicit faith in her pilgrim.

In spite of all this, Tinker had bewildered her by his actions when they met—white of face, unable to control trembling hands, snapping his fingers repeatedly. Then he quieted, seemed to emerge from a state of shock and relapse into gloomy calm. After a brief, and unsatisfactory, exchange of questions and evasive answers he shocked her by launching into a rambling description of Walter Tenny's troubles.

And again she found herself believing him, fantastic as the tale of robbery and disappearance sounded. His honesty backed every word. It was not until he returned unexpectedly that evening and begged her to accompany him to an unnamed place, for an unnamed though assertedly helpful purpose, that her confidence wavered. Now, in the Silk Hat, doubts which had surrendered to his matter-of-fact assumption that she would agree began to stir again, reinforced by the squalor of the surroundings and the worried frown of her escort.

"It's getting late, isn't it?" she asked.

Tinker rolled his arm to glance at his watch. "Yeah—but the fellow will show up." With a flickering thumb he indicated that his concern was not for the delay but for the simple black taffeta cocktail dress which she had selected as suitably inconspicuous. "Maybe you should have dolled up more," he muttered.

"I'm sorry." She covertly scanned the overdressed women around them. "I had no idea where you were taking me, Mr. Tinker."

"For Pete's sake—call me Johnny!" He too surveyed their fellow guests. "It don't matter, I guess. Even if you'd got yourself up like these broads, anyone would know you didn't belong."

"Why, thank you," she smiled. What more she might have said gave way to a gasp of alarm as a man dropped into the chair between them.

Wide-eyed she stared at him. A black suit, shiny with wear and grease, hung on a body several sizes smaller. The unbuttoned coat showed an equally dingy T-shirt bearing a blue emblem too faded for recognition. Rough brown hair, darker where it was wetly plastered low on his forehead; grotesquely long, juvenile-delinquent sideburns; unnaturally black brows; and a sickly copper hue on the cheeks.

The girl's first dismay fled in a deep breath of relief. The disguise might confuse someone who did not know him well, but at this close range she could see how grease paint thickened his brows, and the grains of tan powder caught in the stubble of beard. And no disguise could hide the golden glint in Walter Tenny's eyes when he grinned at her.

"Heavens!" she laughed. "Are you made up as a gypsy, Walter?"

Tink's hand shot out to tap hers. "Easy on names," his whisper warned. "This is *Joe Curry,* one of Ace Daley's sparring partners, if anyone asks. Stick to that." He nudged Tenny and nodded toward the girl. "Satisfied?"

"Sure," said Tenny impatiently, and smiled at her. "Sorry to drag you here. Tink's description sounded like you, but I had to be sure. I couldn't take a chance and go to your apartment."

"I don't mind, Walt—Joe. It's educational, anyway."

"I'll bet!" Tink muttered unhappily. "I don't like this setup. I shouldn't have brought you; let's not waste time. Where's Ace?"

"Watching the back door where I came in. He tried to phone you this afternoon, but nobody home, so he telegraphed." Tenny leaned closer to the girl and whispered rapidly. "Tink told you about the hold-up?" She nodded. "At first I wasn't sure who rigged it, but now I know it's a man named Kramer. I'm in Boston because he's here, and he probably has the bonds with him.

Guess he only intended to hold them until I'd been jailed—to let me see what it's like. His idea of revenge, or all he'd have the nerve for. But I'm still free, so that puts him in a hot spot."

Tenny slid a glance around to make sure he was not being overheard.

"Kramer's too yellow to keep the loot, and it's getting late to produce it and look innocent," he explained.

"Why did he follow you to Boston?" she asked.

Tenny shook his head. "I followed him. He came up for the fight; he's the manager of Nelson, who meets Ace Daley next week."

"That's the last you'll hear of Nelson," Tinker promised. "Or of Kramer! Holy cats! A crooked manager, in with the racketeers. Just the type to stick up a guy and then try to pin the rap on *him!*"

"Now *you're* wasting time," Tenny cautioned, and turned to the girl. "Two things I want to find out from you. Will you stick it out where you are until I can trap Kramer? I know it must be unpleasant for you, but it helps. He and his thugs have been so busy watching you, trying to figure where you fit into the picture, that they haven't given me much thought since they left New York."

There was momentary hesitation before the girl answered. Each day the burden of uncertainty and loneliness grew heavier, and a preview of prolonged seclusion and secrecy made her heart ache. But what of that? She would be helping someone who needed her, putting to unselfish use a life which so far had accomplished nothing worthwhile. "I will stay as long as you wish," she agreed, and added with resignation, "After all, it doesn't matter where I am."

Tenny caught the unhappiness in her words. "I'm sorry—"

"I shouldn't have said that. It has nothing to do with your problem. Is there anything else I can do to help?"

"Couldn't you get a message to—" again Tenny lowered his voice—"to someone we know? A letter from me, I mean. She's moving so often—"

The girl flinched as a wadded ball of paper struck Tinker's shoulder and bounced across the table. Tenny swore softly and slid from his chair. "Someone's coming, Tink," he muttered. "I've got to get out fast!" Stooping, he sidled between tables and into the crowd of dancers.

Curious, the girl moved to pick up the paper wad.

"Let it lay!" snapped Tinker. "Just a signal, I guess." Leaning back, relaxed, he hooked one elbow negligently over the chair back and smiled at her.

Above the smile, she saw with a stab of panic, his eyes had turned hot and shimmering, like molten steel. "What should I do?" she whispered.

"Nothing. Bringing you here was my dumb idea, all the way; I'll look after you. Don't move and don't look to see who's coming. Whatever happens—you sit still."

In the night club lobby Scott surrendered hat and coat to a heavily made-up and brazenly blond checkroom attendant. Walking into the hall he was forced to classify it, with all the charity in the world, as a third- or fourth-rate establishment.

"Silk Hat? Crumpled Derby would be a more suitable name," he derided, taking in garish decorations, littered floor and the coarse faces dimly visible in the near gloom. "Rough, tough and nasty!" was his appraisal of the patrons. All in all, this seemed as near the gutter as he had ever been. John Tinker must be crazy to bring a girl like Maureen to such a place; if after all it *was* Maureen he was bringing. Anxiously he scanned the tables for a sight of the two. Surely they wouldn't be mingling in that boisterous crowd of dancers! The haze of smoke made reconnaissance difficult, so he started slowly between the tables on the right of the room.

A touch of his arm, a hoarse whisper, "Hello, Captain!"

Scott whirled to find a slender, stooping man alone at a table. Yellowish hair, silvered in streaks, sunken eyes which might have been blue but showed colorless in that twilight room. From their corners radiated lines of strain; more lines creased around the drooping mouth. Thin, blue-veined hands worried one of the Silk Hat's paper napkins, crumpling and twisting it. With a shock Scott recognized Daley's brother, the Gent.

The weary eyes fell before his incredulous stare, shifted to the dancers, to nearby tables, to the door. Meaning to reassure, Scott said cordially, "Hello, there —" and stopped in confusion. What was the poor fellow's first name? Ace had never spoken it. "Daley" would be too formal and unfriendly from an older man, but should a comparative stranger call him "Gent"? Avoiding a decision Scott asked, "Are you here alone?"

The man looked at him, then away. "I'm on watch."

He spoke so low that Scott leaned closer. "On watch —for what?"

Another shifting glance, this time with a faint spark of interest. But there was no change in the sepulchral whisper that made Scott think of creeping ghosts. "Ace says you're O.K.," said the Gent softly, "so I guess it's all right to tell *you*. Ace is working in the tunnel—I'm on watch. He says we ought to finish digging our way out and make our break *tonight*." There was heartbreaking anticipation in the word. The Gent licked his colorless lips, twisted the napkin in evident indecision, and at last faced Scott. His voice shook as he asked, "You want to come with us, Captain?"

Scott felt a warm surge of pity and admiration. The man whom Daley claimed was one hundred per cent improved still suffered through spells of reliving the frightful months in an enemy stockade. Still knew the agonizing hope of escape, relying on his only friend. And yet, with all this he was unselfish and brave enough to multiply the risks by taking another prisoner with him. That quality in him which had won Ace's devotion tugged at Scott's heart.

But why was he in this place? Had Daley come here to meet Tinker? The telegram *had* been signed "D." Suddenly Scott picked out Tink's blond head at a table not ten feet away. Beside him sat another man—not Daley, by his build—and the princess!

She had changed from her costume of the afternoon; a black dress brought out the highlights of her face as she talked to the stranger whose face was hidden. All three leaned close over the table in the pose, Scott thought impatiently, of a trio of conspirators.

As he straightened to move toward them the Gent gripped his wrist with a muttered, *"He's here!"* His other hand snapped the wadded napkin in a quick arc to glance from Tinker's shoulder. In a flash the stranger slunk away among the dancers. Tink and Maureen remained at the table, both sitting straight, the girl white-faced.

Scott twisted his arm from the Gent's grip with an angry jerk. The man had made a fool of him! Planted there to watch for Scott's approach and warn his friends, the ex-prisoner had put on an act so convincing that it had almost made Scott forget his errand.

The idea was driven from Scott's mind when a bony elbow dug into his back and a man crowded past and headed for Tinker's table. Even without the blue Homburg Scott recognized the newcomer, who leaned across their table and glared at the girl, as his hand fastened on her shoulder.

Scott charged forward, but there were sprawling patrons in his way. It took him seconds to weave between them.

Those seconds were packed with action. As Blue Homburg touched the girl John Tinker brought his right hand up off the table in a lightning slash at the man's throat. The thug's head snapped back; with a strangled cough he bent forward, clutching his neck. Tink's left hand flashed up and chopped down below the man's ear. He crashed to a writhing heap on the floor.

Two men at the next table sprang up and charged Tinker. The girl gasped a warning, then shut her eyes and sat rigid, white as death. But Tink needed no alert from her; he was on his feet and waiting. He ducked a wild punch from the nearer man and continued the motion by driving his shoulder into the unprotected stomach of the second, who promptly folded over and sank to his knees. Like a steel spring Tink bounced off and spun to finish his other assailant.

But Scott had arrived in time to block that man's

lunge, clamp a grip on his arm and twist it behind his back. "Hold it, Tink!" he commanded.

The orchestra had screeched to a halt in the midst of a tune and the hall was in an uproar of shouts and screams as dancers surged across the floor to join the milling crowd near the fray. A waiter, built like a mammoth, made a clutch at Tinker, who slid under his arm and started the same judo slash which had crippled Blue Homburg.

"Tink!" Scott's sharp word stopped him in time and, as he backed away, Scott thrust his own helpless victim into the waiter's arms. "Hold him till he cools off," he ordered with such authority that the bewildered waiter instinctively grappled with the guest.

"The trouble is all over," Scott informed waiter and gaping crowd. "That thug"—he indicated Blue Homburg, who had struggled to his feet and was weaving toward the rear of the hall—"insulted this gentleman's friend and got what was coming to him. That's all."

Without waiting for comment or question he took the girl's arm and urged her through the ring of spectators. The orchestra came to life; reluctantly dancers drifted back onto the floor.

Tinker elbowed his way alongside Scott. "Sorry that happened, Captain. I thought it would be O.K. to pop in here for a minute."

"I'll take this up with you later," growled Scott. "You *knew* there might be trouble, or why did you plant the Gent to watch?"

"Is *he* here?" Tink's surprise seemed genuine. "Ace must have brought him, then—"

"See that he gets out all right. I'm taking this young lady home."

"Yessir." Obediently Tink dropped back.

When they reached the entrance lobby without further incident, Scott sighed his relief. "You wore a coat?" he asked. When the girl nodded, producing the check, he retrieved his own things and accepted a glossy mink coat from the attending blonde. Her practiced eye assayed coat and owner.

"You really got something there, big boy!" she approved huskily, watching him wrap the fur tenderly about the girl's shoulders.

As Scott hurried his princess to the open air she murmured, "This is the first chance I've had to catch breath enough to say, 'Thank you again, Pilgrim.' How glad I always seem to see you turn up. I was terrified that Johnny would be hurt, until you took over."

"Johnny?" His exclamation mingled impatience with amusement. "My dear—my dear girl," he amended, "I wasn't *rescuing* John Tinker, believe me! I was trying desperately to save some innocent bystanders from getting killed—and painfully killed, at that. Luckily Tink was pulling his punches." He turned her down the alley where he had parked his car. "Get in," he ordered.

"Yessir!" she mimicked Tink's response. When Scott took his seat she darted a furtive look at his set jaw. "Home, James," she commanded.

"We're not going home." Sensing her dismayed start he added, "Not yet. We'll drive out along the river and back."

For the next few moments not a word was spoken. His thoughts kept pace with his heart, which raced with eagerness. What did he care for shrouding mystery and suspicion? Even though the girl had not confided in him—had told him nothing about herself or her background—Maureen was the girl he loved. That ought to be enough for any man; it was enough for him. He would insist that she accept his help in clearing her brother, a task he was ready to assume sight unseen. When she was finally clear of any shadow from that mess, things ought to be a lot different.

As he drove up onto the Harvard Bridge he broke the silence, his voice taut with emotion. "Princess, we need to straighten out a few matters. I don't know whether you realize the danger you were in tonight—"

"I, Pilgrim? Your friend, John Tinker, was in that fight. I was only an onlooker—a frightened onlooker—"

Scott interrupted. "Forget the fight. I'm perfectly serious in saying that Tinker was in no danger. Good Lord! If you'd ever seen him in action against the enemy—" He clipped the sentence off. "Thank goodness, you never did! But I'm talking about the man who grabbed you—the same one who followed you at the museum. This afternoon you forced me to make a promise, but there was a string attached, remember. Evidently you *are* in danger, so that promise is canceled. You'll have to answer my questions—and I mean *now*. Why were you at that dive tonight?"

At the blunt question the figure beside him stiffened. "Just *why* must I answer your questions?"

"Because I love you. Because sometime—you're going to marry me."

The girl caught her breath, but recovery was instant. In a tone of mocking incredulity she declaimed, "Is this possible? Is one of *the* Pelhams—to quote your cousin —asking a girl like *me* to marry him? Beware of entangling alliances, O Pilgrim! I am taboo! My—" she stumbled over a word.

"I know all about your brother!" Scott's interruption was abrupt and forceful. "He is Walter Tenny, late salesman for Edson and Randolph, now a fugitive from the law—but innocent."

The girl fixed sober eyes on his face. "Is that what you—do you really believe that?"

"Of course!" Assuming that the breathless question referred to his faith in Walter Tenny, Scott attempted to bolster her confidence with some slightly untruthful boasting. "I know all about it, knew of it before you outlined that suppositious case against 'a jewelry salesman' this afternoon. You asked my advice then; I'll give it to you now; go straight to William Randolph and—"

"Oh, no!" The cry was pure horror. "Not to *him*—ever!"

Scott's hands gripped hard on the wheel to repress the rage that blazed in him. So Hapgood was right when he suggested that Maureen Tenny might have left her job because of Randolph's unwelcome attentions! That rotten playboy—if he ever met him—"

Too shaken to drive with safety he swung in to the curb. Beyond a black stretch of water loomed the shadowy bulk of the stadium. Here at this hour there was little traffic. He killed the motor and set the brake. His voice was rough with intense feeling as he suggested:

"All right. If you—if you have reasons for avoiding Randolph, go to the other partner. One way or another we are going to get *you* out from under in this, and not let it drag along all winter."

"I can't go to either," the girl whispered. Wide eyes implored his understanding. "We can't think only of me—there are others involved. And I've promised—" She bit her lip, stopping further revelations, and looked away. Her hands twisted the evening bag.

Scott frowned at the averted face. *Others involved—I've promised*—Forgotten, scarcely noticed scraps of incident, of conversation swirled to the surface of his memory. Tink's warning against the girl in Number Three, Tink squiring her to the Silk Hat, and her alarm when Tink was attacked. "Johnny!" she'd called him. Scott fumed. "Why can't you confide in me?" he demanded harshly. "Won't Tinker allow it?"

"Tinker?" There was a touch of hysteria in her laugh as she asked, "Johnny?"

Scott winced as she repeated the name. "That's what I said! How long have you known him?"

The freezing quality which had jolted Scott before was back in her voice and manner. "Do you realize that you are extraordinarily impertinent, Pilgrim?"

"I realize that I am extraordinarily in love, Princess."

"Is this your usual approach—method—of love—of—"

Scott laughed at the encouraging tremor and fumbling. "Steady your voice, my dear, and come right out with it; say 'love-making,' because that is what I'm trying to do. I have no usual method; this is my first experience. Now, why not reward that humiliating confession by answering my question?"

A smile lurked in the eyes which at last met his. "Yes, now that you are properly humble," she announced, "I will grant your request. I have known Mr. Tinker for—for some time."

"That," grumbled Scott, "is about as indefinite an answer as you could invent. We'll let it pass. Why did he take you to that dive?"

"Pilgrim, you are hopelessly archaic. Thousands of nice girls go for that sort of thing—atmosphere, seeing all sides of life. Personally, I've never enjoyed it—"

"Another gold star for you—from me. However, I refuse to be sidetracked into an argument over the merits of night clubs. *Why* did he take you there, I repeat."

"He said that—that I could help someone. Someone I care for."

Scott brushed aside the camouflage. "Your brother."

"If you insist on brass tacks—my brother." She flashed another glance at him and dropped into Miss Wheeler's bittersweet drawl. "And of course to find some atmosphere for my new novel!"

"Did you help?" Scott kept firmly to his subject.

"I hope so. But I was to receive a message to deliver which I didn't get because of that awful brawl. I'm afraid I didn't show up very well when that started. I could only shut my eyes—"

"You did quite right," Scott assured her, and started the car. "Lord!" he snorted, "did you think you were supposed to leap to Tink's side swinging a beer bottle? I thought you showed surprising nerve."

The girl relaxed, lifting her face to the night wind. "You make me feel better about the whole affair."

"Don't misunderstand me, I still think you were foolish to go near that place. The next time friend Johnny approaches you with any philanthropic scheme turn him over to me."

The ominous suggestion in that made her offer lightly, "I will agree if you promise not to scold him for tonight."

Scott nodded grudging assent. It had already occurred to him that he would be on awkward ground if he pursued his first angry impulse to rake Tink over the coals. The little man was not answerable to his employer for his personal life. Unless Scott declared his unreciprocated love for Maureen, hardly a proper move to his servant, what excuse had he for telling Tink whom he should take out or where they should not go? And after Maureen's assurance that she knew Johnny, questioning him would be showing lack of faith in her. No actual harm had come of that expedition; better let it drop.

They crossed the river and whirled down the moon-silvered road onto Storrow Drive. The Basin shimmered with lights reflected from the Cambridge side, few and widely scattered at this hour. When they reached the apartment buildings Scott spoke, his voice serious.

"Tomorrow I have to go out of town, perhaps for a week. A new project for Uncle Phil in Pittsburgh. I want you to promise that before I return you will communicate with Mr. Edson about those securities. Tell him the whole story—"

"Why won't you understand?" the girl begged. "I *can't!*"

Scott opened the car door for her. "In the bright lexicon of youth," he quoted smiling, and paraphrased, "there's no such word as 'can't.' " His face became serious. "I warn you, Princess, if you haven't contacted Edson when I get back—then I shall."

"You wouldn't dare!" She faced him defiantly.

His ardent eyes met and held hers. "I would dare anything to free you from this mess. Winning your love has all the hazards of an obstacle race, tripping over mystery, balked by lack of knowledge. But I have made the start, and, like you—I don't give up. *Nothing* is going to stop me!"

THIRTEEN

SCOTT returned from his Pittsburgh expedition with the satisfaction afforded by a solid week of productive work. Not only had the different surroundings enabled him to concentrate on business, but removal from the storm center of suspicion and uncertainty for those few days had ironed out most of the wrinkles in his disposition. For the first time in weeks he whistled while he planned and sketched in his workroom, hurrying to note down every detail discussed on his trip.

Even in this absorption, however, a corner of his mind devoted itself to the peculiar reception accorded him by John Tinker, who had given every indication of being thrown completely out of gear. Pale-faced and glassy-eyed he stared at Scott when he arrived, instead of leaping to carry his bag and briefcase to the bedroom.

"I thought you—you said you'd be on the noon train," he stammered, following with snapping fingers as Scott took his luggage to the room.

"I worked late yesterday, so I had a good night's sleep at the hotel and hopped an early plane. Everything all right here?"

"Yes, *sir*—everything's swell, no kidding!" Tink's enthusiasm drew a surprised glance from Scott, at which the little man flushed brick-red and hastily slung the suitcase onto its rack. "Sure is good to have you back. I just wasn't expecting you—not so soon, see? But everything's O.K."

Scott felt a twinge of unpleasant memory; that night at the Silk Hat, Tink hadn't expected him. But he refused to look for trouble, and in silence unstrapped his briefcase to shuffle through its contents. "Loads of work here, all rush," he said. "I'm getting right after it. No calls and no callers, if you're going to be here."

"Well, sir—well, honest—" Tink's voice cracked, his forehead creased in an anxious frown. "I was going out, just for a while—I *got* to, Captain!"

"Go ahead. I won't answer any calls, then." Scott headed for the workroom. Carefully he ironed all eagerness out of his question, "All well with Miss Tenny, too?"

"Miss—Tenny?" It was a strangled whisper.

"Miss Tenny—in Number Three." Scott waved a hand toward the next apartment and eyed Tink curiously.

"Oh!" The man's face reddened again. "Sure, she's O.K. Yeah, she's swell!" He edged toward the door. "Well, if you don't need me—"

"Scram!" was Scott's smiling order. "I've work to do."

Three hours later, his projects well outlined, he remembered that he was due for lunch with Philip Pepperell at their club. Still an hour's leeway, but he stacked his papers, forgoing more desk work in favor of a fast walk in the open air and a chance to organize his report to Uncle Phil.

As he crossed Storrow Drive by the pedestrian bridge he thought that even on a December day the Esplanade could be a thing of beauty. The sun did its wintry best to flood the land with warmth. Couples and groups made shifting patterns of color on the walks and around the frozen lagoons, motionless splashes of color on the benches. From the rainbow arch of the Hatch concert shell the Basin, unfrozen, swept upriver in a sun-splattered curve of the deepest ultramarine.

Intrigued by the maneuvers of the soaring, diving gulls, Scott collided violently with another man. His hasty apology ended in a laugh as he turned to find that his victim was Patrolman Walsh.

"Fred, I run into you—and I do mean just that—every time I take a walk," he jested. "Off night-duty now?"

"Yes, sir; you know how our tours alternate. Sorry we crashed—I wasn't looking, myself. Know why?" Walsh aimed a thick finger at a distant bench. "Get a load of John Tinker, with a *dame!* God bless the lad, it's time he began taking notice of 'em again. He's broken his heart over that boyhood crush long enough."

"Tink with a *girl?*" Scott stared at the couple Walsh had indicated. It was Tink, leaning forward, elbows on knees, talking. Amused surprise was swept away, his throat tightened as though a sinewy hand had closed on it. The girl with Tinker wore a blue suit—like a hundred others—and a green hat with a tilted brim and a cocky little feather!

Unreasoning anger set Scott's pulse racing until the blood roared in his ears. Without a word he left Walsh and headed back toward the drive, fighting an impulse to torture himself by looking again at the bench.

How much can happen in one short week! he marveled. Maureen had confessed that she was lonely, ready to grasp the first friendly hand. His own offers of help were rejected; perhaps her friend "Johnny" was more persuasive. Very well, with Tink and his pugilistic cronies to watch over she hardly needed Scott, so he could bow out of the picture.

Once more in his living room he tried to see a sunnier side to the decision. By now Lucy Wheeler must have broadcast her story of his rendezvous on the avenue. There would be embarrassing questions from Nancy. They *would* have been embarrassing because he could tell her practically nothing about Maureen. Now he need not worry about that; he could simply say that he wasn't seeing the girl any more. Then he had only to accustom himself to life without Maureen. "You fool!" he accused himself bitterly. "You know you can't!"

He looked at his watch; time to meet Uncle Phil yet? No. Or had he said one o'clock? Scott went to his workroom to check the engagement calendar on his drawing table. Half a dozen outdated sheets, for the days he'd been away, riffled through his fingers. He ran past the proper date, then stared in consternation at a day heavily ringed with red crayon. It couldn't be *this* Thursday! His annual Youth Banquet—and no preparations in train. That proved how his mind had wandered, these past few weeks, through a maze of dreams—pleasant and perturbing.

It was time now to make certain of one important element in the big night, and he went down the stairs of The Pilgrim and up the stairs of The Princess in a hurried trot. At Mrs. Beddle's door he rang the bell and waited impatiently.

When Mrs. B. answered his summons her mouth opened in surprise, her plump face wrinkled and her white curls trembled. "Lor,' Mr. Scott—it's *you!*" she exclaimed. "I was expecting—someone else!"

"If you are expecting a guest, Mrs. B., I won't—"

"Oh, no, sir! It's only—only a young person who arrived this morning from England. Do come in, Mr. Scott—come in near the fire." She poked the glowing coals remaining in the fireplace. "I'll build it up—though I suppose you don't mind the cold. Young blood, I mean, you know," she chattered.

Obediently moving to the hearth Scott wondered what had so ruffled the usually placid Mrs. B. Not the visitor from England; the housekeeper's warm heart was forever taking in new arrivals—young, inexperienced relatives of old friends—who stayed with her until they learned the ways of America.

"Another nestling?" he asked smiling. "For you to teach and send forth to battle with life?"

"Why, sir—" Mrs. Beddle gulped and veered away from an answer. "I do try to help them, Mr. Scott; my heart yearns over young people. They have so much to learn, and in a week they're chattering slang and turned so highhanded about letting an old woman tell them what's proper. And they still so ignorant."

Scott made no reply. He was scowling at a glove on the floor beside the fireplace chair. A yellow pigskin glove—with a gaping hole in one finger. Last seen on the avenue. "Have you tried to help the girl in Number Three?" he asked with strained casualness.

Mrs. Beddle sighed. "Indeed I have. One look at her and I knew well she was eating her heart out with loneliness—or worry. Very likely both. So I've dropped in now and then with a bit of something to tempt her appetite, or for a little chat. And I tried to get her to come here sometimes, instead of keeping so close in that apartment. But she wouldn't come. Not until—I mean—" She hesitated.

Scott picked up the glove. "Until today? Isn't this hers?"

"Yes, but where—? Oh, she probably dropped it when—"

"When she left with Tinker? I saw them on the Esplanade."

"Oh." Mrs. B. followed the monosyllable with a lengthy examination of Scott through glistening spectacles. "Well, if you saw them, why—?" Her eyebrows arched. "You don't mean you're annoyed because Mr. Tinker is walking out— going round—with a young lady? I'm sure he doesn't neglect his work. Not like so many of the young folk these days. A lick and a promise, and 'When do I get my pay?' A steady worker he is, and that obliging."

With difficulty Scott stemmed the flood and brought up the original subject. "How long have Tinker and the prin—the girl in Number Three—been going out together?"

"Lor', sir—never!" If the housekeeper was not sincere, her shocked surprise was a superb performance. "Not that I know of, that is. Why, he'd never laid eyes on her until one day last week—the day I did up your rooms, Mr. Scott. He made me take him up to see her."

"You mean he didn't know her?"

Mrs. B. shook her head. "Not he. I mind how he stood outside her door, nervouslike, snapping his fingers like Christmas crackers. I introduced them, she asked him in, and I went back to my work." She hesitated, then reproved, "I'm sure you didn't come to gossip, Mr. Scott."

Abashed, he acknowledged defeat and forced his thoughts into proper channels. "Quite right, Mrs. B.," he smiled, "I came to invite you to the formal dinner party I throw each year for my niece, Ellen. She wouldn't consider it complete without you—and your delicious scones." He bowed. "I do hope you find this Thursday evening free?"

The housekeeper chuckled, her cheeks pink with delight. "What a one you are for poking fun at a body, Mr. Scott! You know very well I've no engagements at all, and I'll be happy to come."

At the door he discovered the yellow glove still clutched with a deathlike grip. "Perhaps you'll return this?" he asked, and then frowned. The glove suggested many things—one in particular. "Mrs. B., what is a—a La Tour model?"

The brown, dovelike eyes twinkled. "What a question from *you*, Mr. Scott. It's a hat, of course. Did you think it was a motor car?"

"A hat? Are you sure?"

"Indeed I am. At my last place in England—Carrick Hall, it was—the young ladies had all their hats from La Tour in Paris."

"They must be rather expensive?"

"Never a model under twenty pounds. That would be in American money—let me see—about sixty dollars? Then there would be duty to pay, of course." She pursed her lips. "A dreadful price for a hat."

"Dreadful is the word," agreed Scott soberly. "Good-by, Mrs. B." He went down the hall thinking what a steep price it was indeed for a secretary, or a book cataloguer.

The staid welcome of the doorman at his club, the sober elegance of its hall, the dignified quiet of its lounge seemed an oasis where Scott could relax. He had encountered enough disturbing events for one day, and here at least could anticipate a restful hour, since nothing about his successful trip to Pittsburgh should upset Uncle Phil. That hope for peace lasted exactly thirty seconds.

Having made sure that Mr. Pepperell was not in the lounge, he scanned the occupants of the main dining hall. The long room, whose ceiling beams were darkened by age and decades of smoke from the two fireplaces and from uncountable thousands of cigars and pipes, was comfortably filled. But no Old Pep. Instead Jim Selwyn beckoned urgently from the table where he was seated with a man and woman Scott did not know. Unsuspecting he walked over.

"Join us, Scott, if you're alone." Selwyn rose to greet him and make introductions. "Old friends of yours—or at least one old friend." Turning to the couple he beamed. "Sally, behold my bachelor brother-in-law. Sally Randolph—Scott Pelham. And Scott, do you remember Bill Randolph?"

Completely taken aback Scott stared at the man who stood up with hand half extended. This was Randolph? The Don Juan who hounded secretaries from their jobs? He looked older than his years, slender and pale, white-haired. Scott glanced from him to the pretty woman with a tragic face. They had split up in a storm of ugly scandal, yet here they appeared together. In the moment that he puzzled over this contradiction he was aware that Mrs. Randolph put her own interpretation on his silence. She flushed and dropped her eyes.

Courtesy drove him to relieve her embarrassment with the whitest of lies. "Bill Randolph!" he mumbled, shaking hands at last. "Please, Mrs. Randolph, don't think I'm mentally deficient. It was so unexpected, meeting your husband after so many years." He managed a smile at the white-haired man. "I haven't seen you since those old gatherings at the Pepperells'—reunions of 'Patty's boys.' You probably don't remember me."

"I think I do," corrected Randolph, as eager as Scott to bridge the awkward chasm of silence. "Weren't you the Peps' small nephew, even then on fire to be an architect?"

"This is the boy," Jim Selwyn declared. "And right now he is one of our brighter shining lights in the building game. Sit down with us, Scott, we haven't started lunch. This is Bill and Sally's first trip to Boston in years; it should be a celebration."

"Sorry. I'm meeting Uncle Phil on business." As Scott spoke, Jim's carefully casual remark flashed sudden enlightenment. The Randolphs must be attempting a reconciliation. The wife's agonized wait for Scott's initial reaction suggested that they had met hostile looks already, here where Bill had been so well known. Jim Selwyn was standing by them, of course; no force on earth—or the devil himself—could swerve Jim from a friendship once given. Not a bad pattern to follow, Scott admitted, and surrendered.

He drew out the chair beside Mrs. Randolph. "I'll keep you company until Uncle Phil shows up," he offered, trying to sound agreeable. As the other men sat down Jim's hand brushed his shoulder in a stealthy pat of approval. Encouraging, but not helpful. Scott fumbled for a topic of conversation, plunged at random. "In spite of Jim's accolade," he said, "my 'bright and shining' architecture at present is trying to force ordinary stone and steel to reproduce the inspired, but impractical, visions of Philip Pepperell."

"Don't tell me," scoffed Randolph, "that Old Pep has descended to *building!* What's become of the double-P tradition? Sally, you remember his famous System?"

"But I also remember Uncle Phil," she answered with attempted lightness. "I'm sure that he is clever enough to make building fit in."

Scott nodded. "Exactly what he did, worse luck." He intended to tell them, with appropriate scorn, the names conferred on his work, but thought of The Princess engendered a bright snapshot of Maureen, fanning to new life his dislike of Randolph. He'd better avoid that—

The hurrying waiter drove the thought out of his mind. Having placed an iced grapefruit before Mrs. Randolph he turned quickly with Selwyn's portion. Too quickly. The glass fruit bowl skidded, tilted, and poured a jet of ice water into Sally's lap.

With a hissing gasp she pushed back her chair. The color drained from her face, dark eyes contracted to chilled steel daggers.

Scott, remembering her reputation for hysterical outbursts, braced for an explosion and saw Randolph stiffen with the same apprehension. Even the waiter halted his hasty attempt to mop her dress and drew back warily.

The woman opened her mouth, then clamped her lips and quickly bowed her head. For an instant only. When she looked up her cheeks were hotly red, the brown eyes fixed on her husband. Slowly she smiled at him, at the apprehensive servant. "It did no harm," she said, "don't worry about it." Giving her napkin a casual brush across her dress she picked up a spoon and began on her grapefruit. "How is lovely Aunt Patty, Mr. Pel—Scott?" she inquired.

While he answered he was aware of the glance exchanged by Randolph and Jim, and the latter's admiring nod. He added his own silent applause for the woman's exhibition of self-control. Had her husband made a similar effort to change his nature?

"Prescott! You slicker!" The booming accusation heralded Philip Pepperell's charge across the room. "When I say one-thirty I don't mean two o'clock! I've combed every room in the place, including the bar, and here you're hiding in the dining room!"

Scott excused himself and turned to intercept the advance, not sure how the choleric old gentleman would conduct a meeting with the notorious Randolphs. He and Aunt Patty had sedulously avoided any mention of them since their disgraceful publicity. "Where did you think we'd eat—in the bar?" he jeered, knowing from experience that his only defense against Old Pep was prompt counterattack. "I tired of waiting for you, so I sat down with Jim. Let's get a table."

"Jim Selwyn?" Pepperell lowered his head to peer over his glasses. "Who's that with him?"

"The Randolphs, Uncle Phil. Here's a quiet spot in the corner—"

"Randolphs? Bill and Sally? Good God! Why didn't you say so?" He headed for them at a shambling gallop. "Bill!—Sally! Damn—*darn* your eyes, why didn't you let me know you were in town? Great to see both of you!" His pumping handshakes left no doubt of that. "Hi, Jim!"

"This was a flying visit," Selwyn explained for the flushed Randolphs, his voice low-pitched, confidential. "Bill had business with me, and Sally came along. That other—misunderstanding—is cleared up now—"

"I should hope so!" Uncle Phil trumpeted. Obviously he saw no reason to hide the good news. He clapped Randolph on the back. "Cheers for both of you! Knew you had too much sense to split up. Told Patty so. Didn't need to tell her—she knew it all along!" Catching sight of an acquaintance nearby he beamed. "Hi, Wilbur! Look who's here—Bill Randolph. You remember him—you ought to, he took enough money from you at golf!"

Wilbur, thus pilloried, flushed while he waved. "Bill! Sorry I didn't notice you come in. Hello, Sally. Nice to see you again."

"Sure is!" Uncle Phil regarded them fondly. "Could you make it for dinner tonight? Patty'd love to have you."

"Next trip we will—word of honor," Randolph assured.

"Great!" Pepperell scowled at Jim Selwyn, who was talking quietly to Scott. "What are you two whispering about?"

Jim laughed, and Scott heaved an exaggerated sigh of resignation. "We'd better confess, Jim, or suspicion will spoil his appetite. Sir," he explained with mock deference, "we took the liberty of arranging a plan. Jim was supposed to drive Ellen to a school party at the skating club, then on to tea at a certain Pepperell mansion. Mr. Selwyn, however, having business to transact, asked if I would—"

"You can't!" growled Old Pep. "I want you this afternoon."

"Hold everything, Simon Legree!" Scott soothed, and to the others said with an expressive shrug, "See what it means to be a slave? Now, Uncle Phil, relax. I'm going to dispatch Tink on this errand—which he will enjoy as much as Ellen—and then I'm completely at your mercy—I mean, service."

Laughter blew away the last of the tension in the group, already more at ease because of Pepperell's outspoken acceptance of the Randolphs. Before he and Scott adjourned to their own table two more former friends paused on their way out to greet Bill.

"The Rubicon is crossed, the Randolphs seem to be in," Scott remarked as they sat at their table. "Thanks to you, Uncle Phil."

"Poppycock! Everyone likes Bill and Sally and is glad to see them together again. People, my boy, are always willing to give a hand to someone in hard luck. Only sometimes"—he indulged in a typical Old Pep impish leer—"it takes a little dynamite to start things rolling."

FOURTEEN

SCOTT left his uncle to place their luncheon orders while he called his apartment. Apparently the Esplanade outing was over, because Tink answered promptly. A thoroughly satisfactory outing, to judge from the lift in his voice—a vibratory happiness which Scott had not heard for months. Cheerfully he accepted the responsibility of delivering Ellen Selwyn to her various social engagements.

The call reminded Scott of his promise to Tinker, and over the succulent oyster cocktails for which the club was noted he brought Uncle Phil up to date on the young man's plans for the future.

"It's all very much in the air," he ended, "because Tink has no idea how to set up a physical-culture studio, if that's what you call it, and not much money saved up. Not that he spends any, but he's never let me pay him a decent salary. And he's so independent that I doubt if he'd let me back him. But he has great respect for you and was pleased when I said I'd ask your advice. So if you get a chance to think about it—"

"Don't need to think about it!" Pepperell stood up to survey the dining room. He saw the man he wanted and called, "Lawrence, come here—got something for you!" Sitting down he grinned at Scott. "Lawrence, as you know, runs this clubhouse, and at the last meeting of the governors he reported that the man who's been in charge of our gym, squash courts—everything like that—wants to retire. What's the matter with that job for Tink? Great chance to learn the ropes and save some money toward his own setup."

When Mr. Lawrence arrived with a respectful greeting, Old Pep pulled him down to a chair and plunged with his customary vigor. "Got a man for the gym yet?"

"Oh, no, Mr. Pepperell. The type of man we want can't be picked up overnight. I am—"

"He can be," snapped Uncle Phil, "if you know where to pick him up! We've got him for you. Tell him, Prescott."

Keeping his enthusiasm in hand, Scott gave the club director a detailed description of John Tinker. Mr. Lawrence, making copious notes, was visibly impressed, not only by the list of virtues, but even more by Old Pep's frequent and forceful confirmation. He took Scott's phone number; he would arrange an interview at once.

"That's that," said Uncle Phil when Lawrence had gone. "Now let's get down to business." He speared one of the brook trout offered by the smiling waiter and held it impaled while he glared at Scott. "You still narrow-minded about names for the new apartments?"

"Let's not tangle over that now. If you're so hipped on your System, why can't you be satisfied because you are building them in Pittsburgh—Pennsylvania?"

"M'm." Pepperell chewed slowly, digesting the thought. "Maybe you've got something, Prescott."

Encouraged by this small and possibly temporary victory, Scott launched an account of his negotiations with the Pittsburgh contractors, and the conference proceeded smoothly.

Leaning one elbow on the mantel in the Selwyn living room Scott puffed his pipe and dreamed whirling thoughts. Not of the satisfactory talk with Uncle Phil. That had raised certain legal questions which they felt should be referred to Jim Selwyn, so Scott caught him before he left his office and rode home with him, obtaining encouraging counsel on the way. Now he waited to return in his own car when Tinker delivered Ellen from her social round.

Tinker! Scott frowned unseeingly at his sister, who was reading a letter to Jim. And to him as well, had he been able to pay attention. Instead he considered John Tinker—and the girl in Number Three. The unusual note of happiness when Tink answered the phone. Could Maureen have such an effect on the solid Tinker? Scott winced. Why not? She had that effect on *him*, didn't she? More each time he met her in fact. Still, that cheerfulness might have been relief; perhaps "Johnny" had succeeded in persuading her to give Edson information about the missing bonds. The week which Scott had allowed her for that was ended. If she made no move—he would!

Nancy Selwyn looked up. "Did you speak, Scott?"

"No."

"I thought you said, 'That's that!' with great finality. My mistake. But it would have been an apt comment just the same." For a moment she studied him with the speculative eye of an anxious sister. "In case you weren't listening, this letter is from Jane Randolph, Bill's sister. Remember what I told you about that tragic mix-up?"

"I remember." Scott exchanged a glance with Jim.

Intent on the letter, Nancy missed the byplay. "This is from London, but she says 'sailing for Buenos Aires tomorrow.' I infer that Faith is with her, although Jane never says so, naturally. She writes:

"Keep our secret a little longer, Nan. We have accomplished something by our disappearing act. I hear Faith's parents were shocked into realization and reconciliation. I hope it will endure. Poor little Faith, shamed into exile when she ought to be having the happiest time of her life. She adored her father, but his faithlessness has embittered her; always something of a Puritan, she argues that if he would not be true and honorable, who would be?

"Of course that mood will pass. She will make good; a golden thread of courage is woven through her spirit. By the way, did you know that the Randolphs are planning a memorial building to their son and are looking for an architect—"

Nancy interrupted herself. "Jim, why not recommend Scott to Bill?"

"I've already done it. Bill brought it up this afternoon—"

"Jim," Nancy cried, "have you seen Bill? Why didn't you let me know?"

"They asked me not to. They are naturally sensitive about their notoriety. This was a trial trip to see if their friends had crossed them off their lists. Fortunately, Scott and Old Pep started the ball rolling and I think things will work out."

Jim gave Nancy a brief description of the episode with the careless waiter. "A real triumph for Sally. Bill praised it afterwards, Scott, when she wasn't there. He says they are both making themselves over, as their only hope of winning back their daughter."

"They can do it," Nancy asserted, "if they act like normal people."

"Well, they're trying." Jim ground out his cigarette and sat forward, elbows on knees. "I had quite a session with Bill; you noticed how keyed up he was, Scott?" His brother-in-law nodded. "Alone with me, he let himself go. Grim as death, white faced. Words pouring out as if there were no end to them. The gist of it was that Sally would never again have cause to doubt his loyalty. Admitted he had been to blame, the wifely tantrums got on his nerves. But he insists that he never was the utter profligate that her lawyers made him out. And he wanted you to hear all this, Nan, direct from me. Because he still thinks a lot of you and wants your respect."

Nancy laid her hand on his and kept it there.

"Then he said that he's learned a lesson; that life is a battle which hurts more when you try to evade its responsibilities than if you face the firing line and take what comes. He ended by apologizing for boring me with his troubles. Tried to end, that is, but he couldn't stop talking. I suppose it was having a sympathetic listener. Lord knows, I was that. Because he had been my best friend, but also because he sounded completely sincere and almost out of his mind with worry."

"Worry—about Faith?" Nancy guessed.

"Yes. What finally had pierced his armor of selfishness was something she said at the lawyer's, in a passionate outburst that triggered their reform. That they had ruined her life, because no decent man would marry a girl whose parents had been so disgustingly exploited in the papers, by their own doing. 'Ruined her life.' That was what broke Bill's heart and has gnawed at him ever since—the fear that she may believe a decent life is finished for her and tie up with some man—without marriage—because of that."

Jim took out a handkerchief and wiped his forehead. "I've been torn by some stories in court, but not like this," he said with an apologetic smile.

"Has he so little faith in his daughter?" demanded Nancy with indignation. "Couldn't you reassure him, Jim?"

"What could I say? Nothing but, 'Don't be a damned fool, Bill, she'll come through.' "

Nancy patted his hand. "I can't imagine a better way to help him."

"I guess it did, at that. He settled down and changed the subject to a different problem." Selwyn relaxed and lit another cigarette. "It would seem that one of their salesmen has disappeared with a bunch of bonds. Bill is convinced that the man is not a thief—that there is another explanation for his disappearance. Edson, Bill's partner, is positive that the salesman is guilty."

Scott sat down and leaned forward tensely. Jim eyed him curiously before going on.

"There was a big reward posted, of course, and Edson is sore at Bill because he feels that it would have brought a solution of the case if he hadn't interfered. The suspected salesman has a sister, who was in New York at the time, so naturally the police started after her for questioning, but couldn't locate her. Then Bill announced that the reward offer was null and void if she was shadowed, interviewed or brought into the case in any way."

"How odd!" Nancy began, but Scott was on his feet.

"Does Randolph know where the sister is?" he asked.

Jim smiled. "Come to life at last? You've been so quiet I began to think my monologue had put you to sleep. It happens that I asked Bill that same question. He assured me that he had no idea. During the summer, while the girl was doing an excellent job cataloguing his books, he recomended her to the Jordan girls, who wanted the same thing done to theirs. He thought it was all set, but then they wrote that they were staying in Italy for the winter and would postpone the job. He assured me again that he hadn't seen the girl since she left him."

"Did you tell him," Scott asked, "that they must have changed their minds, because someone is doing it?"

"I did not. Why worry him about that? He's upset enough over the missing securities. He came up here to Boston to ask me to check up on Quigley, the private detective who's working on the case for them."

"Checking here?" was Scott's shocked exclamation. "What's he—"

The question was trampled into dust by the tempestuous entry of Ellen, as usual engulfed in the joyous scrambling of the boxers, Major and Minor. When she pulled off hat and coat and squatted before the dying fire, the dogs sank panting on either side.

"What a day, Mother! The skating club was divine—" She leaped up to favor Scott with a resounding kiss. "Old sweetie! Thanks for letting Tink drive me, and in your super car! The girls simply died! And when he touched his hat and opened the car door for us—! Only he spoiled it by winking at me."

"I'll reprimand him tonight."

"Don't you dare—I loved it! And he was so nice to all the girls; they're simply mad about him. The most fun I've had for ages, and I think he enjoyed it too. He acted so happy and just like a boy, all the time. He's usually sort of sober."

Scott felt that twinge which was anything but happiness. One hour with Maureen to cure years of hopeless waiting?

"And that car!" Ellen bubbled on. "Daddy, why can't *we* have one like that?"

"My dear child!" Jim waved his cigarette. "You are too flattering. A maroon convertible of that particular make, complete with every luxury, may be possible for a rich and carefree playboy like your uncle, but for a hard-working lawyer with a family—I ask you!"

"I can always hope." Ellen gave him a sly grin. "Oh, Uncle Scott—we had one bad break today; had to change a tire. I mean, Tink did. Leaving the skating club he took a side road to go to Uncle Phil's, and a spike a foot long went through the right rear! And oh, while he was changing it—I was sitting on a little fence watching, because he wouldn't let me help—these three men came running up. At first I thought they were college boys out for exercise. You know, jogging along in T-shirts and sneakers, only they didn't look like college—they were older men and sort of rough.

"They didn't see me, I guess, and one of them yelled, 'For the love of Mike, there's old Tinker on his knees at last!' They all laughed and galloped over to him, but he jumped up, red as a beet, and pointed at me. 'Beat it boys!' he yelled, sounding quite mad. And they beat it. But I had a good look at them—"

Ellen paused to wrinkle her brow and run a tongue over her lips. "One of them—the little one—" She hesitated again.

Scott watched her, puzzled by her reaction to meeting, he was sure, the Ace Daley entourage.

"What's the matter, honey?" Jim Selwyn asked.

Ellen rubbed one hand across her eyes. "Nothing. I just felt queer, now, thinking about him—the same way I felt when I saw him. I don't know why, but he made me feel like crying. The other two were different."

"How were they different?" her father asked.

"Just ordinary men—but tough. Tink said they were prize fighters. One of them looked like the ones we see on television."

"Prize fighters?" Nancy exclaimed.

"They didn't—get fresh, did they?" Jim demanded.

"Oh, no. They didn't even speak to me."

"It's all right, Jim," Scott smiled. "I know them—two of them, anyway, and they are perfect gentlemen. Ace Daley is a boxer and an old friend of Tinker's; the others were his brother and probably a sparring partner. I suppose they go out by the stadium for road work."

"Did you go to the Pepperells' then?" Nancy asked, and when Ellen nodded silently, studied the girl's sober face. "Wasn't it fun?"

"Well, I liked it—some. Dear old General kept bringing in food and everything was super, but—well, of course we had tea in the Gun Room and—it was the weirdest thing, Mother." Ellen swallowed hard and dug her heels into the rug while she attempted to explain.

"All the time I was there I kept thinking of Ken Randolph. Remember how I used to listen in when he and Uncle Phil talked guns? And today, no matter how fast I ate or who was talking, he kept coming into my mind. It was sort of spooky." She shivered and tried to cover it with an embarrassed laugh.

Scott could appreciate the uneasy look exchanged by the elder Selwyns. For a turbulent youngster who preferred dungarees to skirts, and any pet to any book, Ellen sometimes revealed disturbing emotional depths. A passing figure, a chance remark, had been known to float her away on a sea of imagination or memory, often to return from the voyage with a totally unexpected cargo.

Once, on her first dinner party at the Ritz, she startled Scott and her family by asserting that she knew the headwaiter—had seen him many times—somewhere. Falling into one of her trances she followed his every move with the vacant gaze of a sleepwalker. Not until weeks later did she electrify her family with proof positive, the picture of President McKinley in her sixth-grade history book. The likeness was beyond question.

The present situation, however, held no element of humor, and Nancy hurried tender reassurance. "Kendall was in your mind today, dear, because I received a letter from his Aunt Jane, and asked you if you remembered him. That explains it, so don't think any more about it. Who else was there?"

Ellen cast off her pall and flashed to mischievous sparkle as she cooed, "*Dear* Lucy Wheeler was there, gorging cakes and shooting poisoned darts as usual. She snuggled up to Uncle Phil and said, simply dripping sugar, 'Have you met Scott's *chawming* girl friend in the La Tour model?' " Ellen would have been blind indeed to miss the slow flush in Scott's cheeks. Before lightning could strike she asked demurely, "Mother, what's a La Tour model?"

"La Tour is a very famous designer of hats," Nancy informed her, and smiled with sisterly cunning at Scott. "Why don't you bring your friend of the expensive chapeau out here for sherry some afternoon?"

"Don't rush him, Nan," Jim cautioned.

Scott managed to produce a wry smile. "Thanks, Nan, but as Jim says, don't rush me. Especially," he fictioned, "since you know perfectly well that Lucy has always dramatized the ordinary."

"But Scott," Nancy urged, "if you do want to bring—"

"I have no one in mind, I assure you." Scott thought bitterly how true that was, unless he intended to invite Tinker to bring his girl!

When he was leaving, Ellen held his coat. Unheard-of-courtesy! Hoping to divert her piercing regard he asked, "You haven't forgotten that Thursday night is our Annual Dinner?"

"Forgotten? Not me! I can hardly wait."

Her enthusiasm sounded genuine, but she still impaled him on what Scott called her 'Fee-fie-foe-fum, I smell the blood of an Englighman' expression.

She nodded slowly. "Jeepers creepers!" she announced softly. "I'll bet I've struck the trail of something! What Daddy said—after what the Witch said to Uncle Phil. She's found out that you're crazy about that girl at The Princess! *Whoopee!*"

Her howl of delight brought the boxers charging to her side, and Scott made his escape in the confusion.

FIFTEEN

AS SCOTT went down Commonwealth Avenue he strode through a world of pearl-gray mist, with the houses only deeper shades of gray. Rain swept against him in stinging sheets saturated with the salty tang of the east wind. The broad walk was deserted for its entire length; only Scott and the fog-wreathed statues braved the elements this late in the afternoon. Far across the Public Garden and the Common, lighted windows in the buildings on Park Street peered down through the gray curtain like hundred-eyed Argus, watchdog of the gods, keeping his vigil on cloud-wrapped Olympus.

Scott pulled up his collar, jerked the brim of his hat down to meet it. Hands thrust deep in the pockets of his Burberry, he hurried toward home and drier raiment. He would have taken a taxi, but naturally, on such a day, no empty ones were in sight. And it had not been raining with such determination when he started. This was turning into a real northeaster. Rain, with Christmas only two days away!

Ahead, through the beating storm he saw the bronze statue of Garrison. It brought to mind Lucy Wheeler's caustic appraisal of Maureen's expensive wardrobe, and the companion memory of the gold cigarette case and the mink coat. Beyond the reach of a secretary, surely.

Unless she had been in on the robbery, and was cashing in her share for luxuries—Scott shook his head savagely. Absurd!

He halted in the lee of Garrison's pedestal to catch his breath and button his collar more securely. There were flecks of snow in the rain now, a sharper bite to the wind. What a night for his party! Lucky that Mrs. Beddle would not have to leave the house to attend or even her sturdy courage might have balked. Ellen was to be dropped off by her brother on his way to a hockey game; a raging blizzard wouldn't deter either of *them.*

Taking a deep breath Scott swung around the statue and plowed onward once more, head down and hat brim flattened against his eyes.

Crash!

A head, bowed like his own, drove into his chest with such force that he staggered. The other figure stumbled. He shot out his arms and caught it. Steadied it. Before he could brush up his soggy hat brim enough to see, a gay voice challenged:

"Pull over to the curb, Pilgrim! Speeding in the fog—where's your license?"

"You!" Scott stared unbelievingly at the girl who had so filled his mind, and the last trace of uncertainty whisked from his heart on the driving wind. Away with suspicions, jealousies and hesitation. Each time he saw her he loved her more. He would make her return his love—or die trying!

The mischievous sparkle in the eyes that met his, the glowing color in her face, the vivid lips curved in beginning laughter were a spark to his smoldering resolution. Without consciously willing the act he pulled her close and kissed her—a kiss of more than friendly duration. Was it his delirious imagination or did she seem to respond?

His hopes were dashed when she jerked free and faced him, chin lifted and brown eyes flint hard. "*Really,* Mr. Pellham!" she said with regal disdain. "Is that your customary greeting for a mere acquaintance? Or could this be a case of mistaken identity?"

Scott's throbbing exultation was proof against her anger. With a laugh he brazenly admitted, "It may have been a *mistake*—but not in identity!" Then he was lost in admiration of the slim figure in an almost transparent raincoat of misty green, its skirts whipping gaily in the wind. From under the pointed hood curled dark wings of hair, intriguingly flattened on wet cheeks. In spite of her twentieth-century costume, perhaps all the more because of it, she seemed the embodied spirit of the storm. Scott made a gallant bow. "No, I was quite sure who you were. The princess!"

She relented enough to smile as she straightened the disarranged hood. *"I'm* not sure it is really I, after that collision. I left my apartment to get a breath of air, but there is more air—and water—than I bargained for and I bowed to the blast, just as you did." The words trailed off into a heartfelt chuckle. "You look so funny. There is a most becoming rivulet trickling down the middle of your nose." She laughed outright, a quick burst of merriment which set his heart aflame—and died when she saw the blaze in his eyes.

With almost a sob she wailed, "Don't look as though you were ready to rend me limb from limb. That's the first laugh I've enjoyed since—I mean, for months. Can't you smile for the lady?"

The tremor in the sweet voice stilled Scott's racing blood. She wanted a friend, not a lover. For the present she would have her wish, but she could not hold him off forever. Making a valiant effort at a purely platonic tone he assured, "I certainly can smile. Will you have the tentative twitch of the lips or the full, cheek-creasing, ear-to-ear grin? Come along and walk back with me."

He slipped his arm through hers and, when she seemed to resist, warned, "Don't! You need a guiding hand to keep you from colliding with another seafarer, you careless mermaid."

Bending to the storm they plodded forward. The girl glanced sideways at the uncompromising set of his jaw and drew the wrong conclusion. "I'm sorry I laughed at you," she offered humbly.

"May you always—I won't say laugh but—feel happy when you see me," Scott prayed. He had an inspiration and pressed her arm firmly against his side. Sternly he announced, "However, you did make fun of me and must be penalized. Tonight my little niece—and Mrs. Beddle, I should add—are dining with me at my apartment. An annual celebration. I want you to join us. Won't you? I command it—or beseech and implore it, whichever is most likely to be effective."

"Oh, I couldn't!" She halted and drew away. "Thank you, but—"

Scott recaptured her arm. "Don't stand still, you'll get soaked, and so will I. *En avant!* Now, as to the soiree—Mrs. B. will call for you at six-thirty, to show you the way. We tie on the feed bags, in Niece Ellen's colorful phrase, at at early hour—she being at the ravenous age. I have planned the dinner with care—"

"Spare me the menu! It's a terrible temptation and sounds like loads of fun, but I must not go—"

Scott interrupted in turn. "As I was saying when some trivial intrusion intruded, we are to have squab with mushrooms, served *en cloche*—those delightful glass bells which my grandmother *would* call 'cloaches'; she was from Cape Cod and scorned the veneers of civilization—as well as countless other deicacies, exotic and preferably out of season." He was delighted by a chuckle from his companion. "My niece, you see, clings to the belief that I am a *bon vivant*, a veritable man-about-town, a—a—"

"One of those 'gilded lilies' you once mentioned?"

"You remembered that! I *am* flattered—although appalled at your elephantlike memory. I must take warning and be circumspect when we—" He snapped short that intended mention of the future. "Anyway, that's Ellen's picture of her uncle and I wouldn't disappoint her for the world. Coming?"

It was impossible for the girl to resist his infectious good humor. "It sounds, and I probaby quote your niece, like quite a clambake. I—do you really want me?"

"Want you? Shall I beg on my knees? These trousers will have to go to the cleaners anyway."

She laughed, and there was a reckless timbre in her voice as she declaimed, "Why shouldn't I come? A hundred years from now what difference will it make whether I—" She was silent, plodding along beside him. She looked up into the storm. "I can't look to the stars for guidance now—"

"Why not?" Scott encouraged. "They're still there, above the clouds, ready to give you counsel."

"So they are! What a comforting thought that they are always twinkling messages of hope, no matter how clouded one's own world. Thank you for reminding me, Pilgrim. Away with musty books and their cataloguing for a night—I will come to your party, kind sir."

"Promise?"

"Doubting Thomas! I'll come, no matter what! For this one evening I'll desert that hardheaded old counselor Caution and follow the merrier message of the stars. And I warn you, don't be surprised, Pilgrim, if in honor of your niece I wear something a little different from my working clothes."

Peering past the hood Scott examined all he could see of her averted face. Was there a hint of hysteria in her gaiety? "Calm down, little water sprite," he advised. "I feel as though I must hold you tightly to keep you from riding off on a rainbow, melting into the mist—or indulging in some other mythological stunt."

He was surprised to find that they were entering their foyer. "I have your promise, see that you keep it," he said as he ushered her to the entrance of The Princess and flourished a soggy mass of felt hat. "Until six-thirty—"

Back into the storm he went, scarcely noticing that it was now entirely snow and the wind was dying. With an eagerness which reminded him of more youthful expeditions he entered the nearby florist shop. Inspecting their stock in a pervading aroma of blossoms and evergreens he emerged at last with a large box under his arm. Then on to Mrs. Beddle's apartment.

He rang twice before the door was opened. Engrossed with the evening's possibilities he was quite unprepared for the blond beauty who appeared. The gray maid's uniform heightened the golden glow of her fair complexion. If this was another of Mrs. B.'s "young persons" she had picked a winner.

"Mrs. Beddle," Scott requested.

"She is dressing; may I take a message?"

A low-pitched voice, keyed perfectly to match the uniform, he noted. No trace of Scotland, though, or any distant land. She couldn't be a new arrival. "Tell her Mr. Pelham is here, please. I'm sure she'll see me."

The blue eyes leaped to his face at the name, then fell. "Yes, sir," she murmured.

At that moment Mrs. Beddle burst out of an inner room and advanced, clutching modestly at a dressing gown resplendent with huge red roses. Her cheeks were pink, her eyes shining with excitement. "Don't tell me the party's postponed, Mr. Scott! Miss Ellen can't come in this storm?'

"Nothing could stop Ellen," Scott laughed. "Everything is all set and I invited—the young lady in Number Three to join us. I came to ask if you would call for her and bring her over."

"Indeed, I'd be glad to. It's nice of you to get the child out of that apartment—a party will do her a world of good. I'll go for her in plenty of time, she may need help dressing. But don't fret," she called as Scott departed, "we won't keep Mr. Tinker's dinner waiting."

Tinker! For the first time Scott's enthusiasm cooled enough to allow sober thought. He had put his foot in it this time! He had forgotten, in the delightful companionship of their walk, that Tinker had been—been—well, dating her, hadn't he? And apparently to their mutual pleasure. And now Tink would be forced to wait on her, like any servant! What a mess! Scott ignored the elevator for the stairs to give himself time to think.

Wasted effort; no solution presented itself which would not be more embarrassing than the *status quo*. Too bad, but better break the bad news at once. He unlocked his door and strode to the kitchen.

Tink looked up from the salad he was preparing. "A rough night for Miss Ellen to come in town, sir."

"She won't mind the weather."

"Nope. She's a good sport." Tinker stowed the salad in the refrigerator. "Hey, that reminds me—she was a sport the day I chauffeured her. I told you I had to change a tire; those tubeless are good but they wouldn't stand that. Well, while I was changing it, along comes Ace and gives me a yell. Didn't see Miss Ellen, sir, or he'd never have done it. He was out doing road work with the Gent—"

"Ellen told me," Scott interrupted, cravenly relieved to postpone announcement of his intended guest.

"Oh?" Tink rubbed his chin and sighed. "Sorry, Capt—sir, I should have told you before she did. I don't want you thinking I don't take proper care of her, mixing her in that gang."

"I know that she's as safe with you as with me, Tink."

"Thanks, sir—and you can bet on it." He grinned at a memory. "Don't think they worried Miss Ellen, though. At first she was kinda popeyed, staring at them, but then did she ask me questions! About them, and prize fighters, and had she ever seen any of them on TV. Of course she hasn't because Ace has never fought before the network cameras." He chuckled. "She got real excited when I told her what goes on in Mason's Gym, where they train."

" 'Gym' reminds me," Scott said. "I told Mr. Pepperell about your wanting a real job now that you're O.K., and as you might expect from him, he pulled one out of the hat—*presto!* Mr. Lawrence, the manager at my club, is looking for a man to run our recreation facilities: gym classes and so on. He'll call you."

"At *your* club—no kidding!" Tink's eyes bulged. "Why, it sounds swell! I'm sure obliged to you and Mr. Pepperell."

"Then don't let us down. We gave you quite a build-up so, when you see Lawrence, don't go modest with him."

"O.K., sir—and thanks." Tink's eager smile narrowed to a calculating grimace. "I'll bet they pay enough so a guy could plan on getting married—after a while?"

Scott experienced a chill around his heart. "I imagine so," he agreed gruffly. "But get the job first."

"Yeah—sure!" Tinker glanced at his watch and jumped. "Right now I'd better get this dinner party rolling!"

"I'll leave you to it." Scott took a deep breath—and took the plunge. "Set *four* places; I have another guest coming."

Tink beamed. "Good work! A real party will do you good; you ain't looked too happy lately. Hey!" He cocked an eyebrow with infinite meaning. "If it's a lady you should've given me a chance to polish the family silver. They notice things like that."

"I'll do that next time. Build a good impression gradually. Take this box of flowers, Tink. Violets for Mrs. B., sweet peas for Ellen, and the orchids are for the young lady in Number Three of The Princess." Having maneuvered to the door during these directions, Scott closed it on Tink's amazed, *"Holy cats,* Captain! No kidding?"

After Scott had showered and adorned himself with dinner clothes and a royal-purple cummerbund he paced restlessly about the living room. Snowflakes spatted against the windows and door of the balcony, where Tink had hung wreaths. Tall red candles already flickered on the gate-legged table. Its central decoration brought an appreciative whistle from Scott.

A winter scene. A little snowbound red house, set among miniature fir trees, with a properly rotund Santa Claus halfway down the chimney. His sleigh and reindeer waited patiently, standing aslant on the drifted roof. Scott bent to study it, amazed at the delicate details; there were even tiny hoofprints and runner tracks behind the sleigh. A gently exploring finger satisfied his curiosity; the trees came from a toystore, the snow was that foamy white plastic so like real snow. Everything else had been painstakingly sculptured from soap and artistically painted.

"That Tink!" he marveled. "Another architect in the family!"

The door chimes! Scott listened. Tink opening the door. Then his voice in stilted imitation of the Pepperells' butler, General. "Good evening, Miss Ellen; we're honored to have you here. Won't you deposit your wraps in the guest room? Mr. Pelham will greet you in the living room when you're ready." Ellen must have flung off her "wraps" without delay, for Tink's normal voice whooped, "Hot dog!" and then lowered to a muted but unmistakable wolf whistle.

Scott quelled an inclination to echo it when his niece appeared. The transformation which he once prophesied to Nancy was accomplished. Ellen had burst from her chrysalis. Her tangerine dress billowed over rustling crinoline, the once tangled hair was brushed to a sleek ponytail of burnished copper. Her lips, Scott felt, could do with a little neutralizing; she must have smeared the orange lipstick on surreptitiously in the car. Dripping exotic earrings touched her shoulders. Obviously from the dime store, cheap, absurd—but, surprisingly effective.

Instead of the usual boisterous hug he received an extended hand and a languid, "Good evening, Uncle Scott. So nice to be here." Then she dropped the pose and grinned. "When do we eat?" Before he could answer she counted the places at the table. "Who's the fourth? Mother's in New York and Jimmy's gone to the game—Not *Dad?* He'll watch me like a hawk for fear I'll do something awful!"

Scott shook his head. "Mr. Selwyn will not be present."

Ellen moaned in horror. "Don't say it's Lucy Wheeler? I saw her heading this way when Jimmy let me out."

"Perish the thought! She was probably hiking to her bosom friend Molly, in The Princess; she haunts the place. At ease, my dear. I asked Mrs. Beddle to bring a young lady who is—"

"Oh, one of Mrs. B.'s 'young persons'? I won't mind her." She giggled. "Maybe I can help her if she's fork shy at such a ritzy party."

"Please be nice to her—"

"Mrs. Beddle!" announced Tink from the doorway, once more impersonating the sonorous General. "And Miss Number Three."

Scott glared suspiciously, but there was no trace of mockery in the smooth pink face. No emotion visible. Then the guests entered and Scott forgot Tinker. By the overwhelming relief that flooded him he knew that subconsciously he had been afraid Maureen would not come.

She was even lovelier than he had realized. A deceptively simple white evening dress shimmered with sparks of golden light. Sparks twinkled from the brilliants set in gold hoops of earrings, flashed from stones in the pendant above a plunging neckline, even glittered from the buckles of her slippers. Circlets of ruby and emerald glowed on the hand holding an evening bag.

Scott quaked inwardly. Diamonds, emeralds, rubies! More of the ill-gotten gains from those bonds? Surely not paraded so publicly! But it was natural to wonder, wasn't it? Every time he made up his mind that this girl was beyond reproach, something came up to confound him.

Martha Beddle, her brown silk muted to obscurity by such jeweled splendor, led the girl forward with the maternal pride of a hen who has hatched a swan. "Here we are, Mr. Scott!" she beamed. "And Miss Ellen! It's a real pleasure to see you, miss!" To a whisper she returned a smiling, "Surely, I remembered the scones."

The instant Scott turned from Mrs. Beddle to her companion his voice departed—his gray matter with it. As he struggled for speech he realized that Ellen was staring at him. He must introduce his guest—

The hand he had seized in welcome and clung to in desperation was gently extracted from his. Its owner smiled at Ellen. "Your uncle said his *little* niece was coming! Isn't that like an uncle, they never do let us grow up. Are you at home from college for Christmas?"

Ellen went limp with adoration. "I wish my family could hear that! They, as well as Uncle Scott, think I'm still a child. I'll tell them that—what did you say your name was?"

The question revived Scott. Evidently she had missed Tink's introduction. So much the better, one of her lightning calculations might have recalled the remarks of Lucy Wheeler. Would anything switch her present basilisk stare? Inspiration struck. "We'll call her 'the princess' tonight, Ellen. She's an author."

"And that is my nom de plume," the princess smiled.

"I know—that means 'pen name.' " Ellen regarded the celebrity with awe. Slowly her forehead wrinkled in a frown. "You know, there's something about you—have I seen your picture in the papers?"

Scott heard the faint gasp before his guest said fervently, "I should hope not!"

"I mean," Ellen muttered, still groping, "where they show the author of a new book or something?" She shook her head. "No, it wasn't a picture, I'm sure. But somehow—" She frowned harder. In the portentous silence which descended on the room the sudden exultant clap of her hands burst like a shot. *"I know!* You remind me of one of Tink's friends we met on the road. The prize fighters!"

SIXTEEN

AT ELLEN'S bizarre announcement Scott's look flashed to the princess and found her eyes on him. Amazement predominated in them, he decided, but there was also a tinge of amusement, and a question. She was expecting him to take charge, while he floundered in a nightmare of uncertainty. What could he say?

Tinker saved him by appearing suddenly with the crisp suggestion—almost an order—"Dinner is served, sir." Tension evaporated.

Scott watched him politely draw out a chair to seat Mrs. Beddle. His face wore its habitual good-humored calm, except for the nervous flush induced by his responsibilities as cook, and heightened tonight by the guests' admiration for his table decorations. Nothing remained of the surprise he had shown when Scott named his fourth guest. Perhaps he and Maureen had found an opportunity to confer before she entered the living room. She, too, appeared indifferent to his role as waiter. Her head was bent over the orchids.

Quite recovered from her fit of abstraction and unaware of its consequences, Ellen pinned on her own corsage. "These make it a real party, Uncle Scott. Thanks loads!" Without pause she transferred her attention to the cherrystone clams, dousing them liberally with sauce.

Under cover of his own preparations Scott studied her with mingled emotions. The child's strange faculty for recognizing a likeness, however remote, must have been working overtime if it could connect a sweating prize fighter with tonight's glamorous princess. Then a stunning explanation rocked Scott's laboring brain.

According to Tink, Ellen had seen Ace and the Gent—according to her story, there had been three men. And Scott, when Tinker returned from New York, had felt sure that it was Walter Tenny who came with him, using Sergeant Daley's identity papers. Now he must be masquerading as one of Ace's helpers: the third man in the group. And Ellen had noticed some resemblance when she met his sister! Scott eyed his clairvoyant niece with respectful admiration.

While the three adults politely mingled conversation with dining, Ellen devoted all her faculties to satisfying a thriving appetite. Not until Tinker served tawny meringues bulging with ice cream did she condescend to take time out from eating and focus her wide-eyed stare on the princess. This time, however, to Scott's enormous relief, the look was reverent.

"You don't look like an author," she observed frankly.

"Oh, but I really am!" Laughter mingled with wonder in the musical voice. "I wasn't sure of it myself, until tonight. But at last I am!" She drew a letter from the bag in her lap with excited fingers. "Listen to this!" She flashed an apologetic smile around the table. "I was so thrilled that I had to bring it with me, hoping, of course, that I would get a chance to boast." Her smile was all for Scott as she exulted, "Some day you may be proud to think that you once entertained a celebrity."

She blushed as Scott's eyes held hers for a disturbing moment. Then she lowered them to the letter and read:

"Dear Madam:

"We take great pleasure in accepting your cleverly illustrated story, 'The White Crane's Husband.' Our check will go forward as soon as you inform us to whom it should be made payable. You must agree with us that The Princess, Care of Mrs. Beddle, etc., etc., while it may suffice for postal authorities, would create a minor panic in banking circles.

"We beg to remain—"

"So you see"—with a smile for Scott—"I did adopt a nom de plume."

"A check!" Ellen whooped. "Hot diggety! But why not tell them your real name?" Her forehead puckered, a sign which her family dreaded. "You're not ashamed of it, are you?"

Scott intervened promptly. "Exciting news! And on the night of our annual banquet. What is the story about?"

"A white crane in Franklin Park." The breathless author was as anxious as he to switch the conversation. "I haunted that aviary before—when I first came here; the strutting, skipping birds fascinated me, and their terrific Latin names appalled me as well."

"Appalling is the word for Latin," Ellen agreed. "Deliver me!"

"I simply ignored them to concentrate on watching and sketching." Having distracted the girl's attention from identities, she dared a quick smile at Scott, who circled thumb and finger in approval. "I'm sure, Ellen, that my drawings for this story would make the pilg—your Uncle Scott—writhe in artistic horror."

Ellen sighed. "I wish I could go hunting atmosphere with you sometime, but I suppose a real author wouldn't be bothered with me. Cousin Lucy Wheeler wouldn't; she's the only other writer I know. She's always hunting for atmosphere—that's what *she* calls it, but it's just plain snooping for gossip and—" She saw Scott's rebuking frown and hesitated. "What I meant to say was—I could show you lots of places in Boston that simply reek with atmosphere.

"You'd love Memorial Hall at the State House, with the battle flags of the Massachusetts regiments and the places they fought, all the way from Bull Run to Appomattox. I always cry there—I hope you won't mind—it's so sort of final, all those torn and bloodstained banners." Closing her eyes she began to call the dreadful roll in a dream-haunted murmur. "Antietam . . . Chancellorsville . . . Gettysburg . . . the Wilderness . . ." Her eyes popped open, sparkling.

"Wilderness reminds me, I could take you to see Uncle Phil's collection of old guns. And I could show you T Wharf, where clipper ships came in with tea and spices and silks from far Cathay. That's China, you know. I could get Jimmy to drive us around. Jimmy is my brother. You'd like him," she finished, quite out of breath.

Scott heard the girl beside him draw in a sharp breath. Was she thinking of her own brother, now a hunted man? If she was, she covered it bravely with a smile at Ellen.

"I'm sure I would, I—I think brothers are wonderful. What is he like?"

"Well, he's handsome and has nice manners—and he teases me until I want to murder him! He'd keep a promise if it killed him." She nodded toward the portrait above the fireplace. "Jimmy just has to be fine, you know, not to disgrace *him*. He was our great—how many 'greats,' Uncle Scott?—grandfather, and His Excellency, the Governor of the Commonwealth of Massachusetts! We all have to live up to him, Mother says."

Scott sensed increasing tension in Maureen and switched the theme somewhat clumsily. "Have you seen the monkey lately, Ellen?"

"No. He's gone."

"Gone? From Uncle Phil's? Where did he go?"

"Gosh, don't be so jumpy, Uncle Scott!" Ellen chided. "I don't know where he went. General just told me to say goodby, because he was leaving. I wept buckets when I kissed his little black nose! Oh, do you suppose the man who left him there came back—"

Tinker was at her side, suavely suggesting, "Another meringue, Miss Ellen?" By some wizardry he had the confection ready.

"Oh, I couldnt!" she groaned. "But doesn't it look delish! No, thank you, Tink. Definitely, I'm through!"

Scott's pulse quicked to double time when Tinker served the coffee. Ellen never drank it and Mrs. B. refrained out of respect for the god of sleep, so he proposed, with a casualness he was far from feeling, "If you want a look at the new Pittsburgh apartment sketches and other things, Ellen, they are in my workroom. Help yourself."

With typical perception, Mrs. Beddle twinkled a glance from him to Maureen and rose from her chair. "May I come with you, Miss Ellen? I should like to see how an architect begins work on a new project."

As they left the room Scott intercepted the girl's attempt to follow. He dropped a hand on the chair beside the fireplace. "Sit here, Princess, and enjoy your coffee. I'll give you a private showing later." When she complied he sat on the arm of the couch.

For a time she kept her eyes on the blazing logs. Then, as though slowly conscious of the absolute quiet in the room, she looked up and surprised his eyes fixed on her with unguarded tenderness. Hastily she said, "I'm a fire worshiper, as well as a stargazer. Those flickering, leaping flames put a heart and soul into this lovely room." She glanced up at the portrait. The eyes of the gentleman in velvet and gold seemed to be studying her. "His Excellency is awe-inspiring; I feel him X-raying my spirit! Ellen's mother—your sister—thinks a great deal of family background, doesn't she?"

"In a way. Nancy has brought up her children to believe that, because of their background, they owe the world a little extra in the way of character and behavior. I think that she is right. But Nan is no snob. If she likes a person, it makes no difference what that individual has in the way of background—or money. Least of all money."

"I love your voice when you speak of your sister. Is she beautiful?"

Scott set aside his coffee cup with a sheepish grunt. "What a question to ask me! Aren't brothers notoriously blind?"

"Can you imagine her," the girl probed with heightened color, "going to a dive like that night club?"

"Yes! If she had as good a reason for going as you did. And that brings up a question I want answered. Have you communicated with Edson about those missing securities?"

"No. I—I—"

"Remember the alternative?" he prompted grimly.

"You have no right to interfere!"

"I have the right which any man has to save the girl he love, when he sees her involved in a dangerous situation." He stood up to move toward her, but she slipped past him and sat at the piano.

Running a hand over the keys she watched him hesitate, then follow. "You shouldn't keep bringing love into the picture, Pilgrim! I'm in trouble enough without having unrequited love added to the burden."

"Am I never to tell you that I love you?"

"Never. I don't like men; I don't trust them. I wouldn't marry an angel from heaven if he laid his halo at my feet!"

Scott frowned. "If you dislike men so much, how could you accept me for a friend?"

"Because I was so desperately lonely that I grasped your hand—as a drowning man proverbially clutches a straw."

"Thanks for the delicate compliment. The same sort of despairing clutch at Tinker, I suppose?" In his agitation Scott missed her laughing "Oh, Johnny!" and went on, "You talk about men as though you were a thousand years old!"

She smiled. "You have accused me of that advanced age before. And you are right—I am, in my heart." Abruptly sober she warned, "The flippant girl you met in the rain this afternoon was—was a couple of other people!"

"Do the 'couple of other people' like men?"

"No! They don't trust them, either."

"Then you're overfed on tabloid newspapers and TV

thrillers. The average man is a law-abiding, decent citizen—"

"The average man!" she scoffed, and in a magical transformation threw off her gravity and became the adorable, the tantalizing princess of the avenue. "Who wants an average man? I deserve a *superman*—I'll settle for nothing less!"

When Scott took an impulsive step forward she shrank away, bringing one hand down on the piano keys in a commanding yet harmonious chord. "Don't move! And don't pay any attention to my foolishness. I told you that acceptance of my story has gone to my head. And this gay, friendly party, after all these dreary weeks shut up in that apartment—Stay where you are, *please!*"

The panic in her voice sent his spirits skyrocketing. Was she afraid of her own emotions if he took her in his arms? It was a temptation to put his theory to the test, but he locked his hands behind him. "We'll arbitrate," he offered. "Play for me and I'll stay away."

"Consider yourself pledged to disarmament." Her eyes were brilliant with laughter. Then she sobered and improvised a slow introduction. Scott retreated to the balcony door and watched the thinning snow while she played and sang softly:

> "Now the day is over, night is drawing nigh,
> Shadows of the evening, fall across the sky. . . ."

As the final note of the fervently rendered song died away the girl choked, dropping her head on outspread arms. With an exclamation of concern Scott turned, but before he could move she was on her feet, a protesting hand extended.

"Don't scrap our treaty!" She spoke gaily although there were tears in her eyes. "Here's one that ought to really send you!" Back at the keyboard she began a rollicking samba that was currently popular. The tears were gone when she finished and looked to Scott with mischief in her eyes at his silence. She rose with a theatrical bow. "The storm of applause is overwhelming!"

The silence was electrically charged for the instant before he protested, "Play fair, Maureen, or I break that treaty! Come over here." Instead, she retreated behind the couch. "Don't be afraid, I shan't touch you. We'll clear up your brother's trouble first; then I'll ask—"

"Oh, here you are, Scott!" Jim Selwyn's voice interrupted. With a sibilant gasp the girl gripped the back of the couch, her frightened eyes on the man at the threshold. He flushed, but gave no intimation that he knew her, and after the briefest pause continued as casually as though interrupting tête-à-têtes were a daily custom.

"I came for Ellen. As Jimmy left the car at the office I thought I'd save you the trip. Randolph and I had supper together and he decided to stop off and talk memorial plans with you. Come on in, Bill."

As Selwyn stepped into the room the man behind him saw the girl as she backed slowly toward the piano. Randolph's face went blank with incredulity and paled almost to the whiteness of his hair.

Watching Maureen, Scott caught the curious glow which lighted her eyes. Love, he suspected in savage resentment. She was still in love with that—that—Before he could select a name detestable enough he saw her face stiffen to a disdainful mask.

Randolph glared from her to Scott and back to her. "What are you doing in this apartment?" he demanded.

"Don't answer, Miss Tenny!" Scott snapped, striding forward.

Her eyes were like ice as she stared at him. "How dare *you* advise me? You—you spy!" With bitter scorn she added, "You traitor!" and slipped past him to the balcony door. Hands behind her she matched furious glares with Randolph. "You thought with *his* help you'd catch me!" she taunted. "You haven't—yet!" One hand appeared gripping the door key. She jerked the door open, stepped out, slammed it. The lock grated.

"My God!" Randolph started forward. "What's out there?"

Scott backed against the door, lifted fists ready. "None of your damned business, Randolph!" he blazed.

SEVENTEEN

IN THE fast-building crisis Jim remained the calmest of the three. A speculative smile touched the corners of his lips as he surveyed the closed door and its aggressive defender.

Randolph moved closer. Anger thickened his voice. "Open that door, Pelham!"

"Hold everything, Bill," Jim counseled.

"That's good advice, Randolph!" Scott growled, contempt making every word sting. "You're too old to play knight errant, and I don't feel like *playing*."

Selwyn put in a quieting, "You take it easy, too."

"Then get him out of here!" Scott waved toward the hall—and bit off what more he would have said. "Oh, Lord!" he breathed instead.

"Why, *Daddy!*" Ellen's protesting wail heralded her entrance. "When did you come? I wanted Uncle Scott to take me home!" She flounced to his side, pulling Mrs. Beddle with her, and stared at the frozen group. "How funny you all look. Where is—"

"Surprise, honey!" Selwyn put an arm around her shoulders, linked his other arm through the housekeeper's and drew them both into the hall. His low whisper was important enough to hold his daughter, at least, spellbound. Mrs. Beddle, with the wisdom of wide experience, kept her back primly to the living room.

Randolph stared as though hypnotized at this influx of the gentler sex. Then he flushed crimson and turned back to Scott with a sheepish smile. "My abject apologies, Pelham. Jim did tell me that his daughter was dining here, but surprise at meeting—at seeing—Miss Tenny, who has been among the missing, knocked the fact out of my mind. I'm afraid I have no other excuse for making such a scene." Still red-faced he fumbled to button his overcoat. "We can talk business some other time, if you still care to."

He called, "Jim, I'm going to drop in on the Pepperells before I catch the eleven o'clock train for New

York." He consulted his watch. "I have plenty of time. And, Pelham, again I apologize for intruding on the festivities. Good night." Including Ellen and flustered Mrs. Beddle in a courteous bow he went down the hall.

"Ellen, get on your things," ordered Jim, following him.

"Come along, child," Mrs. B. urged. "Don't keep him waiting."

Alone in the living room Scott twisted the balcony door handle and rapped on the glass. "Maureen!" he called guardedly. "They've gone. Unlock the door. Hurry!"

Shielding his eyes from the inside light he peered through the glass. The balcony seemed deserted. With frightening clarity he remembered the girl arguing that, in an emergency, a person could climb down. Good God! Had she attempted it—on a night like this?

In panic he snatched up a small chair and drove its back against the glass beside the lock. The pane shattered to the rug. Glass crunched under foot as he reached through the hole, groping for the key. He pulled the door open and stepped out.

Slender footprints led to the railing where the snow had been brushed aside, and where two silver slippers stood neatly aligned, their buckles glowing like tiny beacons. Scott's heart plunged in a sickening nose dive.

Clutching the shoes he leaned to look down—but there was no need. On the opposite balcony, too, snow had been swept from the rail. Through the grillwork he could see footprints leading to the door of that apartment. His heart leaped and choked him. She had swung across—she was safe!

Followed the inevitable reaction. What a crazy stunt—everything slippery with snow! She needed a guardian. Suppose her foot had skidded— He shook off the thought; she hadn't slipped, so why torture himself with imaginings—why stand here wasting time? Make sure the crowd had left his apartment, then have it out with her. *Spy and traitor,* indeed!

It appeared, as Scott had unwillingly suspected, that Randolph was as responsible as her brother for this hiding out. Growling imprecations he went in. He was righting the battered chair when Jim re-entered the room. Selwyn grinned as he took in the broken glass, the silver slippers and his brother-in-law's unhappy face.

"You swing a nasty chair, boy!" he commented genially. "Must have been in a hurry."

Scott knew he was flushing. "I was afraid that she—she might have gone over the railing," he muttered sheepishly. He noticed the slippers in his hand and hastily set them on the nearest chair. "She didn't, thank God!"

"They usually don't, outside of the movies," was Jim's dry comment. "I hope you appreciate that highly diverting monologue I delivered, after my inopportune entrance. A slight thing, but mine own. I know how an actor feels when he enters on the wrong cue. Ad-lib like mad. At least it gave you and your friend time to get some of the color back into your faces." He twirled his hat carelessly. "Was—er—that girl here at dinner with Ellen?"

"She was—with Ellen and Mrs. B. Got anything to say against that?" demanded Scott hotly. When Selwyn only studied him without comment he snapped, "Listen to me, Jim! Maybe Randolph hired you to check up on her, but your espionage stops at *my* door!"

"What gave you the idea that I was checking on her?"

Scott's temper boiled. "You're a good bluffer in court, Jim, but I'm not buying any of that. If you're not shadowing Maureen Tenny, explain why you ducked into her apartment—"

"Maureen—" Selwyn made a bewildered gesture toward the balcony door. "You mean—*her* apartment? Are you crazy? I never saw the girl before tonight!"

"You didn't go to Number Three at The Princess, I suppose—the night of Nan's birthday dinner?"

"Why, yes." Jim sounded genuinely perplexed. "What's that got to do with—" He paused, and his eyes suddenly brightened. "So *that's* the girl who's been cataloguing!" Then sharply, "How did you know I'd been there? Doing a little sleuthing yourself?"

"No! But Lucy phoned Nan that she saw you come out. Laugh that off!"

"The Witch?" Jim's lip curled in disgust. "And Nancy never questioned me—what a woman! Believe it or not, I went there to get a book," he smiled. "Bill wrote, asking me to send him a certain volume the Jordans wanted him to sell when he found a buyer. Warned me to keep mum about it, you know how collectors are. Mrs. Beddle let me in, which Lucy neglected to mention! But I saw no girl there. That Wheeler pest ought to be shot!" he growled.

"That," Scott said, "is one point we agree on. But we certainly don't see eye to eye on Randolph. He had a nerve busting into my apartment and blowing up like that!"

"Was he the only one? Your attractive guest supplied a few fireworks, too." Selwyn's voice was amused. "Considering the situation, I can't blame either of them. A salesman named *Walter Tenny* disappears, and *Maureen Tenny* shows up here. No wonder Bill was stunned and the girl thought you had lured her here to hand her over." More soberly he added "If you see her again, tell her Bill says she needn't worry, she is safe from any interference by him."

"I'll see to that myself!" Scott began angrily, but got no farther.

Ellen swept into the room with as much dignity as a too-long overcoat and flapping overshoes permitted. Her pockets bulged, and behind her trailed Mrs. B. with a florist's box.

"A perfectly lovely part, Uncle Scott, especially the eats—and so exciting!" she exclaimed. "Do you know why Daddy dragged me into the hall? To tell me that he's getting me a movie camera for a surprise present and to see what size I wanted! Isn't he the best! Where's the princess? I must say good-by—" She noticed the wrecked door and gasped. "Why, what happened?"

"The glass got broken," said Scott, and regretted the idiotic answer at once.

"What *have* you in your pockets—and that box?"

interposed Jim helpfully. "You must have hit the jack-pot on a give-away program!"

"I only have some marrons!" Ellen feigned indignation. "And some scones, and my flowers—and that last meringue I didn't eat." Virtuously she added, "If we get stalled in this storm a bite to eat may save our lives. Good night, Uncle Scott, thanks loads for everything."

As the door closed on the Selwyn's, Mrs. Beddle laid an imploring hand on Scott's arm. "Where's the young lady?" she whispered, darting a worried look at the scattered glass.

"She left before that happened," he reassured her. "Those men coming in so unexpectedly upset her. She climbed over to her balcony."

"The reckless child! Suppose she had fallen!"

Even the thought recurring shook Scott. "She didn't—so let's forget it." He paced nervously. "She's furious with me, though; thinks I'm responsible for something unpleasant that happened. I'm not! I'm going over to her apartment and tell her so. Right now!"

"I'd best go with you," suggested Mrs. Beddle. "I'm sure I won't sleep a wink tonight unless I know she's all right. Do stop raging up and down, Mr. Scott, like a wild animal in a cage. I mind how Mr. Beddle used to carry on when he was in a temper. Doesn't do a bit of good, so let's go and see how she is."

Their exit from the apartment was observed with conflicting emotions by the girl they sought; she retreated around a corner of the corridor when they appeared. Unseen, she watched them enter the elevator and descend, and congratulated herself on finding the coast clear—now she could contact Johnny without trouble. No doubt Scott was squiring the housekeeper back to her rooms; how like him to remember that courtesy in spite of what he had just gone through.

Her own part in those hectic moments gave her no satisfaction. Almost as soon as she had locked his balcony door she began to regret that furious denunciation of him as a traitor. He could have had no part in Bill's arrival, his surprise was as complete as hers. But she had screamed at him like a shrewish fishwife! Her cheeks burned at the memory and at the realization that her overwhelming disappointment over his fancied deception proved her depth of feeling for her pilgrim. Unneeded testimony, if she faced the truth; the whole evening had been a struggle to prevent her stern resolve from melting under his smile, the unmistakable hunger in the steady gray eyes.

In the morning she would ask humbly to be forgiven. Painful to her pride, but not so painful as losing his friendship. If she knew her pilgrim, he would understand when she explained that the shock of seeing— She hesitated. Better not mention Bill, perhaps—Scott obviously had taken an instant and active dislike to him. Maybe she wouldn't go to Scott tomorrow. Let time cool his anger—

"Heavens!" she rebuked her thoughts aloud. "You are swinging as wildly as a weathervane in a tornado! And you've all night to make up your mind, but only minutes before he comes back!" She ran lightly down the hall and pressed Scott's bell.

Tinker answered; his face flushed and his eyes popped in surprise.

She slipped in. "Close the door quickly!" she begged with an excited laugh. "I thought I'd never get here. I started out of my apartment, imagined I saw someone duck out of sight in the hall and shut myself in again. Shows the state of my nerves, doesn't it? When I finally screwed up my courage and came here up the stairs I almost ran into Mr. Pelham and Mrs. B. So here I am."

"Yeah? What for?" Tinker sounded worried. He scowled at her peppermint-stick dress and orange sweater.

The girl giggled. "Disapprove of my intrusion or my costume, Johnny? Sorry, it is rather gaudy for a slinking female, but I was soaked by my trip and threw on the first things at hand. I came back for my bag and slippers. The bag may be on the piano, but I left the shoes on your balcony when I climbed across to mine."

"You *climbed*—!" Horror in the yelp. "Holy cats! No kidding?"

"No wonder you're shocked. In the best society a lady doesn't leave a dinner party so unceremoniously—

but I had to." The girl's light touch failed her at last. "You know who came here?"

"Sure, I know. But *you* know Walt would give himself up before he'd let you risk your life—"

She repressed a shudder. "Don't talk that way! Nothing happened. Let's find my things." As she followed him to the living room she said, "I had such a curious feeling when I slid over that slippery railing. As though my real self floated in the air, watching my struggles, and found them absurd. Not tragic after all—just funny." She sighed. "But you can't understand that—"

She stopped because Tinker stopped. He was frowning at the broken door and scattered glass on the tan rug. "Holy cats!" he muttered. "What's been going on?" Shaking his head he drew the heavy curtains tight across the door. "I'll have to get some of the captain's drawing board and tack it over that hole till I can put in new glass." He eyed the girl. "Did you do that?"

"Of course not! I thought I might have to on my balcony door, but it was unlocked. Here's my bag, it has my apartment key in it, that's why I came back for it. And here are my slippers!" The easy success of her trip put a quiver of excitement in the girl's tone. "I'll feel safer with that key; I snapped off the lock on my door and left it ajar, so I could get back in if I didn't make it here and find you. Thanks for everything, Johnny. I'll vanish now."

"I guess you'd better." He preceded her to the hall and reached for the doorknob. The musical chimes stopped his hand in mid-air.

Petrified, the two stood breathless. Her fingers fastened on his arm. "Oh, Johnny!" It was a despairing whisper. "I was crazy to come—!" A warning shake of his head silenced her.

Through the door filtered the muffled, but unmistakable, tones of Philip Pepperell. "By thunder, Lucy, if you've dragged me here on a wild-goose chase, I'll—" Inability to nominate a punishment fitting the crime left him speechless.

"Don't you believe it!" The Salem Witch's strident soprano pierced the solid panels clearly. "You'll find this place *rifled!* I didn't tell you over the phone, but I saw it happening. Well, practically! When I left Molly's upstairs, I stopped across the street—to admire these buildings. I'm using them for atmosphere in my new book," she interpolated quickly. "Suddenly the balcony door here flew open! A *woman's* figure stood vignetted against the light of the room. She climbed across the balcony of The Princess."

"Rot!" exploded Old Pep, with a vigor which shook the door. "Think I'm soft in the head to believe such stuff?" He prodded the bell till its chimes were a frantic jangle. "You've been having a nightmare!"

"No, *really!* Then there was a crash of glass and a *man* dashed out. In my excitement I stumbled off the curb; when I looked again the man had gone; followed his accomplice, I suppose. Scott's suite was being robbed. 'What should I do?' I asked myself."

Pepperell's snort of derision brought a hysterical giggle from the listening girl. Tink motioned for silence, his face worried.

"By thunder," Old Pep rumbled, "I know what you *should* have done. Minded your own business instead of calling me! Why the devil doesn't somebody answer? You've got me hopped up with your wild story now, if that's any satisfaction! I'll have to use my key to ease my mind."

Tinker dragged the girl away from the door. She shook her arm from his grip. "I'll go across the railings again," she offered faintly.

"Over my dead body!" Tink looked vainly around. "If I hide you in the Captain's bedroom or workroom—that would really give that old battle-ax something to squawk about!"

At the sound of the key turning the lock he abandoned futile planning and pushed the girl into the kitchen. Closing the door he backed against it and stared wildly at her.

She smothered a laugh at his expression, and in perfect imitation whispered, "*Holy cats!* No kidding!"

EIGHTEEN

IN SILENCE Scott led the way along the corridor of The Princess, gave the bell a commanding jab and waited, engrossed in thought, trying to plan the coming interview. How to keep calm—

Mrs. Beddle jerked him back to reality with a breathless "Look!" and a shaking hand pointed at the door.

It was ajar—it was moving! Scott saw the dark crack widen slowly, and as slowly narrow. He blocked the door before it closed, swung it open and back against the wall. Somewhere in the unlighted room beyond the entrance hall sounded a whispering rustle.

His face paled as he crossed the threshold and stood listening. Mrs. Beddle's breath at his shoulder made tremulous puffs. The sound came again out of the darkness, a soft crackle like dry leaves being crushed by stealthy feet. Groping along the wall inside the doorway he pressed the switch and blinked in the sudden glare of light.

"That's better, I must say!" Mrs. Beddle sighed. There was no touch of pink in the wrinkled cheeks now.

"Wait outside, if you'd rather," Scott suggested, and was irritated to realize his hushed tone. Anxiety and mystery were certainly taking their toll. He closed the door firmly and called, "Anyone at home?" so loudly that the housekeeper jumped.

No answer, save another rustle of the dry leaves. Scott snapped on a light in the right-hand room. Mrs. Beddle was almost stepping on his heels. On the floor lay a soft drift of white, the dress which Maureen had worn to dinner. Shed in haste, by the look. The housekeeper tiptoed into the bathroom and reappeared. "No one there!" It was an incredulous whisper. "Could she have gone out—this late?"

"Lord! Don't whisper—talk!" Scott urged. "We'll

check the whole place to make sure. She might have fallen asleep."

As they approached the living room the weird rustle became more distinct. He pressed the light switch and stood tense, trying to locate the sound. Not an easy room in which to note something amiss; it was cluttered with the Jordans' loot from all over the world. Antiques beyond price, the tall mandarin chest, the Phyfe desk far too valuable to be used as a mere desk, clean-lined mahogany chairs, Limoges enamels, Renaissance candlesticks. And of course the books—on shelves, guarded by heavy plate glass and locks, even on the wall, where a rare dime novel of the early eighties hung in a gold frame, its lurid cover fitting perfectly into Scott's mood.

Only one jarring note. On an antique knee-hole desk stood an electric typewriter, its looping cord plugged into a nearby lamp, as out of character with its surroundings as a jet plane in the Roman Forum.

A sudden current of air ruffled the loose pile of papers beside the machine. Two of the sheets sailed off and fluttered to the floor, settling on other displaced sheets with a faint crackle.

Scott looked down at his companion with a grin. "That's what we heard. Creepy enough to give me goose pimples!"

"What was *that?*" she quavered, and stared back down the hall. "I heard a door shut! Perhaps the young lady has come back."

"We would have heard her unlock it. I noticed the catch was off and snapped it before I closed the door. Wait here, Mrs. B."

"I'd rather go along with you, Mr. Scott, if you please. I'm not afraid, really—why, I mind one castle where we were quite proud of our ghost—but I didn't like that open door when we came."

Scott heard her apprehensive panting behind him as he walked down the hall. The entrance door was ajar again. Scott knew he had not left it like that. Whatever breeze was ruffling the papers in the living room might have moved it while they waited outside, but it could not have blown open a locked door.

"Maybe a sneak thief got in, and slipped out when we went in the living room," Scott suggested. He opened the second bedroom door. "We missed this; he could have ducked in here as we entered. We'd better look around, see if anything is disturbed or missing. Maureen might have left a note, so look for that, too. You start here, Mrs. B., and I'll begin in the living room and work back to you."

As he walked over to the typewriter desk to gather the fallen papers, something hard squeaked under his shoe. He picked it up, a shining half-moon of black stone or enamel, broken off a larger piece, for the straight side was jagged. Complete, it would be the size of a dime, but much thicker. He weighed it in his hand, puzzled.

An icy draft stirred against his face, moved the papers on the desk. Something open, of course; he should have realized that before. Slipping the unidentified black object into his pocket he moved to the balcony door and pulled the hangings aside. The glass door, which they had held partially closed, swung wide and deluged him with cold night air. Behind him the pile of papers swooped in wild flight. He locked the door and retrieved the sheets again, stacking them on the desk.

A heavy dictionary stood propped open behind the typewriter; that would anchor the papers securely. He picked it up—and recoiled as if a cobra had struck at his hand. Removing the book exposed a small leather portfolio. The name "Edson & Randolph" stamped on the flap seemed to explode in his brain.

"No!" he groaned. "My God, no!"

His hand shook as he picked up the case, unbuckled its strap and drew out a sheaf of crisp papers. The missing securities! He felt physically sick as he leafed through them. *Some* of the missing loot, anyway— If Maureen had been cashing them in—

"Hold it!" he muttered savagely. Where was his faith, to condemn her simply because he found the bonds here? They had been planted in her room by someone; someone who stealthily opened that door and startled Mrs. Beddle a few moments ago? Believe that!

"Mr. Scott!" the housekeeper called. "I don't find any note and I'm sure nothing is missing." She was coming along the hall.

He slipped the leather wallet inside the waistband of his trousers. Buttoning his dinner coat helped to hold it in place; there was no noticeable bulge.

Mrs. Beddle trotted in, chuckling, completely recovered from her attack of nerves. "What a to-do over nothing, Mr. Scott; now I remember Miss Tenny came in all wet and muddy from her walk this afternoon, so I took her skirt to press it. She's gone to my apartment to get it, I'm sure."

"I hope—" Scott swallowed the rest at an electrifying peal of the doorbell. Maureen returning? She wouldn't ring. Someone else—

Whoever it might be, Scott realized, had better not find him with that incriminating case under his coat. "Mrs. B.," he whispered, "I don't want anyone to think I've been snooping in this apartment. I'll go home by the balconies—"

"Lord, Mr. Scott, don't you risk that!"

"I'll be O.K. After I've gone, you open the door—but don't tell a soul I've been here. *No one,* understand?" He gave her an encouraging pat on the shoulder, stepped out onto the balcony and closed the door. Then he flattened against the building to peer past the edge of the curtain. He watched Mrs. B. trot out of the room—and waited. . . .

The storm had blown itself out; hardly a flake drifted down from a sky where the moon made a wan patch of light behind ragged clouds. Before long that moon would be bright enough to silhouette Scott glaringly against the pale wall.

The housekeeper returned to the living room, stopping just inside the doorway to turn and address the man who followed her. Scott could not hear her words, but judged from her folded arms and jerking head that they were emphatic.

The man pushed past her, glanced around the room and scowled. Then he faced the little woman, towering over her like a massive boulder. Hands on hips, chin jutted forward, he appeared to ask a series of questions. His fat jaws chewed slowly after each answer.

Scott grinned. "The very model of a modern private sleuth or maybe a police detective," he muttered. "I had a feeling, when that bell rang—and I was so right!" Behind the detective and the housekeeper a shadow moved in the hall: another man keeping in the background. "This," said Scott softly, "is my cue to get far, far away."

The journey between balconies was surprisingly easy although unpleasantly damp. He slid his hand through the hole in his door and turned the key. Inside, he drew a breath of relief. So far, so good, but it had been a close call. Before he finished that thought a sound from the hall threw him back into uneasiness. Steps advancing, a deep, growling voice and a shrill one. For a wild instant Scott thought it sounded like Lucy! His nerves were undoubtedly wrecked tonight. They disintegrated further when the Salen Witch strode into the room.

She chattered as she came. "Where shall we look first? Isn't this *thrilling*—" The sight of Scott choked her off and sent a painful flush over her sour face. "Oh! Here he is!" Her disappointment was comic.

Pepperell sank into a chair. "Thank God, you're all right, Prescott!" He puffed heavily, fixing Lucy with a baleful glare. "By thunder, woman! If you ever rout me out again because your screwball mind has gone off the hooks—!" An explosive snort promised dire consequences.

"Don't bark at me, Uncle Phil; *I* was worried about Scott, too—and I was right!" Triumph whetted the Witch's bleat to a razor edge. "Look at his face! Look at the snow on his shoes! He's been somewhere. He can't keep the truth from *me!*" Her voice cracked on the last word and she flounced down on the couch as though nothing less than an earthquake would budge her.

Scott seethed with impatience. Why, when everything was going haywire, must this prying monster camp on him? Outwardly he managed a fairly carefree laugh. "Why this midnight visit, Lucy? Of course I've been somewhere. Going through an empty apartment with

Mrs. Beddle, as a matter of fact." Rather neat, he thought; how far could he truthfully carry that story and make it believable? "Never know when some friend will ask me what's for rent, you know. And the snow?" He glanced at his shoes. "Such sharp eyes, Cousin! I did step out on the balcony over there, to check on the view. A view which would surprise you," he added, grinning.

Miss Wheeler glared. "There's more to this—"

"Keep quiet, woman!" roared Pepperell. "Just hold your tongue for the next hundred years and we'll all be happy!" More moderately he explained to Scott, "She insists that she saw a female, pursued by a man, on your balcony—"

"I didn't say 'pursued,' " Lucy corrected, but a fiery glare silenced her.

Pepperell grunted. "Look, Prescott, I want to explain my actions. This—this *she* had a brainstorm, imagined there was at least a robbery afoot, and routed me out of my club. When I got here after a wild ride in a taxi there were lights in your apartment, so naturally I expected someone would answer my ring." He hesitated in embarrassment. "Well, nobody did answer, so I used the key you sent me. I wasn't prying, boy! I was afraid something had happened to you."

Scott dropped an affectionate hand on his shoulder. "You couldn't be unwelcome here, no matter why you came." He glanced coldly at Lucy. "Novel writing must have stimulated our cousin's imagination to the boiling point tonight. Just to cool it off, I don't mind making a tour of the premises to reassure her." As she started to rise he snapped, "No, Lucy, you're not coming with me! You've made me ridiculous enough."

"You're such a tyrant, Scott!" She subsided with a snicker which was like a saw drawn across his nerves.

"No tyrant, just careful. If someone *is* here, *you* might get shot!" He went down the hall, opened the doors of his bedroom, Tink's room, and the hall closet. He had no intention of making any search, but he ought to stall long enough to satisfy her. What the dickens had become of Tinker, that he wasn't on hand to let Old Pep in? Wondering that, he opened the kitchen door, revealing a scene which struck him dumb.

At the sink stood Tinker, carefully washing his way through a mountainous stack of dinner dishes. He turned his cherub face and innocent blue eyes on Scott, gestured a salute with the dishmop and passed a cleansed plate to his assistant. The Princess, her sweater and skirt protected by one of Tink's white coats, received the plate gravely and began wiping it.

Scott glared at the tableau, his face going red. "A touching domestic picture!" he growled.

Tink's cheeks glowed brighter pink, but Maureen bobbed a curtsy. "Thankee, sir," she simpered in an approximation of Mrs. Beddle's accent. "I was only minded to give the lad a hand." Then she nudged Tinker with the plate. "Is it the squire himself?" she demanded with pretended awe.

After the last hour's storm and stress Scott was in no mood for comedy. Not, certainly, with Uncle Phil and Lucy still on the premises. "Don't let me interrupt," he said coldly, backed out and shut the door. He returned to the living room, crossed to the balcony door and parted the curtains to peer out. Then he confronted his guests.

Pepperell gave him a long, appraising study and hauled himself out of his chair. "Come on, Lucy!" he barked. "I can tell from the boy's face that it's just what I figured all along, your suspicious mind on the loose again. Didn't find anything missing, Prescott?"

"Of course not! Lucy had only one grain of truth in her bushel of chaff." He pointed to the broken door. "I suggest that Tink had this open to air out the room, the wind blew it shut and smashed it. The man she saw would be Tink sizing up the damage. And if he went to the basement for glass and putty to fix it, he couldn't let you in."

"Of all the wasted effort—and worry!" Old Pep glowered at the woman. "I said, *come on!* We're leaving!"

"Oh, no, we're not!" she shrilled. "How about the girl I saw? Was she going after putty, too? Don't be childish, Scott Pelham—you're not fooling me!"

"Lucy!" It was not a name, it was a leonine roar delivered by Old Pep. "You've got more human cussedness in your carcass than I ever saw before, but you'd better listen to me! Wipe this evening clean out of your mind! If one word about it drips off your forked tongue—look out for me! I have some influence. Even in the dingy circles you frequent, and by the Almighty—I'll use it! This family has put up with your vicious gossiping long enough, and *I'll* stand for no more of it! Now get up on your feet and get moving! Out!" He ended red-faced and panting.

Even the Salem Witch was cowed. "I'm sure it shall be as you wish, Uncle Phil," she stammered, moving hastily to the door. "Good night, Scott. We really must be going."

"Yes!" muttered Old Pep savagely as he followed. "We must!"

Scott ushered them out with nervous haste. The delay made his task no easier; those men from Number Three might see his footprints and be over on the jump. He must move fast, but first he must make his position clear to Maureen. He owed her that, to make up for his momentary doubts of her. Even though she was unaware of them, they lay heavily on his conscience.

He walked into the kitchen, again interrupting the dishwashing, and without preliminaries, jerked a thumb over his shoulder. *"Tink!"* he snapped. "Outside."

Tinker eyed him and dried his hands on his apron. There was no misreading the severity of Scott's face. "Yes, Captain," he said, and went out, shutting the door.

Scott unbuttoned his jacket and held up the leather wallet. "See this, Maureen?"

The girl stared. She could read the gold name on the case and exclaimed in delight, "The bonds? *Where* did you get them?"

"On the desk in your living room."

She went white. She bit her lip while she studied him, her dark eyes enormous in the pale face. *"My* living room?" she whispered.

Scott's throat tightened; he ached with the desire to ask for an explanation, to hear her deny all knowledge of the evidence and reassure his love. But asking her to justify herself would admit his suspicions, suspicions he fought blindly against at every turn—and conquered for a time at least. They were gone now, when he looked into those enchanting eyes—He drew in a deep breath. "I'm not asking how these stolen securities got into your room," he stated quietly. "I ask nothing."

Some of the color stole back to the girl's cheeks and her eyes glowed. "Then you don't believe—"

Scott shook his head. "As far as I'm concerned, Maureen, you had nothing to do with them. Because I know that *you* could do nothing wrong."

The glow in her eyes was a shining light. "I thought I understood what 'having faith' meant," she said softly, "but I never really knew before!"

"Then you have never known a man truly in love." Scott gave a wry smile, at himself as much as to her. "Call it faith—or the stubbornness of love. Later, I shall probably welcome explanations, but they must be voluntary, not forced. Right now, I am going to return these securities to Randolph as fast—"

"Please!" She flung out an imploring hand. "Not to him! Give them to Walter—let him return them. Don't you see, it is the only way he can surely clear himself!"

Scott considered her request, slapping the wallet gently against his palm. "You are so sure of his innocence?"

"I am sure—or I would not risk destroying the trust you have in me," she reminded. "If your faith will stretch so far."

Scott sighed. "Apparently there are no limits to it." He slipped the wallet into his coat pocket, opened the door and called, "Tink!"

"Yessir!" Tinker was in the kitchen with the word.

"I'm taking the stolen bonds to Tenny. He's still with Ace?"

Tink's eyes popped at the news, but discipline allowed no questions, only required answers. "Yessir."

"Take our friend over to Mrs. Beddle's, quick; she is to *stay* there." He glanced at Maureen, who nodded acquiescence, although confusion was plain in her expression. "Then come back here, Tink. There were a couple of men—detectives, I think—nosing around Number Three. They'll be knocking at my door next—never mind why. Just keep them out. But no rough stuff!"

"Yes, *sir!*" A dancing flame in his eyes belied the promise.

"Just one question, Tink. *You* believe Tenny is on the level?"

"Captain, sir, I know it. Why, I grew up with him—he was one of us Battlers, that club I told you about, remember? He's straight as they come."

"Which seems to make it unanimous." Scott repeated his orders: "Get over to Mrs. B.'s, then whip back here and keep those lads from pushing down the door."

"I hope they try it!" said Tinker, watching Scott snatch a coat from the hall closet and charge out the door. "Holy cats! What a night!"

NINETEEN

NUMBER *17* BREEN STREET was even more dingy and odorous by night than on Scott's first visit. He kicked the snow off his shoes, mounted the narrow stairs and knocked on Daley's door. Noticing that the transom was open, and remembering that former call, he wondered if he would again hear the surreptitious opening of a window which suggested someone's hasty departure. But a sound from below distracted his attention.

Had the street door opened and closed softly? He had given no thought to being followed here. Craning over the stair rail he could see no one in the shadowy hall. His frayed nerves were playing tricks on him; other people lived in this house, didn't they? He turned to find Daley's door thrown wide, but with Ace blocking it, a statue of truculent readiness. When the light from the room disclosed Scott's identity the fighter relaxed.

"Oh, it's you, Captain Pelham! Step in." He shut the door and locked it. "Grab a seat, sir."

The room was the same carefree clutter of living and training accessories. Ace was the same, scarred, formidable, but watchfully polite. The Gent was slouched on the chair in the corner, as on the first day, but now, instead of a ledger, a monkey occupied him. He was scratching the little, grizzled head and whispering.

Scott was jolted by a sudden inspiration and a compelling urge to laugh at his own density. Here sat Walter Tenny, disguised so the most brilliant detective would never recognize him. First as an outraged sergeant traveling from New York with Tink, now as a pathetic derelict of the war. What a make-up, and what an actor! Scott recalled his own flooding sympathy when the man, sitting forlorn in the Silk Hat, chilled him with that nightmare voice from the prison camp. . . . Now, vacant-eyed he played with the monkey—

Scott came down to earth with a thud, his brilliant discovery tumbling around his ears. The Gent had been here long before Tink's trip to New York. He and his monkey were wandering under The Pilgrim balcony weeks ago. The Pepperells spoke of him and suffered with his displaced pet shortly after that.

"Hey!" said Ace. "You all right, sir?"

How long had he stood there gaping? Scott tried to collect his stumbling senses, but succeeded only in mumbling, "So you have Dizzy back home?"

"Did you come to see *him?*" Daley asked pointedly.

"Sorry, Ace, I'm a little unstrung, I guess. I've had a wild evening, and—"

A resounding knock on the door clipped off the sentence. Daley's blue-green eyes were slits as he stared at Scott. A jerk of his head signaled him to the side of the room before he unlocked the door and pulled it half open. Through the crack at the hinges Scott glimpsed a blue coat and a darker blue Homburg hat. The rasping voice was familiar, too.

"Hiya, Daley!" said the new arrival. "Want to talk to you."

Ace grunted. "Lefty Moss, huh? Talk fast, I'm busy."

"Come off it!" sneered Blue Homburg. "You ain't too busy to talk to me. Kramer sent me; we want Tenny, and we know you've got him hid. I'd have grabbed him the other night, if them pals of his sister hadn't horned in."

"Figure to turn him in?" asked Daley with deceptive gentleness. "You'll get laughed at. The cops can't hold him—"

"That's what you think. I hate to upset you, but the missing bonds have been found—in his sister's apartment. All we want now is Tenny." Moss pushed the door to open it wider.

Daley's fist moved too fast for Scott to follow it, but he heard the *smack* of the blow and a grunt of pain. Daley stepped through the doorway, his other fist cocked, but there was no need. Retreating footsteps beat a rapid tattoo down the stairs. Ace came in, locked the door and rubbed his knuckles.

"Kramer must be off his nut," he remarked casually. "If he really wanted Walt he'd have sent more than that yellow punk. He's got plenty others to send. I guess it was a bluff."

The Gent spoke, still petting the monkey. "That's the man who came to the night club, Ace. And I signaled to Tink and Walter, just the way you told me to."

"You done it perfect," Ace assured him. "I knew we could count on you, that's why I put you on guard." He turned to Scott. "O.K., sir. Now what's on your mind?"

"That man who was just here—"

"Lefty Moss? He's tied up with Kramer in some racket, and must be in on this Tenny deal, too. Maybe he helped stick up Walt."

"He's certainly been mixing into it since 'way back, watching the apartment and following Miss Tenny. I saw a man who looked like a detective over at her place tonight, and there was someone with him I didn't get a clear look at—maybe this Moss. Anyway, I came—"

Ace darted out a silencing hand. He had been giving Scott only half his attention, and now he stepped soundlessly nearer the door and cocked his head. He put one hand to the knob then withdrew it. A grin creased his battered face as he moved over to the couch.

The Gent looked up. Ace put a finger to his lips, still smiling, and held out his hand. A wraith of laughter flickered on the Gent's pale face as he transferred the monkey's clinging paws to Ace's arm.

"I'm telling you, mister!" Daley's voice rumbled full strength, but he winked at Scott. "I'm getting fed up with that Tinker and his pals! Sending you guys round here, day and night." Walking lightly as a cat he approached the door. "He must think I'm running a hotel!" He raised a long arm until Dizzy was within reach of the open transom. The animal swung onto it, peered out and down. He slanted a round-eyed, innocent blink at Ace and without warning dropped from sight.

A yell of unadulterated horror gave way to thrashing and terrified curses. Feet pounded down the stairs. Stumbled. A heavy body bounced the rest of the way. The front door slammed. Dizzy climbed back through the transom, paused to scratch himself absently, and rejoined the Gent in two elastic bounds.

"Now that we're alone, sort of," Daley said, "what's the pitch, sir?"

"That eavesdropper," said Scott, "was probably one of the detectives I saw at Number Three, if they *were* detectives. They followed me here because they suspect that I found the Randolph bonds. Which, incidentally, I did."

"Yeah?" Daley's bicolored eyes gleamed. "Where are they?"

"Here." Scott patted his chest. "Miss Tenny and Tink insisted that I bring them to Walter."

"Swell!" Ace whirled to the couch. "Gent! Open the window and signal to Walt! We've got to step on it!" To Scott he muttered, "This'll *snow* Walt, for sure; he'd almost given up." He pulled the door open a crack, peered out. Satisfied he closed it.

A blast of wintry air from the open window swept a tall man in off the fire escape. He was shivering, blowing on his hands.

"Captain Pelham," introduced Ace, "shake with Walter Tenny."

Scott frowned at the smudged face, bushy eyebrows and ragged sideburns. An unwholesome-looking character who would fit better as a hoodlum than in the offices of Edson & Randolph. No faintest suggestion of any likeness to his princess! Scott's heart pounded. What kind of a flim-flam had he let himself be talked into?

Tenny smiled at him. "Glad to meet you, Mr. Pelham; I've heard nice things about you." He put his hand to his face. "Excuse my appearance. I've been understudying one of Ace's trainers, and this is the way a second-rate fighter is supposed to look. The Gent says you have located the stolen securities. I won't attempt to thank you."

Scott's spirits rebounded from zero. There was refinement in voice and diction; beneath the dirt and artificial coloring, if he looked closely, showed clean-cut features and an expression of calm self-reliance.

"Don't thank me," Scott said. "And don't ask me where I found these." He produced the case of securities and passed it to Tenny. "Could you check to see if they tally?"

"Easily. I have a list, of course, but as you can imagine I've had time to learn it by heart." Running through the certificates he nodded. "All present. Believe me, I appreciate what you've—"

"Skip it!" Ace interrupted. "And get moving, Walt. Get on your horse, pal—don't hang round or we may lose that stuff again. I'll trail you, in case them dicks of the captain's get nosy."

"Wait, Daley!" Scott protested. "Where's Tenny going?"

"To New York! Walt, get in touch with Randolph the minute you hit town—but steer clear of that frozen fish, Edson. You'd better—"

"Hold everything!" Scott broke in again. "That's not the way to handle this, Ace. If those men *did* follow me and are outside—"

"I can take care of them!"

"Probably," Scott agreed dryly. "With a rousing brawl, and lots of spectators, and maybe an arrest for assaulting an officer, and more trouble. Besides, Randolph isn't in New York. He's taking the train from here tonight."

Tenny stepped forward. "Then I'll catch him at the train."

"*If* you make it," Scott reminded patiently. "You can't go running around this city with those bonds in your pocket. Suppose something happened—anything—and you're picked up. It would be the finish for you. Who would believe you were only returning them to him? No, we've got to be cagy. Pipe down, all of you, and let me think!"

He paced the room, unaware that he had reverted to the tone and manner of a company commander directing his men. But the others felt it, accepted it, and stood silently waiting.

"Ace, have you a car?"

"Yes, sir. In the back yard, up the alley."

"That helps. Listen, now; whether Lefty Moss is alone or has others with him, we've got to scatter. I'll take the bonds, go out the front door and up the street fast. Whoever is watching may figure that I've turned the stuff over to Daley, so I'd better run; that should worry them. At the same time, Ace and the Gent follow me out but go around back and get the car, driving *down* the street. The idea is that any of us may be heading for Walt Tenny in some hideaway, so they'll split up to trail us—I hope—if there is more than one of them.

"If it's Blue Hat alone—Lefty Moss, to you—he's going to be so busy trying to make up his dumb mind which to follow that he won't think beyond that. So, Tenny, the minute you hear the car clear the yard you go down the fire escape. Can you get out at the back of the yard?"

"I've done it often," Tenny smiled. "Over the fence to the next street."

"Do that, then." Scott consulted his watch. "You have about twenty-five minutes to reach Back Bay

Station. Know where that is—across Copley Square and behind the Sheraton?"

"I'll find it."

"The New York train leaves from the South Station, but stops at Back Bay, down below street level. I'm going to the South Station, buy a ticket and berth, get on board, and ride to your station. I'll be at the forward end of the last car. You hop on there, I give you the bonds and the tickets, and you locate Randolph on the train and make delivery. Check?"

"Sure, I'll find him."

"We don't want any slip-up on this," Scott warned. "If you don't get there, I'll stay aboard and see Randolph myself, and try to sell him your story."

"I'll make it."

"I think you will. Let's get the show on the road, then. All set, Ace—Gent?" He snapped his fingers. "Here's an idea, Daley. Why don't you head for Fred Walsh and have him pick up Kramer before any word gets to him about this deal?"

"I'll do just that. Fred knows the whole story; he's been waiting for word from us to grab that crook. Let's go, Gent."

Their exit from the house, Scott thought, could not fail to attract attention. As he ran up the sidewalk he heard the other two pounding along the alley. Something interfered, there was a hollow clang and the noise of confused scrambling, and Daley's voice roaring cursed. Fell over an ash barrel, Scott deduced, suppressing a chuckle. He looked back, slowing his pace. No one following; no one in sight.

The car churned out of the alley, battering a way past something which resisted with metallic clamor. The same ash barrel? The noisy motor faded down the street. Was that another car starting up? Sounded like it, above the muffled thudding of Scott's feet on the new snow. Tenny should be on the fire escape by now—

Scott reckoned he could make the South Station easily if he found a taxi. He speeded up, rounded the corner by a small variety store and—

"*Hey!* Hold up there!" A policeman turned from trying the door of the shop. When Scott slid to a halt the officer strolled over, tall, wide and suspicious. "What's the rush? Who are you?"

"Scott Pelham." Impatiently he presented his wallet. "I'm running for a train."

"Is that so?" With maddening deliberation the patrolman extracted the identification cards for closer study. "Any trouble back there?" He nodded down Breen Street. "Sort of noisy."

"No trouble. I've been calling on Ace Daley, the fighter. A party of us; you heard the others leaving in their car."

"I'll say so!" The officer looked from Scott to the card in his hand. "Deputy Director, Civil Defense, with a real nice picture of you, Mr. Pelham. That's good enough for me." He returned the wallet. "Go ahead, sir; hope I didn't hold you up too long."

"I'm trying to catch the eleven o'clock at South Station," Scott threw over his shoulder as he walked rapidly away. "Hope I find a cab!"

It was the wrong section of town for taxis. Minutes later he hurried along Beacon Street, heading for the Common. The Park Street Church clanged a solemn quarter-hour warning. Better give up hope of a ride and cut straight across to Tremont, then down Winter, on foot. At the head of the Guild steps, which led from Beacon Street onto the Common, a jovial hail forced him to pause again.

Philip Pepperell, having finished his interrupted evening of bridge at the club, was wending his homeward way and in the mood for friendly conversation. "Here you are again, Prescott! And looking as though you'd been stealing sheep. What in thunder's going on tonight?"

Seething at further delay Scott waved without halting. "Have to see someone in a rush. Good night—for the last time tonight, I hope!"

He raced down the steps and past the festively lighted Christmas displays on the white slope. The stable, the waiting Magi, the reverent shepherds and their flocks stood caped in sparkling snow. The little groups of Dickensian statuettes seemed determined to carry on their caroling in spite of the smothering white blanket, and on Tremont Street every building was iced as though by a master confectioner.

It was five minutes before eleven when Scott reached the ticket window; less than a minute to go when the yawning clerk gave him ticket and sleeping-car reservations. Even at this hour the concourse was thronged with holiday travelers. He dodged through the crowd. The New York train was moving out as he swung aboard the last car.

A grinning porter pulled him up the steps. "Your bag, sir?"

"Picking it up at Back Bay," Scott panted, and held out his tickets. "I'm Number Nine, Car One Twenty-one—but I'll wait here to get my bag."

He had recovered his breath by the time the train ground to a halt in the cavernous depths of the uptown station. He leaned from the steps, searching for Tenny. Not many passengers boarding here, but a few wanted his car. He dropped to the platform to clear the way. No Tenny! Had someone caught up with him? Far up the track the conductor waved; the wheels began to turn slowly.

A flying figure appeared suddenly from behind a rumbling baggage truck. Tenny, thank the Lord! *"Here!"* Scott yelled, trotting along beside the moving car. In the vestibule above him the porter unlatched the door to close it. "Wait a minute!" Scott begged. "Someone coming!"

Tenny dashed up, gasping and speechless. Scott thrust bonds and tickets into his hand. "Everything's there—hop on!" He aided the breathless man with a vigorous shove up the steps. The porter hauled him to the top and slammed the door.

Scott watched the red lights on the train dwindle in the night, to sparks, to pin points, to nothing. He drew in a long, satisfying breath, the first for hours. "And that," he muttered, "is that!" Five minutes at the most for Tenny to locate Randolph and then—justification and freedom. Exit Ace Daley's begrimed "sparring partner," enter Walter Tenny, Edson & Randolph salesman.

Nor was Scott's satisfaction merely altruistic; his own burdens, real or imagined, were vanishing with the speeding train. Maureen was free and clear now, so that his love could openly work to win her love in return—

A hand clamped on his shoulder and spun him to face a thick-set, heavy-jowled man whose cheeks quivered with rhythmic chewing—the stranger Scott had seen questioning Mrs. Beddle in Number Three. Behind him hovered an even less welcome apparition—Lefty Moss, not so immaculate as usual. The blue coat showed signs of having rolled on the dusty stairs at Breen Street, a purple lump disfigured his jaw.

Scott knocked the restraining hand from his shoulder. "Whats the idea?" he snapped.

The heavy man grimaced. "You amateur crooks give me a laugh! You hollered 'South Station' at that cop so loud and innocent I couldn't help wondering if you were pulling a fast one. On at South—and off at Back Bay, I tells myself. And here you are." He resumed his sober chewing.

"Very bright of you, Sherlock," Scott jeered. "So what?"

"So, questions, bub—plenty questions." The man preserved his air of cool satisfaction. "I know you're a friend of that girl in the ritzy apartment. I know you lifted the bonds *out* of her apartment, hopped across to the next balcony and beat it to Daley's." He paused to chew.

"I can hardly wait for the next installment." Scott's sarcasm was wasted on the stolid man. "Where were you when I left Daley?"

"In a doorway up the street—expecting you to pull a razzle-dazzle getaway. You sure did, bud. But I've still got a lot of questions. Like, for instance—" he extended a pudgy hand—"how's for handing over the stuff now, without any trouble?"

Scott shrugged. "So sorry, no have got, *bud*." Then he abandoned humor, his face hard. "I've thought of a few questions myself, and you'd better have good answers. Like, for instance—" he mocked, "just who the devil are *you?* One of Kramer's bully boys—?"

"Uh-uh!" with a slow shake of the head. "Ernie Quigley, private detective, employed by Mr. William Randolph." He rolled the wad of gum in his mouth visibly. "Want to answer my questions here, or step around the corner to Police Headquarters?"

Scott indicated the hovering Lefty Moss. "If you'll bring your pal along that's the smartest suggestion I've heard all evening."

TWENTY

THE INQUISITORIAL SESSION at the Berkley Street Police Headquarters began badly for Scott. A bald and florid Lieutenant Jenner, his black brows frowning till they met over his sharp nose, put through a phone call to the New York train and made certain from Randolph himself that he had the bonds, that Tenny was with him and that he was completely satisfied.

Lieutenant Jenner was not. He took a sour view of Scott's frank admission that he had personally removed the securities from the living room of Number Three. The two sergeants who were assisting at the proceedings were equally displeased, as they showed by the vigor of their questioning. It was the unexpected intrusion of Lefty Moss into the drama which saved Scott from further grilling.

Lefty, his Homburg once more at its rakish angle, had no intention of helping "this mug, Pelham"—his unflattering description of Scott. On the contrary, he hoped to add to his troubles. Pushing to the front he leaned both hands on the lieutenant's desk and commenced a rasping account of the difficulties, mental and physical, which Scott had continually thrown in his way.

Inattentive to the boring recital, Scott let his eyes wander. They fixed on the massive onyx signet ring adorning Lefty's finger. Its gleaming black stone showed a ragged hole. Scott sat up with aroused interest and fingered a small object in his pocket.

"You, Moss!" he interrupted brusquely. "*You* were in that apartment with Detective Quigley. In the living room."

Lefty sneered. "Not me. Only in the hall; I never went near that room. Ask Quigley." He straightened to appeal to the detective. "He can't rig me in on this—"

"Only in the hall?" Scott repeated. "Show your hands! Lieutenant, look at his ring!"

With an oath Moss spread his hands on the desk. "Yeah, look at it—the stone's cracked. And this guy did it! I started to speak to his girl in his car, one day at the museum, and he roughed me! Pretty near busted my hand!"

"I may have cracked the stone," Scott growled, "and I wish it had been your jaw! But you've lost part of it. Right, Lieutenant?"

Puzzled, Jenner gripped the man's wrist. "I see there's a hole there, what of it?"

"Take a look at this." Scott slid the black fragment he had picked up in The Princess across the desk. "A perfect fit, isn't it? I found that on the floor by the desk in the living room where the bonds were hidden. And that was *before* this crook and Quigley came into the apartment."

Like famished hounds on a fresh trail the three policemen transferred their torrid questioning to Mr. Moss. The unequal contest lasted less than five minutes before Lefty collapsed. Well, he admitted reluctantly, he *had* put the missing securities in Miss Tenny's room, yes. But only so she could find them and return them to her brother—honestly! He had been watching when she came out and snapped the lock on her entrance door, so that gave him a chance to slip in and do his good deed, see? But Pelham and the housekeeper almost caught him. He didn't want to explain to them, so he ducked into a bedroom and then slipped out when they weren't looking, see?

Pressed as to why he didn't present the bonds to the girl in person and receive her thanks, Moss stumbled among evasions to the contemptuous amusement of the questioners. And when it came to the problem of where he had obtained the bonds in the first place, he so perspiringly entangled himself in contradictions that even the saturine Quigley joined in the laughter.

At the lieutenant's suggestion his assistants removed Lefty for further interrogation while Jenner returned to Scott's case. The latter's declaration that he had interested himself in the affair because the sister was convinced of Tenny's innocence drew a snort from Jenner.

"This gets fishier every minute!" he grumbled. "You, Quigley—do *you* think the girl wasn't in on the deal?"

"I know she wasn't. She's worked for Mr. Randolph and he liked her. He wouldn't have her shadowed—"

"He must have *liked* her! Or was he afraid she'd spill something about *him?*"

Scott's anger flamed at the insinuation and he started to answer hotly. But Quigley flapped a pudgy hand at him for silence.

"You're off the beam, Lieutenant," the detective declared. "Nothing like that. Mr. Randolph's fair, that's all. The minute the papers got hold of the news everybody started after the sister. He was sure she had nothing to do with the job, and fairly sure that Tenny was the fall guy in some dirty work. So he stuck that 'lay off the sister' rider on the reward offer, which pulled the heat offa her just as he expected it would, and hired me on his own."

"So that relieved us of any responsibility?" Jenner's sarcasm was pointed. "The heavyweight Private Eye takes charge—for a fat fee!"

"Now, Lieutenant!" Quigley protested mildly. "In case you have the idea that I've been sitting round reading the racing forms and collecting from Mr. Randolph, listen to what I *have* been doing."

Scott's estimate of the gum-chewing detective underwent a sharp revision while he listened. Starting with Walter Tenny's past Quigley learned of the disgruntled sergeant who had sworn revenge and identified him as Kramer, the manager of a prize fighter and intimate of small time racketeers.

Armed with a newspaper picture of Kramer leering proudly beside his fighter, Quigley scoured the neighborhood of Edson & Randolph's office. Eventually he located a small restaurant on an alley which Tenny often used as a short cut, a restaurant whose proprietor clearly remembered Kramer, a silent patron who had sat at a certain table overlooking the alley so frequently as to be noticed. It was remarkable that Kramer had never been seen there since the day of the robbery.

"Then," explained Quigley amiably, "Kramer came to Boston with his man, for the fight with Ace Daley. So—this overweight sleuth," he grinned at Jenner, "came up to your neck of the woods."

Since he had learned that Daley was an old friend of the missing salesman, Quigley was not surprised when Tenny appeared, not taken in by his disguise. His coming seemed to presage a showdown with Kramer, whose nerves were giving way at the long delay in his plan for revenge, so Quigley acted first. He let it be known, where he thought it would do the most good, that he was interested in acquiring the bonds.

At seven o'clock on the preceding evening, an anonymous phone call informed Quigley that the caller would meet him on a corner near The Princess at ten o'clock, ready to put the finger on the loot, provided the pay was right and no questions asked. Quigley was on hand promptly—but Moss turned up a little late, no doubt because planting the stuff and avoiding Pelham and Mrs. Beddle took unexpected time.

"And were you shot with luck!" the detective reminded Scott. "If that dope hadn't dropped the stone outa his ring, me and these gentlemanly Boston cops would still have you on the grill."

Further revelations by the Private Eye were cut short by the entrance of Patrolman Walsh escorting a pale and quivering ex-Sergeant Kramer, a hulk of a man, flabby of face and figure. "No trouble with him at all, Lieutenant," Walsh reported disgustedly. "He was just dying to come over here and tell you all about it."

And Kramer told all, a stammering confession of attempted revenge and terrifying consequences. He'd been so careful, all the way. Hadn't touched Tenny—no, sir! Just put the finger on him for his friends to do the job. Then, when Tenny had suffered the humiliations of arrest and jail—he meant to return the bonds with an anonymous message—only something went wrong—the cops never did grab Tenny! Then Boston—still with the bonds burning his fingers—and Lefty Moss, having learned that Tenny's sister was at The Princess, tried to get rid of the incriminating evidence—and flubbed that, too!

Scott wearied of the unpleasant exhibition and with Lieutenant Jenner's grinning dismissal retired from headquarters. It was nearly two o'clock and he was bone tired. He walked slowly homeward, too played out to more than hazily review the night's happenings. Quietly he let himself into the apartment, dragged off his clothes and crawled into bed. Tomorrow would be time enough for all he had to do. Tinker first, then Maureen—Tomorrow? It was here! All right, then—later today. . . . He slept.

The insistent, harrying ring of the telephone dragged him awake. It went on and on. Why didn't Tink answer it? Groaning, he staggered down the hall. That cross-country gallop last night was more exercise than his legs were used to; they twinged in every muscle. He fumbled for the receiver, muttered, "Hello?" and heard his brother-in-law's voice.

"Jim! What's wrong—at this hour?"

"What hour? It's quarter of eight." Selwyn laughed. "Don't tell me you have a hang-over, after *Ellen's* party!"

"No. I was up late, though—"

"Probably," said Jim dryly. "But never mind that. Could you meet Nancy at South Station at eight-ten and take her to the Peps'?"

"Why, of course—glad to." Scott felt dazed by his sudden awakening and the request.

His condition showed in his voice, for Jim asked, "You don't sound very lively; sure you can make it?"

"Don't worry, I'll make it! Nan's the one who'll worry—what's happened to you?"

"A flat—in the garage! We were to breakfast with the Peps—I'll see you there."

Scott cradled the phone. Not too much time! A shame if Nancy had to wander around the station looking for her husband. He gave cheeks and chin a lick and a promise with the electric razor, searched frantically for a clean shirt, dumping the bureau drawer.

"Holy cats, sir! What's going on?" Tinker stood in the doorway.

"Call the garage!" Scott snapped. "Have my car brought around!"

"Yessir!" Tink shot down the hall and began to dial like mad. "What's happened? Didn't you find Walt?"

"Yes. Everything's all right, there. Randolph has the bonds. I have to meet Mrs. Selwyn on the Federal from New York."

Tinker reappeared with Scott's hat and topcoat. "What's happened to Mr. Selwyn? He's always on the job with his wife."

"Flat tire. See you later." Scott departed, shrugging on the coat as he went. No time to question Tink, but when he returned he'd devote the day, if necessary, to getting to the bottom of his friendship with Maureen Tenny.

That purpose hung on the back of his mind an hour later as he sat opposite his sister at the Pepperell breakfast table, but it could only intermittently cloud his appreciation of the heart-warming occasion. Sunshine streamed in the purple-tinted windows, dappling the gem-bright colors of the rare Bokhara on the floor. It lingered lovingly on a Paul Revere bowl which added its own distinction to the priceless mahogany lowboy, and lanced a golden ray through the diamond panes of a corner cupboard to set the Sandwich glass sparkling.

Around the table it fell warmly on Philip Pepperell's bristling crest, brightened the ever-youthful face of Aunt Patty and turned Nancy Selwyn's auburn hair to molten copper. At intervals it played hide and seek with General's white teeth and rolling eyes as he bustled importantly back and forth from the sideboard, filling the air with the aroma of coffee and the fragrance of crisply curling bacon.

Soothed by hospitality and good food, Scott roused himself from the tangle of anxiety and conjecture that seemed forever buzzing in his head. Smiling at Aunt

Patty he asked, "Are any of your old boys coming to your Christmas Eve party?"

"None of my boys will ever be *old*, Scott," she rebuked gently. "They will never lose the qualities we loved in them, so to us they will always be the same." She glowed with excited color. "Yes! Some of my boys are coming—but you'll never guess which ones!"

"Happy Hapgood?" Scott ventured.

"Oh, darn!" Aunt Patty's blush deepened at the impulsive use of her most emphatic oath. "How did you know? It was to be a surprise."

"I didn't know, just hoped. Hap said in the fall he'd try for it."

"Well, now the secret's out, I may as well tell the rest. He's bringing along that big, blond medical student, Dick Paddock."

"Wonderful!" Scott applauded. "Haven't seen Dick for years. I wonder how Happy ever tore him away from his work. From what I've heard, Paddock is a man of note now—one of New York's top-flight nerve specialists. Anyone else coming I should know about?"

Aunt Patty smiled significantly at her husband before she announced, "Yes. Bill Randolph—and his wife."

"The Randolphs!" echoed Nancy. "How wonderful!"

Scott protested, "But Randolph went back to New York!"

His aunt beamed with delight at the sensation she had created. "He and Sally were both going last night. He dropped in here, late, and when I learned that she was in town, too, I made him promise to bring her to the party. Bill had to return on some business, but he is flying up this afternoon. New Yorkers," she remarked with mild amazement, "seem to think no more of a trip here than we do of driving to Newton!"

"I think it's marvelous!" Nancy patted the delicate hand of her hostess. "You and Uncle Phil *would* go all out to help them to a comeback."

"Of course. As I suspected, Sally didn't come here with Bill last night because she was afraid we wouldn't care to see her after—after all that's happened. The idea! I told Bill what I always say: 'Think success—and you invite success!' And they are coming. Bill hopes that you, Nancy, can help to convince Sally that she is as welcome as ever. You *are* glad they're coming?"

"Haven't I said so? It will be a godsend for them, I should imagine. This holiday would have been so tragically lonely for them, their first Christmas without either son or daughter." Nancy's thoughts turned naturally to her own child. "I suppose you threw the usual superparty for Ellen last night, Scott?"

Uncle Phil snorted. "A crashing success, wasn't it, Prescott? And I do mean *crashing!*"

Scott ignored him. "You should have seen your problem child, Nan! Didn't I warn you that she would some day burst out of the dungarees phase? She has! Silks and satins, and near jewels. To borrow a line from the Bard, 'She hung upon the cheek of night like a rich jewel in an Ethiope's ear.' "

"Ellen's all right!" Pepperell agreed. "I wish I'd seen her in all that war paint, but I arrived too late for the party."

His wife arched her brows. "Were you at Scott's last night?"

"Didn't I mention it?" He assumed an air of surprise, then regarded his nephew over the tops of his glasses as he added, "I dropped in. Sort of looking around. Not enough excitement at the club," he explained with another leer at Scott.

Aunt Patty accepted his statement without question, and showed that her mind was on other things. "Nancy, you'll stay and help me get ready for tonight, won't you? There's so much to do."

"I'd love to, but I ought to go home. Even though I've been away only two nights. I'd like to make sure the children are all right."

"Just the *children?*" demanded Jim Selwyn, making a dramatic entrance. "How about me?" His wife's welcome allayed any possible doubts as to his importance. "Ellen's in the hall—she stopped to beautify! Darling," he hissed, "prepare for a shock—our daughter has been bitten by the glamour bug!" He grinned at Scott. "But it's a wonder she can stop talking about the princess she met at your party long enough to accomplish anything!"

Silently Scott told himself, "Hold on to your hat—here it comes!"

"A princess?" Nancy stared from her brother, who was absorbed in lighting a cigarette, to her husband, who was equally engrossed in a hot muffin he had filched from Scott's plate. "What princess—"

"Hi, everybody!" Ellen strolled in, her eyes sparkling, her lips a cupid's bow of violent crimson. She dropped her hauteur like a discarded cloak to give her mother an enthusiastic hug. "I missed you frightfully, angel!"

"I am flattered, but skeptical. Missed me, while partying with Uncle Scott? Of course you had a wonderful time?"

"Just *mar*-velous!" The girl propped her elbows on the back of a chair and sighed dreamily. "There was the most adorable girl there, Mother. A princess!"

Nancy's face expressed utter bewilderment at this repetition of the news. "At Uncle Scott's? What country is she from—"

"Not a foreigner! She's as American as we are! She came with Mrs. Beddle, and I couldn't take my eyes off her all evening. The most *mar*-velous voice, velvet—with spangles on it! And a gorgeous dress—and such jewelry!" Ellen sighed again. "I was dying to ask her where she picked it up, because I didn't see *anything* as nice where I got my earrings, and *they* cost two dollars!"

Jim Selwyn laughed. "Honey, that jewelry was the real thing."

"Real?" Ellen squealed. "Honest? Good grief, Mother, they were real diamonds and things! *Jeepers!*"

In the stillness following her outburst Scott enjoyed all the sensations of a man standing on a ticking bomb. In a moment—

"I still don't understand," Nancy confessed.

"Well," Ellen explained, "the princess isn't really a princess, she's a writer. That's her nom de—the name she writes under. But she's not a nasty, stuck-up author like the Witch—I mean, Cousin Lucy." She darted an apprehensive look from her father to her uncle and hurried on. "She looked more like a movie star, really. And she talked books, and psychology—I think—with Uncle Scott. They thought all I cared about was the food, and it was the *most*, but I listened, too. And I'm just *dying* to hear all about her from Uncle Scott!"

"So am I," Nancy agreed enthusiastically, and all eyes centered on Scott.

He rose slowly from his chair, paused dramatically while he ran a cool glance over the expectant faces. "It seems to me," he announced, "that you have been brought completely up to date on *l'affaire* princess. If you still pant for thrilling details, I suggest that you contact Cousin Lucy—she's never at a loss for gossip." With a nod to Aunt Patty he said smilingly, "Thanks for the breakfast, favorite Aunt. And I'll see you all tonight."

He strode to the door and went out, but not quickly enough to escape Ellen's pained wail, "Wow! How was that for a deep freeze!"

TWENTY-ONE

THE SUN was setting among ruddy clouds, peering through to wink a spectacular good night to Boston. A skim of ice around the edge of the Basin glowed like polished metal; the tall white building with its weather signal blushed a becoming pink to carry out the color scheme of its warning "red for snow"; and every pane of glass in the water-front buildings flashed back molten gold. It seemed as though the departing orb of day was forecasting the blaze of light which the myriad candles in countless windows would soon pour out to greet the Christ child on this Christmas Eve.

Scott Pelham turned from the radiant color outside to face the three men in his living room. He had wanted to avoid their eyes for a long moment while he got his voice under control. The sight of tough, punch-scarred Ace Daley with an arm thrown protectively across the Gent's bowed shoulders had melted him with sympathy.

The smaller man stood passive, gazing around the room with a curious puzzled intensity, keener and more alive than his customary vacant stare. Tinker leaned against the mantel, fingers snapping.

"Go on, Ace," said Scott. "Sit down, all of you."

Daley motioned the Gent to the couch and lounged on an arm of it. "There isn't much more to tell that you don't know, Captain. The cops have Kramer and Lefty, and their only problem is how many charges to hang on them bums. They won't bother Walt again for a long time. And he called me at the gym this morning, on top of the world, back on Randolph's payroll with a raise."

Hesitantly Scott asked, "Has—has his sister been told?"

"She sure has!" Daley angled a knowing grin at Tinker, who assumed his most wooden expression. Then the fighter stood up, rubbed his fists nervously on his coat and moved closer to Scott.

"Now that everything's washed up, sir—could I speak to you sort of in private?" He jerked his head to indicate the Gent, who seemed preoccupied with the upholstery of the couch, smoothing the rich fabric as though its touch pleased him.

"Surely," Scott said. "Tink, why don't you take the Gent to the kitchen and give him some coffee—or anything he'd like." When the two went out arm in arm he smiled at Daley. "I suspected that you came here with something on your mind, Ace. Let's have it."

The fighter rasped knuckles across his bristling chin; the unmatched eyes blinked in embarrassment. "Remember when you first come to my place, and offered to help with him?" He rolled his head toward the kitchen. "And I turned you down cold."

"Perfectly all right," Scott assured. "You wanted to swing it yourself. You didn't hurt my feelings."

"Well, I didn't do the Gent any good by it, for all my loud talk. I told you he was pulling himself together pretty good. He was till I set him to watching Walt's sister. About then he started to slip—go off his rocker again, see? I had to get the monk back from Mrs.

Pepperell to calm him down, and that didn't help much."

"Then you'd better take him to a doctor at once."

"Yes, sir." Ace took a deep breath and plunged. "But that's my trouble—I'm broke. And the big money I was waiting for ain't in sight now. The Nelson fight is off."

"Canceled?" Scott asked. "Oh! Because of Kramer's arrest?"

Daley's grin was bitter. "That—and Nelson doing a disappearing act himself. He was in on the robbery, see? So—" he spread his hands helplessly—"until I line up another match—"

"We won't wait for that." Scott spoke decisively, for an idea had presented itself. "Look here, bring your brother to the Pepperells' tonight." He smiled. "I'll bet that Mrs. Pep invited you for Christmas Eve the day you went there?"

"Sure," Daley admitted sheepishly. "Said anyone who's been her guest is welcome on Christmas Eve. A real champ, that little dame! But cripes! I wouldn't take her up on it, sir; her classy friends would faint. Why can't we meet some place else?"

"Because a friend of mine, a doctor who has worked miracles with veterans worse off than your brother, may be there tonight. I want Dr. Paddock to look him over, as our first step. Whether it will mean an operation, or just treatments, don't worry about the money—leave that to me."

"You're the boss now; we'll show up." Daley looked down at his loud suit. "Sorry we ain't got sporting clothes—"

"Never mind that, you'll do. Come about nine-thirty."

"O.K.—and thanks, Captain. That don't say much—"

Scott waved away his gratitude. "See you tonight." He watched Ace stalk down the hall to collect the Gent from the kitchen. "If only I haven't raised his hopes too high," he thought uneasily.

Scott sat on the couch, loading his pipe. Now for a

talk with Maureen, a talk which should clear up much misunderstanding.

At a sound from the doorway he looked up. Tinker stood there, his face pinkly radiant, eyes dancing.

"Captain—I—I wanted to tell you that Maureen and I can never thank you enough for what you did for Walt."

Scott felt all color draining from his face as he echoed stupidly, "*You* and Maureen? What do you mean?"

"Well, holy cats! I thought you were on to us!"

"On to what?"

"That Walt Tenny's sister was the girl I've been gone on, all these years."

"Maureen Tenny?" Tight-lipped, he stared at Tinker.

"Sure!" The delighted grin seemed permanent. "Mrs. B. thought you'd caught on, too, that day you dropped in at her place—the first time I took Maureen out. We'd made her promise not to give us away, but she said when you came in you looked at her so sharp she felt as if she'd been caught red-handed. You remember, sir?"

Not trusting his voice, Scott nodded. Disconsolately he crossed to the tobacco jar beside the couch, knocked out his freshly filled pipe and reloaded it with meticulous care, completely oblivious of his actions. Through his paralyzed brain swirled the picture of a girl in a blue suit and perky green felt hat sitting close to Tink on that Esplanade bench. Huskily he muttered, "I suppose that you—and she—plan—"

"Yeah! We're getting married, as soon as you can find someone to look after you here. If I get that job at your club—O.K., we'll be sitting pretty. If I don't, we'll make out. Maureen isn't afraid to start small, and she hasn't any family to boss her now; they moved to the coast a while back. She promised to name the day the minute Walt was cleared, so we're all set."

Scott puffed his pipe with what he hoped appeared stoic calm. "I wish you could have told me some of this before."

"I would have, Captain! But first Ace ordered me to clam up, on account of not wanting *anyone* to know about the mess and start talking—and then Maureen wouldn't hear of it. She said not *you* of all people. I dunno why. Women get funny notions, don't they?"

"Seem to. Will she go back to New York until—the happy day?"

"Nope." Tink chuckled. "She's going to finish up the books in Number Three, says we can use the money." He jerked to attention at the sudden ring of the phone. "Want me to take it, sir?"

Scott brushed past him without answering, and lifted the handset. "Scott Pelham—*Happy!* When did you arrive? . . . What do you mean, 'Who's dead?' . . . Oh, I've got a cold coming on, I think—makes me sound gloomy. . . . You're at the club? Great, I'll be right over—Did you bring Dick? . . . Good work, Hap! This will be the greatest Christmas ever! Aunt Patty was bubbling this morning because you two were coming. . . . Be there right away—good-by!"

He hung up and hurried to the hall closet. Tinker followed, looking concerned. "Did you catch cold last night, Captain?"

"Nothing to worry about." Scott pulled on his coat. "My very best to Miss Tenny, Tink. Tell her I say she's a lucky girl to get you. I won't be back until late. Take her to supper—to a show—on me. Have fun."

At the club Hapgood and Paddock greeted him hilariously. They had shed all cares and responsibilities, bent on enjoying their holiday to the hilt. Scott made a superhuman effort to play up, but beneath his assumption of gay reminiscence, heart and mind lay frozen.

Maureen—and Tinker! It wasn't possible. And yet, why not? Tink was pure gold. Yes, but he was unashamedly a tough character, uneducated, and not particularly worried by that—A girl would overlook a lot, if she loved him. *Loved* him—the princess love Tink? It couldn't be true! And Scott was back where he started.

He felt a sense of relief when, after dinner, the three walked to Beacon Hill. In the darkness he could scowl over his torturing thoughts without attracting attention.

Snow fell softly as they went past houses whose windows were ablaze with lights—the steady glow of electric candles, the wavering fire of wax candles in towering pyramids, candles in wrought-iron holders which branched like miniature trees. Garlands on every door, and a mammoth tree lifting its blossoms of sparkling lights high above the dark Common.

As the friends reached Louisburg Square the snowfall dwindled to feathery daintiness, lying like diamond dust on their shoulders. The Hill was an enchanted world where snow transformed ordinary iron fences to fantastic convolutions of glittering white, clung in swan's-down drifts on roofs and spires and perched a furry white cap on every chimney-top. Here again candles gleamed and flickered in wreathed windows, casting a ruddy glow on the groups who stood looking out, bringing more sparkle to the colored balls and tinsel on Christmas trees in the shadowed rooms behind. Hospitable doors swung open, releasing a cheery odor of fir and balsam as friends came laughing in.

Carolers trooped down the street, their voices swelling in a paean of joy:

> "Peace on earth, good will to men,
> From Heaven's all-gracious King.
> The world in solemn stillness lay
> To hear the angels sing."

The swaying crowd in the wake of the singers formed a rhythmic pattern interwoven with splashes of barbaric color and harmonies of sound. Snow frosted the processional cross of ebony in the van of the choristers. The beauty and mysticism of the scene thrilled Hapgood and Paddock to silent wonder as they merged with the crowd. They linked arms with Scott to keep from being separated, seeming not to notice that he walked in bemused silence.

At the Pepperell home General bowed low in greeting. His eyes and teeth took on an extra sheen when he recognized the visitors. "I'll be dogged! It's Mr. Happy an' Mr. Dick! We've surely missed you gentlemen!" Then he bethought him of his responsibilities and resumed the dignity of office. "Madame is receiving in the red drawing room, upstairs, sirs. But, Mr. Scott, Miss Nancy wants that you should step into the Gun Room before you goes up, if you please."

"You and Dick go ahead," Scott told Happy. "I'll join you in a minute." To General he said, "I'm expecting Ace Daley—you remember, he's the one who left that monkey here? He's bringing his brother. Show them into the Gun Room. I'll be upstairs, so let me know when they arrive."

Going down the hall he wondered what Nan could want. For her sharp eyes he must pull himself out of this swamp of misery, lest she discover that his hopes—and, yes, his heart—had been crushed to splinters. He forced his lips to a stiff smile.

The room was lighted only by the fire on the hearth, its walls deeper cherry red under the glow, the ranged firearms gleaming softly. The flames silhouetted the woman who stood with one bronze-shod foot on the fender. A fur coat lay across the chair beside her; two dripping overshoes, which looked absurdly delicate for utility, stood side by side on the hearth.

"General said you wanted to see me, Nan—"

The woman turned—and Scott stopped dead, his gray eyes darkening to piercing black. *Maureen!* He started forward numbly and covered half the distance between them before he could master his voice. Even then it quivered with emotion when he demanded sharply, "What are you doing here?"

Her eyes shone with laughter, her lips were unsteady. The suggestion of suppressed joyousness made Scott grit his teeth. How she must love Tink to look like that!

"Why—why shouldn't I be here?" she almost whispered, raising her hands as though to ward off his formidable advance.

Scott caught her wrists. "Now that you are here, you will take back that *'Traitor!'* you flung at me last night!"

"With all my heart!" Her cheeks reddened. "I'm truly humble—I know now that you didn't—"

"*How* do you know?"

"Because—because Bill—" She caught her breath, her eyes darting past him.

Jim Selwyn walked into the room—and stopped as if shot. Scott dropped her hands, even in his agitation noticing with contrition that she rubbed her red-marked wrists. Selwyn swung hastily on his heel and headed for the door. "Pardon *me!*" he exclaimed loudly. "This is where I came in before!"

Scott ignored the interruption. Lips and cheeks colorless, tense with strain he demanded, "What is Bill Randolph to you?"

His furious inflection lifted her chin proudly, squared her shoulders, but still the laughter lurked in eyes and voice. With an airy wave of the hand, copied from Tinker, and in his most characteristic cadence she announced:

"No kidding, Captain—meet Faith Randolph."

TWENTY-TWO

FOR A LONG, SILENT MOMENT Scott's heart and brain ceased to function. Blindly he groped for a chair and braced himself with a hand gripping the back. The puzzle which he had assembled after so much thought, so many pains, tumbled apart in fragments and then, like bits of colored glass in a kaleidoscope, shifted to form a new design—with Faith Randolph its dominant figure. The outraged daughter he had heard and seen in Hapgood's office.

Slowly understanding flowed into him. *This* was the girl he loved, no matter what her name, and *she* was not engaged to Tink! The color rushed back into his face and his eyes flamed as he took an impetuous step toward her.

Uncertainty drove away her laughter and she drew back against the mantel. Scott halted, ramming his fists hard into his pockets, and the same repression edged his voice when he assured, "You needn't run. I won't beat you, Maur—*Faith*—for fooling me so. Not if you answer my questions."

"What a confirmed bargainer you are," she teased.

Soberly he insisted, "Tell me why you took Maureen's name and her job here, letting your Aunt Jane pretend you were with her."

Hands clasped behind her, she met his eyes steadily, but the diamond pin on her mint-green dress twinkled as though she were trembling. "You know *why* I was going with her to Europe; you heard my defiance in the lawyer's office. I read that in your face as you stood glowering that day. But you couldn't know that my ultimatum was a desperate bluff."

"You didn't mean it?" He was incredulous.

"Oh, I never intended to testify," she explained. "But I couldn't have gone so far away from Mother and Father. I was all they had left, wanted to be near if they needed me, but hoped that by disappearing as though forever I could bring them together. Believe me, it wasn't the impulsive tantrum it must have sounded; I had made my plans before I went to Mr. Hapgood's office. And Maureen Tenny was the ace up my sleeve," she smiled.

"So she was in the plot?"

"From the first. We became friends while she worked at the house, and I knew that she had expected to catalogue the Jordan books as her next job. Then they postponed their return from abroad, so that was out. Out for Maureen, but not for me, because the Jordans being our cousins, I felt sure they wouldn't object to my occupying their apartment for a while."

Scott snapped his fingers. "That's why you rushed to Uncle Phil's office when you reached Boston—after telling the Pullman porter to forget you!"

"Of course. Uncle Phil had been Father's guardian and was an old friend—and landlord—of the Jordan sisters, so my project depended on him. He obtained their consent—" Faith broke off suddenly as Scott's remark penetrated her absorption. "How did *you* know about my arrival?" she gasped.

"You asked about Ninety Park Street right outside my compartment. I seem fated to eavesdrop on your most dramatic moments. But go on."

"Well, I had talked Maureen into taking my place with Aunt Jane on the trip we planned some time before. Aunt was delighted to have a neophyte under her wing on a tour which was old hat to her, and Maureen wasn't reluctant to help me by seeing the world with all expenses paid." Faith sighed regretfully. "We had figured every angle, even to Maureen telling her brother that *she* was going to work at the Jordans' but that he must never mention it to my father. That was so he wouldn't try to reach her there and discover me. Everything was set—and then the atom bomb exploded!"

"The robbery?"

Faith nodded. "Only an hour before Maureen's boat left she heard that her brother had disappeared—and why! She couldn't contact me—I was keeping out of sight until I could board the train—and had to sail or disrupt all Aunt Jane's arrangements. And since I never looked at a newspaper, for fear—" she dropped her eyes in misery—"for fear of reading some new disgraceful action of my parents, I knew nothing of the robbery and lived secure in my incognita until you handed me that warning note. That really shook me, because I didn't realize it was meant for Maureen." She turned toward the fire with a tremulous laugh. "Don't glare at me as though I were a juicy bone you wanted to chew!"

Scott forced his voice to casual friendliness. "Sorry if I gave that impression. My inclination was quite different."

"Now," she announced with an upward flashing glance of delight, "you are being staid and sober pilgrim, thoroughly Bostonese."

"I'm only thoroughly bewildered," Scott sighed, and asked the question which had so long tormented him. "Where does Tink fit into this melodrama?"

"Tink didn't 'fit in'—he barged in," she admitted ruefully. "And almost upset the apple cart. I knew about Johnny from Maureen, but he only knew that Walter had said she was at The Princess, so when Mrs. B. introduced 'John Tinker' to 'Maureen Tenny' I had to talk hard and fast, believe me. Without disclosing my name I explained why we had changed places, and begged him to trust us and play the game."

"And he agreed?" Scott wondered. "Tink is more easily swayed by feminine charm than I thought."

"A grudging compliment?" she suggested demurely. "Undeserved, kind sir. You see, Johnny was on the spot; if he exposed our deception, showing that Maureen departed for Europe immediately after her brother's securities disappeared, it would be seized on as damning evidence against them both."

"True enough." Scott patted the back of the wing chair beside him. "Sit here, Faith, while you unravel more mysteries for your stupid pilgrim."

Instead she chose the one across the hearth. "This is not so close to the firing line," she explained gravely.

Scott countered by moving to lean against the mantel, where he could study her within arm's reach—a tantalizing prospect. With forced calm he said, "You have given me many moments of utter confusion, my dear. When I found you sitting with Tink on the Esplanade bench—"

"I never!" she denied indignantly.

"I saw you there yesterday."

"Oh!" A gasp of amused enlightenment. "But that was Maureen."

"Maureen—here? In your blue suit and La Tour hat?"

"The very same," she smiled. "I felt that the situation was becoming too involved, and too dangerous, so I air-mailed the latest developments to Maureen. She told Aunt Jane the whole story, and Aunt shipped her back by the next plane to take up quarters with Mrs. B. as one of her widely known 'young persons.' "

"The blonde I saw there! But why your suit and hat?"

"That," Faith boasted, "was our last fling at mystery. We plotted to merge into one girl, always appearing in the same costume, to confuse the hounds on our trail. With some success, yes?" she challenged gaily.

"With such success that today, when Tink told me he was marrying Maureen Tenny, my world went black." Scott cast restraint to the winds and bent to grip her hands. "Faith, I've waited as long as I can—" He clenched his teeth on the words and stood erect as a woman with silvered hair swept into the room.

"Faith, dear, here is Mr. Hapgood. And you must come upstairs to see the guests." Sally Randolph hurried toward them, her violet dress swirling with her haste. Her husband switched on the lights as he followed with Happy.

"Why, it's—Scott Pelham, isn't it?" Sally discovered. "He was so kind to us at the club, Faith. I'm glad you have met him."

While Hapgood and Faith exchanged greetings Randolph spoke in an undertone to Scott. "Forgiven me for my exhibition, Pelham?"

"Forget it. But *why* did you call your daughter 'Miss Tenny'?"

"You had called her that," Randolph pointed out, "so I judged that you didn't know who she was." He turned away as Hap spoke.

"Scott, you must rescue Dick from the toils of your niece," the lawyer said sternly. "She may be young, but she has the old Pelham gift of fascination, and Dr. Paddock is rapidly going overboard. Maybe it's the hot toddies we had at the club. Here come the lovebirds now," he announced in a stage whisper as Ellen and the beaming doctor entered.

"Happy, you're jealous!" Scott charged gleefully. His spirits had soared to record heights. How many weeks since he had felt so happy, so confident?

"Mr. Scott, sir!" General spoke from the door. "The gentlemen you expected has arrived."

Behind him appeared the flushed face of Ace Daley, who was whispering remonstrance to the Gent. The smaller man was crowding past the butler. His face was pale, his lips worked soundlessly, his eyes darted from wall to wall at the weapons ranged there. Then he jerked free from Daley's restraining hand and stumbled to the center of the room.

Ellen stopped in the middle of a remark to Paddock and whirled to stare at him. All color ebbed from her cheeks. "Why—it's that fighter who looks like—like the princess!" she whispered. Her lips trembled. *"No!*

It's—" Choking back a sob she flung herself on Scott and hid her face against his shoulder.

The Gent's eyes followed her and there was a light in them that Scott had never seen before, a glow instead of blankness. Slowly they shifted around the room and fixed on Sally Randolph.

She stepped forward, her face transparent in its pallor, her eyes wide with incredulous hope. *"Kendall!"* The hoarse whisper seemed to tear her throat. Then with a hysterical laugh sadder than any tears she cried, "Oh, God! It *is* Kendall!"

The Gent blinked and put out a hand to touch her, a faint smile bringing life to his drawn face. "Naow, Maw, steady daown!" he soothed, with a drawling twang so unlike his usual monotone that Scott shivered. The Gent put both hands on Sally Randolph's shoulders, patting them gently. Then his knees gave way and he sagged forward. Only Paddock's lightning reaction saved him from crashing to the floor.

TWENTY-THREE

DR. PADDOCK, holding the slight figure easily, looked around the room and then laid Kendall on the broad, cushioned window seat.

"There's a long couch in the front room," Scott suggested.

"I want him here when he comes to," the doctor said quietly. "This room stirred his first memories, I believe. Ellen and his mother did the rest."

Scott's throat contracted unbearably as he watched the still form. Sally Randolph and Faith knelt beside Kendall, and Dick Paddock bent over him intently. Randolph stood by the hearth, haggard eyes never leaving his son, clasped hands twisting constantly. Ace Daley's swift catlike steps took him silently to the end of the window seat, where he leaned against the wall, staring with desperate anxiety at his comrade.

The street door opened and closed and laughing voices filled the hall for a moment, then trailed away upstairs where the Pepperells and their guests were gathered, quite unconscious of the drama below.

Kendall's head rolled, his eyes opened. In a clear untroubled voice he said tenderly, "Mother! And Faith!" The blue eyes shifted, found Dr. Paddock, narrowed in puzzled study of the unfamiliar face. "Where—who are you? Where's *Father?*"

Randolph stepped past the doctor. "Here, Ken—" He had to clear his throat, brush mist from his eyes. "We're all here, boy. Thank God we four are together again!"

"But where's Ace?" Ken demanded anxiously. *"Ace!"*

Daley stooped to lay a scarred hairy hand in his. "Right in your corner all the time, Gent. Take it easy. You're O.K. now."

"Sure I am, Ace. Sure." Ken looked at the eager group and smiled. His voice came strong and joyous as he repeated, " *'Together!'* What a wonderful word." His eyes closed and the deep lines in his face smoothed away as he dropped asleep.

Scott caught Daley's eye and led him out to the hall, closing the door gently. In the dining room he pulled two chairs near the window and motioned Ace to sit beside him. In silence they stared out at the passing crowd while Scott smoked a cigarette in tense haste and the fighter massaged his red hair.

At last Scott said softly, "You pulled off a miracle, Ace."

Daley grunted. "I don't think it was me, but Somebody sure did." In a muffled whisper he said, "I'm going to miss that kid."

"You needn't," Scott comforted. "I'll bet Ken isn't going to lose sight of you, and the Randolphs owe you too much—"

"Nobody owes me nothing!" snapped Ace. "I told you before, the minute I seen him I *had* to look after him. Something got me."

Scott nodded. "I know what you mean, I felt it. But why did you claim he was your brother?"

"Aw," Daley shrugged, "it saved a lot of nosy questions. And he did remind me of a kid brother I had who was sort of high-toned and polite all the time. That's why I called him 'Gent.'" Daley stood up suddenly. "Look, sir, I'm going to blow; this is no place for me now. Be seeing you." He was gone before Scott could speak.

Paddock came in then, and Scott asked anxiously, "How about Kendall? Will he pull through, Dick?"

The doctor took the chair beside him and lit a cigarette with professional calm. "He will. He is already normal. Recognition of Daley as well as his family indicates that past and present are both clear and nothing is lost. He will come out of his nap as good as new."

"Has he known all the time that Faith was his sister?"

"Subconsciously, I am sure. Faith told of his watching her in a museum; that was memory struggling to break through. The Gun Room turned the trick. The combination of that unusual room which he used to admire, Ellen's startled recognition—that child has a ghoulish memory!—set the stage, and his mother's hysterical cry broke the spell."

Scott suggested, "I wish you would come upstairs with me when I tell Uncle Phil and Aunt Patty. It's going to be a shock."

"I'd like to." Paddock put out his cigarette. "This sort of shock is a pleasure to watch. We'll let the Randolphs stay by their son for now. I sent the daughter home; from what I hear she's had all the emotional strain she ought to stand."

I sent the daughter home. Dick Paddock's words companioned Scott as he strode rapidly through the snowy streets. Could he see Faith again tonight? It wasn't so very late, and he had so much to say. Back there in the Gun Room she had done most of the talking; now it was his turn. Nothing stood between them now; nothing that he could imagine. He went up the steps to The Princess two at a time. Better check with Mrs. Beddle on his way to Number Three; Faith might have dropped in to give her the wonderful news about Kendall.

The housekeeper answered his ring and the amused understanding in her eyes made his cheeks burn. Before he could frame a question she shook her head with a regretful smile. "She isn't here, Mr. Scott. She stopped to tell me about her brother—who'll dare say now that the age of miracles is past? She has gone up to the roof garden—said she couldn't shut herself in between four walls after all this."

On the roof Scott closed the door of the sunroom behind him. Overhead, the clouds which had shaken out their feathery flakes to whiten the city had withdrawn to pile a long gray bank along the horizon. The stars shone out serene and clear, as has been the way of stars for unnumbered generations. Steady, immutable, their golden beauty spread a limitless canopy of light.

Faith Randolph leaned against the railing of the garden, her face upturned to the sky. At the crunch of his step on the snowy path she turned with a start.

Scott sensed her instinctive impulse to retreat. His face was white as he protested,"Don't go. I hoped to find you here; you told me that you took your problems to the stars."

"No problems tonight—happiness!" It sang in every word. "Knowing that my parents are together again and that we have Kendall! Think of his coming back to us after all this time; it's unbelievable." Her voice lowered in sudden apprehension. "He will be all right, won't he? Dr. Paddock didn't say that just to comfort us?"

"No, he told me the same. And before I left, Kendall had awakened and seemed perfectly normal—and very cheerful."

"How wonderful! I really did believe Dr. Paddock, he makes one fairly tingle with confidence in his judgment. No one but him could have sent me away from Ken tonight." She paused and then whispered with a sob in the words, "I shall never forgive myself for—for failing him that day at the museum. Ellen recognized him, but I, his own sister, not only didn't know him but was afraid of him!"

Scott laid comforting hands on her shoulders. "Don't torture yourself with that, dear; be reasonable. You saw him in an unfamiliar place, completely strange to both of you. Don't you know that Intelligence men and detectives agree that the best possible disguise for a man is to drop out of his accustomed sphere and appear in totally different surroundings? That was the way you saw Kendall. And, after all, how much of a look did you get at him?"

"Not much," Faith agreed. "And one hand was covering his mouth."

"There you are. It's hardly likely that Ellen would have recognized him that day, either. It was the Gun Room setting which stimulated her memory. She had seen him there many times, had sat listening while he and Uncle Phil talked guns. And remember, she saw him before, on the road with Daley, then met you and was struck by a resemblance. Her mind was prepared. Add to that her phenomenal memory—and there you are." With conviction Scott repeated, "Don't blame yourself. Believe Dr. Paddock. Believe me."

Her eyes were misty as she forced a smile. "I do believe you, and thanks. How often I've had to thank my pilgrim!" She turned away, gripping the railing as she looked up at the stars.

Giving her time to conquer her emotion Scott said lightly, "I wish you had been at supper, after most of the guests left. Old Pep was shaking with diabolic chuckles because he alone knew your secret and gleefully watched us all become more and more bewildered over 'the girl in Number Three.'

"And Aunt Patty was listening blissfully to everyone's happiness. In a few days we'll probably hear that the Peps have endowed something, as a thank offering for the miracle of Ken's restoration to his family under their very own roof. Forget the mystery and heartache, Princess. They are all behind you."

"Forget them? Yes!" There was a lilt in her voice as she admitted, "I feel as though I had escaped from a strange, underground life. It wasn't easy; I hate deception. All these last months my spirit has seemed a lonely wraith of impersonation driven relentlessly through a never-ending nightmare." She shook her bowed head. "But I stuck to my plan, a desperate effort to bring Mother and Father together. They were growing older, what was there in life for either one alone? A little freedom, for a little time—but lonely freedom." She shivered at the thought. "Lonely freedom! Can there be any purgatory worse than that?"

Scott took her hands. His tone was vibrant with eagerness. "There is a cure for loneliness."

Without meeting his demanding eyes she whispered, "Yes. All through my nightmare, whenever I looked to the stars—"

"No cure but the stars, Faith?"

For an instant her shining eyes met his, then the long lashes hid them. "There was another," she whispered. "I loved being with you."

"Only *being with me?*" he mocked. Her eyes, her voice, her nearness swept away the iron control he had kept on himself. His arms went around her, crushed her close. With lips pressed against her hair he whispered, "I spoke before and you wouldn't listen, but until the day I die you hear me saying, 'I love you, Princess, I love you!' "

With a sigh of happiness and surrender Faith raised willing lips to his.